Cindy,

More easy reading

Ada

D1506496

Willard

Beyond Batty Catters

by

A. J. Gillard

4th Floor Press, Inc.

www.4thfloorpress.com

www.ajgillard.com

Copyright © A.J. Gillard 2012

All rights reserved. No part of this publication may be reproduced in any form or by any means without the express prior written consent of the publisher and/or author.

This book is a work of fiction. Names, characters, places, and the scenarios depicted are meant to be fictitious. Any resemblance to actual persons, living or dead, establishments, locations, or events is entirely coincidental.

Library and Archives Canada Cataloguing in Publication

Gillard, A. J.
Beyond Batty Catters / by A.J. Gillard.

Issued also in electronic format.
ISBN 978-1-897530-29-0

Published by 4th Floor Press, Inc.
www.4thfloorpress.com
1st Printing 2012
Printed in Canada

www.ajgillard.com

Other A.J. Gillard Books

Available from 4th Floor Press, Inc.

A Matter of Time

Gambler's Cove

Like Coming Home

Maya and Teddy Take a Walk

Murphy's Law

Stories for Andrew: Rantings and Amusements for a Soldier Abroad

www.ajgillard.com

www.4thfloorpress.com

Beyond Batty Catters

by

A. J. Gillard

Batty catters – Barricado – Ice formed in winter by the action of spray and waves along the shoreline of the sea, making a barricade on the landward side – the accumulation of masses and slabs of ice forced up on shore by tides and waves, or grounded near the shore. How does one understand the term if one hasn't lived it? In Newfoundland it's Batty Catters. It exudes enticement, fun and danger, and everyone knows if you make it beyond the Batty Catters you're safe.

Prologue

The toddler fell, then crawled across the brown painted floor. He'd stop and shake his head from side to side, the facecloth dangling from his mouth. Everyone laughed, amused by his antics as he soaked up their attention. From time to time he'd pull himself up, walk a few steps, then fall and continue crawling.

I sat and watched him.

"You look so serious, Kenny. What are you thinking?" Katrina looked at me from where she sat near the window.

"I don't know," I replied. Actually, I knew, but chose not to share it. Instead I looked at my glass. "I don't know why I'm drinking this stuff. It tastes terrible."

"It's an acquired taste, you know." Katrina said, wrinkling her nose ever so slightly as she peered at the low budget beer in her glass.

I shook my head and chuckled. "Maybe we should have hot chocolate instead."

"Try this." She handed me her glass and I took a sip. "I mixed it with a soft drink."

My first instinct was to spit it out, but I made a face, closed my eyes and swallowed. I passed back the glass and held out mine. "Here, mix mine, too. It's definitely better than this."

I watched the child rise and fall, rise and fall, still determined to make it to somewhere else. The room was so foreign and dirty. I needed to be drunk. I needed something to make me forget. "This place reminds me of where I grew up," I muttered, nearly to myself.

Katrina shrugged and shook her head, making her long, blond ponytail swing from side to side. "I can't imagine you growing up in a place as remote as this. Hell, I don't even know what we're doing here, Ken. A cottage in the middle of nowhere? My dad better not find out about this. He'd totally freak. Completely. This is no place for any daughter of B. J. Toms to be…" her voice trailed off with a smile as she thought of her father and glanced out the window. It hadn't taken long for Kenny to figure out that Katrina was a daddy's girl through and through. She loved and admired the man the world knew as B.J. Toms, multi-millionaire businessman. To Katrina, B.J. was simply her dad, the one man in this world she could always count on.

"The weather sure is gorgeous today though," she said sarcastically with a twinkle in her blue eyes as she stretched out her arms. "I'm hoping to get a tan from the sun from this window. Think I can get a tan lying inside here? I need it badly. I'm so white."

Surely I was from another time, another place. This could never have been me.

I took another sip of my beer cocktail and cringed. I thought about my own father. He wouldn't approve. "Perhaps we should be drinking hot chocolate after all." Katrina chuckled lightly.

We had been at the cottage for three days, but already it felt like a lifetime.

We were sitting in the one room, the only room at a friend's cottage, somewhere in Northern Maine. I had no idea where. The weather was mild for March. Katrina and I had been invited for the weekend with our friend Melinda and her mother. Melinda had warned us that it was 'rugged.' Rugged barely described the place.

I walked to the front window and looked out. The lake was still frozen and I looked to the shoreline for signs of spring. There was no ice pushing up on the land—not like there'd be back home. This was different. There were no ice flows or stormy seas to worry the two cross-country skiers that passed the cottage on their way around the lake. Every place has its dangers, but I couldn't see them there that day. The sun was shining, there was no wind, and the water was dripping from the roof. How quickly the year was passing.

The location was everybody's dream of a cottage in the country. The cottage itself was not. It was modest, too modest, even by my standards. However, being only eighteen years old and having a weekend away from university, any place was a welcoming place. Besides I had grown up in a remote area, so remote that painted floors or lack of sewer facilities should not have bothered me.

I was just a freshman at Atlantic University. My friend

and roommate Katrina and I had accepted another student's invitation to spend the weekend at her parents' cottage. The three of us had enjoyed each other's company over the past months and Katrina and I were happy to have someone from the area who could take us "home" occasionally. Melinda was from Halifax. Katrina was from Boston. And I? I was from that other time, that other place. Like so many of the other students we had just discovered the euphoric effects of alcohol and being able to escape for a weekend to relax and guzzle beer was a reward for having survived another week of stress. We discovered, however, that Melinda carried with her a secret—a secret that we now watched crawl across the floor. She was an unwed teenage mother and whenever she got away from the university, she would, not only out of obligation, but out of love, spend any available time with the child who was destined to be a part of her life forever.

I watched him and wondered how long my own secret would remain intact. It was just over a year and, as part of my secret was still a mystery to me, I had no choice but to live in the here and now. I watched him crawl.

Melinda's mom came into the room, picking up the clothes and toys that needed to be packed as she walked. "Kenny, didn't you say you were from the Northern Peninsula of Newfoundland?"

I nodded. It hadn't been quite two years since I had left. My mother died when I was only four. My father had drowned last year. "Yes, I did."

"Have you been back since you left?"

I shook my head. "No, I have no family there anymore. Why do you ask?"

"I just heard about three kids who were swept away from what sounded like batty catters. Does that make sense?"

"It's March. It makes sense."

"What are batty catters?" asked Katrina as she reached beneath her chair to grab a wayward stuffed bear.

"It's hard to describe, really. It's just a place. Just a place on the shore. It's a place where the ice comes in, but it's more. Maybe we'll visit one day and you'll see."

"I'd like that," she said as she handed the toy to Melinda.

But you still won't understand, I thought. You could never understand unless you're from the island. And going back? It won't be for a long, long time, if I ever go back.

Melinda's mom interrupted my thoughts. "You're welcome here anytime, Kenny. You, too, Katrina. Melinda and I come here just to escape, really. Melinda's dad isn't very well. I just got a call. I'm afraid we'll have to go back now," she said as she wiped the back of her wrist across her forehead. I could see the tension had returned to her eyes, the fear and the pain. "But just remember both of you are welcome here or at our home anytime. It's good for Melinda. She doesn't get out much since Nicky was born. I'm glad for university. It gets her away from home and of course she can always come here."

"Why didn't she choose a university in Canada?"

"I guess because of the cottage," said her mom. "We've come here since Melinda was just a kid. It's just a matter of miles to Nova Scotia. Why did you choose to come to Maine University? Why not stay in Canada?"

"It had what I wanted," I said. I didn't really want to tell them the truth of why I had chosen the United States over Canada.

Perhaps I'll come here more often, I thought to myself as Melinda and her mom started packing frantically. I had no home and I had no money. I was struggling to pay for university. I was holding down two part time jobs, but I had to. If I couldn't go back, then I was going forward and if going forward meant coming to this rustic place, then I would. I couldn't look back. It was too painful.

I pulled up a chair near Katrina and watched Melinda pick up the toddler. "Well, I've got to come back here or at least home every weekend," she said. "I've got a major connection with this place. You know, Kenny, you're so lucky. No babies holding you down and your father didn't live long enough to be a problem for you. I love my father and my son, but it does make life hard at times."

Katrina squeezed my elbow compassionately, hoping she could take the sting out of Melinda's comments. I understood though. Melinda probably would have loved to trade places with me. Her father, much older than her mother, was in the late stages of Alzheimer's and Melinda's life was constant stress, having to cope with her father and with a son. She just didn't know the pain I was also suffering.

There was nothing to connect me to my town anymore, except memories that I could only hope time would erase. I watched Melinda open the front door. I no longer had a father like her. Mine had gone, freeing me from any obligation the future might have held. There was no child to shape my life, my dreams. I was solely responsible for myself.

"I know you said you'd like to go back home someday, but you won't, will you?" Katrina asked. Though we had only been friends for a semester, she knew me inside and out.

I shook my head and, doing what I was used to, I fought back the tears. "My father's body wasn't found. There wasn't even a funeral." I sighed and ran a hand over the tight braid I had wrangled my thick hair into for the entire weekend. "There's nobody to go back to. When it comes to family, Kat, you're as close as I'll ever get."

"Then you'll come with me forever," she said without the slightest moment of hesitation "You'll be my sister."

We stood up and hugged each other. The alcohol from our one beer each had made us teary-eyed and we needed to cling to each other. A tear rolled down her face. It was a tear of happiness for what she had found. The tear that rolled down my cheek was of sadness for all I had lost.

We followed Melinda out to the car. My future had just begun.

Chapter One

Every time my car approaches a hill I get numb. It all rushes back to me in a split second—the moment of sheer panic, Katrina's scream on impact, the windshield pushing into my face. All of it. Every time, there's a flash of fear so deep I have to force myself to continue forward. The urge to slam on the brakes makes my right foot twitch. After all these years, I still feel the pain.

As my Lexus crowned another hilltop safely, I sighed deeply, exhaling the breath I had been holding. All around me, I watched the land of my childhood pass by. I hadn't been on the island of Newfoundland in nearly seventeen years and everything about me had changed. The island had not. Dense woodlands covered the landscape to my left as the ocean raced by the right hand side of my SUV. Through the open window I could smell the brine in the air and visions of my past life threatened to cloud my mind.

Tears began to pool in my eyes as I neared the next hill. *What the hell am I doing here?* I thought to myself as my fingers gripped the wheel tightly. *Why did I ever promise B.J. I'd come back?* The weathered sign on the roadside read, 'Englee 10 km.'

There was no one on the road, but what was on the other side of the hill, if anything, still scared me. As I approached the top a Jeep came flying much too close and I swerved, going off the embankment and slamming on my brakes.

My heart was pounding. I put my head on the steering wheel and cried. I didn't look up as my door opened. "Are you okay?"

My whole body shook.

His hand touched my head. "Miss, please. Are you okay? What happened? Why did you swerve?"

I lifted my head. I brushed away the tears. "I'm fine. I just needed to cry and I guess I needed to do it right here." I stared into his face. "I'm sorry."

"Sorry! Well, you chose a hell of a spot! You could have gotten us both killed." He was suddenly angry and his nostrils flared.

"Me!" I pulled off my sunglasses just as he did. "You were the one…" but I stopped as I stared at the man peering into my car. My heart skipped a beat, then started to race faster than I ever thought possible. My hand left the steering wheel and moved towards his face, as though I had no control over its intentions. Lance. Lance Richards.

He drew back, looked at my hand and I froze. His anger disappeared. "You look mighty pale. Are you sure you're okay?" His stare searched my face, as though he'd find an answer in my hazel eyes.

"Yeah, I'm, I'm…" I stammered. There he was, inches from my nose, and he had no idea who I was. The tears threatened to fill my eyes again as we stared at one another. I ran a shaking hand over the brown wig that covered my own long red hair; the action snapped me back into reality. . "Sorry, Mister…"

"Richards. Lance Richards," he said with the caution one uses when approaching a crazy person.

"Mister Richards," I said and cleared my throat loudly. "Sorry, I'm a bit of a mess today. I'm not usually a nervous driver but today I'm a bit shaky. It's been a long trip."

"Did you drive from St. John's?" his voice was deeper than I remembered.

I shook my head. "Deer Lake."

"That's long enough. Are your travels nearly done then? Where are you heading?"

"Englee, just to Englee," I replied, trying desperately to sound normal.

"Right, then, Miss…" he prompted.

"Call me Kay." I offered my hand and relished the feeling of his calloused palm as he accepted. It was the same hand I remembered from all those years ago.

"Well, Kay. You're not far. Englee's just down the road a bit. Sure you're okay to get there?"

"Yeah," I said as I reluctantly released his hand. "I should be able to make it." He looked down the road and pointed. I couldn't believe how little he had changed. The black leather jacket. The blue jeans. The black hair touching his collar. It looked as thick as it always was. He had grown even more handsome over the years.

"Have you ever been to our fair town before, Kay?" He seemed to be trying to lighten the mood.

"Not for years," I said, trying to keep the nostalgia from my voice.

"So, you've been here before? Maybe that's why you look familiar," he smiled as he stared into my eyes once again. "Well, we have a motel now, so if you're looking for a place to spend the night and unwind a bit..." he pointed to my right hand which was still gripping the steering wheel fiercely. "It's called The Park Place Motel, just into town and on the right, you can't miss it."

"Thanks, I think I will check in. I might be here for a day or two," I said lightly.

"Well, that's the place you want then. My brother, Reg, owns it and his wife, Ester, runs the place. They'll be more than happy to have you." I couldn't help but notice that he limped as he stepped back from my door and began to walk back to his Jeep which he had left running on the opposite side of the road. "Nice meeting you, Kay."

I couldn't move. Reg. Reg was still living in Englee. He owned the motel. I don't know what I had expected—that he would have disappeared into thin air, the way I had half a lifetime before. Of course not! Reg would never leave Englee. He'd never be pushed out, the way he had pushed me to run.

Snap out of it, Kennedy, I told myself. *You knew he'd still be here. That they would all still be here. Lance didn't recognize you. Neither will Reg. No one will have any idea who you really are. Kennedy Warren may have run from this town, terrified, poor and alone, but Kay Toms is the one returning. Strong, independent, Kay Toms. Not a frightened schoolgirl.*

I looked to the oval-cut ten carat diamond wedding ring on my left hand and took a deep breath. B.J. had wanted me to come back to my hometown and face my demons. It was his dying wish and I had given my word to the man who had saved my life, my husband. For B.J. I could do anything. I owed him everything.

I slammed the door shut and started the engine once again. I had come this far. I would make it to Englee and say goodbye forever. Finally I would hold my head high and face the demons that waited.

As the taillights of Lance's Jeep disappeared from my rearview mirror, I slowly headed towards town. I stopped on the crest of the hill, pulled to the side and looked down. I needed to remember what I had left behind.

Directly across from me I could see the Richards house standing like a fortress guarding the town. It was on the tip of the island, nestled against the high cliffs of Heights Cove. The thirty acres were guarded by the jagged rocks that swept down to the Atlantic. It hung over the town like one of Ben Gillard's paintings. The closest neighbour was a graveyard hidden behind a wall of trees.

I had loved that house. It wasn't really a fortress. It was a two storey white clapboard house like all the other homes in the area. It was large, though. Much larger than most homes. It had a view that was breathtaking. The deck overlooked Canada Bay, with a view of Devil's Island, the Cross Rocks, and every boat that came into the bight had to pass by the Richards' estate.

I smiled as I suddenly felt myself running through the house, being chased by Lance. He'd catch me in the mud room and there'd be yells and screams as he pulled me down and tickled me. The commotion would bring his mom; she'd smile and leave us alone.

I remember a large den off the big country kitchen. I could feel the soft cushions as I'd lie there and study or just sit around and wait for Lance.

I wondered what had happened to Janine. She was the live-in maid. I don't know if she ever smiled, but she was a great cook. She'd bring cookies to Lance and me when we'd get home from school. But I remember how she'd sternly tell us to take off our boots when we entered.

I closed my eyes and felt it all; the warmth, the love, the home I loved.

I shook off the nostalgia when Reg entered the moment. My heart beat wildly instead. I could feel myself tremble on the inside. I hated to run into him, even though he was Lance's brother.

A car passed me, slowed down and eyed me with curiosity, then continued. I wondered if anybody even remembered me anymore. I wondered if Mr. Richards ever thought of me.

I am not a Richards. I am, or rather I was, the caretaker's daughter.

Nobody in town had a caretaker or could even afford one except Mr. Richards. I think it was because my father had lost an arm in Mr. Richards' sawmill that he hired him. There were lots of things he couldn't do, but he always managed, subcontracting sorta' when he really needed help.

In any case, my father had a permanent job with the Richards' family and since my mother had died when I was very young, Mrs. Richards was delighted to include me in her family. I became the only girl in the family of two boys: Reg and Lance. I had the run of the Richards' house as if it were my own.

I don't know how Mr. Richards had become the most prominent man in the town, but he was. He owned the general store, the fish plant, the sawmill, and as a result he controlled the town. I was soon to find out that he had sold the fish plant after I left, a cunningly smart move. The fish industry was in a decline. The sawmill was no longer in operation. That industry had also died out. I had no idea who owned the mill now or what had become of it.

Mr. Richards always seemed to be one step ahead of everybody. I was soon to find out just how important the Richards were in the town. He now controlled the marina, the bus line, the chip plant, and indirectly through his son, Reg, the crab plant and the only motel in the area. The largest grocery store in the area was his, as was the only pharmacy within miles. These were his holdings that you could see. He probably owned or controlled more than was visible. I was familiar with business now.

There was a lot I knew about Mr. Richards, but there was probably as much about him that I didn't know. I wondered if he knew who B. J. Toms was or if he was aware of the new me. Through my late husband and my own efforts, I had become a part of the financial world. I wasn't famous by any stretch of the imagination, but to those in industry, my reputation was well known. I just hoped that if he was aware of me, he would not see me for who I really was underneath. I couldn't go back as myself, not yet, if ever.

I was still scared, unsure of how I'd be received. I had to find out about Reg. What had happened that night? And I was still unsure of Lance, especially of Lance. Perhaps he had never forgiven me for what was done to him.

I stopped my dreaming, my remembering, took a deep breath and continued down into the town. As I drove towards the bridge the old familiar chill came creeping over my body. As a child it was so exciting to find arrowheads, to find amulets, to know that Indian remains had been found in the town. Somehow, digging up parts of the history had made us special.

But as the chill crept over me, the wisdom and knowledge of being adult replaced the excitement of a child. I shivered as

I crossed that Indian burial ground.

As a child I had no idea why I felt the way I did when I crossed that sacred place. I had no idea I was even walking on a sacred place. We were only children and nobody, not even adults, questioned what happened around us. In a community where there were as many churches as there were families one could only assume that evil lurked. Otherwise, why so many churches?

For a moment I ran a hand over my stomach. In that very place where my eyes now focused I saw the evil that had driven me away. I wonder if what I had witnessed would have even occurred in another part of town. But it all happened in this place I now slowly drove over and I wondered if life had changed, if any other strange occurrences had taken place since I left many years ago. A car behind me forced me to move faster and I changed my thoughts to what would be my home for the next few days.

It didn't take me long to find the motel. It was right where Lance had said it would be. In fact, it faced the General Store and stretched along the road, almost touching the fish plant.

As I walked into the main reception room, I stopped for a moment to take in the decor. Rather than the cheesy, oceanside tourist paraphernalia I had expected, I was impressed to see the tasteful, almost upscale details of the new furniture and soft lighting. As my eyes scanned the modern prints tastefully framed on the tope walls, I couldn't help but smile. It was a little taste of my current home and, while completely out of place in the sleepy town of Englee, a welcomed sight. Then I saw Ester.

Standing behind the marble counter was a tall, buxom, bleach-bottle blond in the tightest velour track suit I had ever seen. I marvelled at the near painted-on effect of the fabric as it hugged her ample curves and flared open at an alarming rate of incline to display an overabundance of cleavage. Over her heart was a shining brass name tag, proudly stating, "Ester Richards, Manager."

As I took all of Ester in, my eyes finally ventured to her face—under the layers of drugstore makeup and fake eyelashes was the warmest smile I had seen in years. Her bright green eyes crinkled at the corners as her lips curved into a genuine welcome that put me instantly at ease.

"G'evening, welcome to Park Place Motel," she said, as her eyes took in my suede coat and Louis Vuitton bag. I shifted the bag behind me and stepped forward to the counter.

"Thank you," I said with a smile as I handed over my credit card. "I'm not sure how long I'll be staying..."

"Oh, well, that's fine. We won't be kicking you out," she giggled and winked a heavily shaded eye.

"I appreciate that," I said jovially. "So..."

"So, just yourself then?" Ester asked as she began typing into the computer. "Not expecting company?"

"No, just me."

"Oh, right then," she said as she skimmed the card through the machine and reached for a key from beneath the counter. "Thank you, Mrs. Toms. If you need anything, just call over and let us know. We'll do anything we can to make your stay in Englee as comfortable as possible. Will you need a map of the sights?"

"The sights?" I said almost sarcastically. "Sorry, um, no, not this evening. It's been a long trip, so I'll just call it a night."

"Help with your bags?" Ester offered, though I noted she didn't move from her perch.

"No, no, that's fine, the room's just..."

"Just out the door, to your left, number eight, can't miss it," Ester pointed and smiled. "Get yourself a good rest and tomorrow will be bright." She smiled as I took the key from her and turned to the door.

Four steps down the pathway to my left, my heart nearly stopped. "God damn it!" his voice boomed. I hadn't heard that tone in nearly eighteen years, but would have known it anywhere. Reg. "Why the hell isn't this done, Charlie?"

I froze on the spot. *Oh God, Oh God*...Reg. I slowly turned my head to look down the narrow gap between the main reception building and the row of motel rooms. There, standing in the alleyway was Reg, towering over Charlie, a man I remembered as slow-witted but sweet. In the fading light of the sunset, Reg's blond hair shone. Charlie's own head, covered in a tight wool toque, was bowed as he stared at his feet and wished to be anywhere else.

"Sorry, Mr. Richards, I was just gettin' started..." he leaned heavily on the broom he held. "I'll get it done, don't you nevermind, you'll see. All done, clean as a whistle." Without ever looking up, Charlie began to move the broom and manoeuvre his way past Reg and towards me.

Behind him, Reg glared with a look of utter contempt. As he noticed me, he snapped his mask back into place and smiled. A cold shiver ran down my spine and jumpstarted my legs. Without a word, I rushed forward to find number eight. At the door, I fumbled with the key as my hands shook. Beads of sweat formed beneath my wig and my heart pounded.

Finally inside, I slammed the door shut behind me and secured the deadbolt. After quickly pulling the curtains closed, I threw my bags to the floor and flopped onto the bed. My mind reeled--the scene with Lance on the roadside, seeing Reg, meeting Ester, seeing the town that had shaped my life, all replayed in my head. *Good God, what have I done?*

Three light knocks tapped on the locked door. My head snapped up. Moving slowly off the bed, I stood, and stepped cautiously towards the door. With one terrified eye to the peephole, I stared at the top of a gray woollen cap. The breath I had been holding gushed from my lungs. Steadying my hand, I unbolted the door and tried to smile.

"Sorry, missus," Charlie mumbled as he looked at me sheepishly. He held out his hand. "You dropped this..." I stared at the receipt that must have escaped my jacket pocket.

"Oh, why, how did that happen?" I said gently, trying to keep my voice steady as I glanced to the empty parking lot behind him. The years had not been kind to Charlie, I noted, as I took in the deep lines that etched his face. Holding his gaze for just a moment, I searched for any sign of recognition. There was none. He had no idea who I was. Obviously uncomfortable with the attention, he shifted his gaze to the ground and turned.

"G'night then, missus. G'night," he muttered as he ambled away.

"Thank you," I said weakly as I shut the door once again. Leaning against the solid oak, I shuddered. The memories of my childhood were so vivid and I needed to find closure with a past I could not forget. All I meant to do was visit the town once more and then leave.

Yet, I was starting to realize that I couldn't. There were fears in this sleepy little town that I had to face, if I was ever going to move on with my life.

I pulled the tight, brown wig off my head. It was one of my favourites, made especially for me. Regular wigs couldn't effectively contain my masses of wild, curly red hair. That red hair and my mother's eyes were the last remaining markers of the girl I had once been. My face had been forever changed by the accident, making me unrecognizable, even to myself at times.

Katrina and I had just graduated university and were starting out on a celebratory road trip when we crested that hill and slammed into the drunk driver who had crossed the double line. I woke in a hospital bed nearly three weeks later to find her father sitting in a chair, praying for me to come around. I couldn't talk, couldn't move my head at all, even blinking was excruciating. I let out a whimper. B.J. leapt out of his chair and rushed to my side.

"Kenny, Kenny, it's okay, try not to move," he said as he stroked my hand. "You were in a car accident. You're in the hospital now and you're going to be okay." His kind blue eyes were filled with tears. I remember through the fog of morphine thinking that he looked tired. I raised my hand; it was heavy. I brought it into my line of vision and saw the cast that held it. Only my fingertips were visible. I brought them to my face and felt the thick bandages that wrapped my entire head.

"You've been hurt, dear," B.J. had said. "It's pretty bad, but you're going to pull through. You're going to be okay." There was determination in his voice, as though the words were a mantra. "You're going to be okay."

A burly nurse rushed in just then, lowered my casted hand back down to my side, and injected a fresh batch of painkillers into my IV. My memories of the weeks that followed are vague, moving images of white coats floating in and out of my line of vision and B.J.'s voice constantly reassuring me. There were surgeries, many, many surgeries.

I paced in the motel room and stopped to look at myself

in the mirror above the bureau. In the ten years since the accident, I had become accustomed to my new face, the one that was reflected back to me just then. Yet, I still felt as though I was walking through life wearing a mask. In many ways, I was. The plastic surgeons had done their best, even managing to make me beautiful in the end. Beautiful, yet different in a fundamental way.

Recovering from the crash, I had to face life without my own face and without my best friend. Katrina had not survived the impact. B.J. and I found ourselves alone in the world, not knowing how to go on.

Kay Toms, as I became known after we married the following year, was a whole new woman. I took to wearing wigs when B.J. and I were in public, so no one from my past would ever recognize me in the slightest. So Reg Richards would never find me.

Yet, here I was. Back in the town I had sworn I would never return to. Staying in Reg's hotel, under his roof, right under his nose. I could feel my resolve strengthening. I was no longer a scared teenager. I was an adult now. I could face whatever he would throw at me.

"Oh, Katrina, I wish you were here right now," I said to the empty room.

I picked up the wig and walked to the mirror. It's been so long, nobody will recognize me. Nobody. I just hope Lance will understand.

My name is Kennedy, Kennedy Warren. I had been told that my mother had adored J.F.K. I can only assume I was given the name for nostalgic or hero worship reasons. I've never known another female named Kennedy. To my friends I was Kenny. Oh, it got misunderstood quite often and I was teased for having a boy's name but that was okay with me. I was, after all, a tomboy.

I enjoyed playing with boys; cowboys and Indians, building forts, fishing, tinkering with boats and their motors. I guess it was because my mom died when I was just four and there was just me and my dad. He took good care of me and I adored him.

I walked to the window and looked out. The last of the day's light glistened on the water. The town looked hushed. I had to stay; especially now. I needed closure. B.J. had known that, long before I ever realized it. From the little I had seen of the town as I drove through it, I thought how much the people needed help. At this very moment it looked like I was the one who needed the help. I had it all, yet I had nothing. One man and his secret from eighteen years ago could eliminate Kay Toms and there'd be nobody to know or even care. Except for Lance, nobody knew I was in town, and he didn't even know who I was.

Chapter Two

The following morning I found my feet leading me to Locker's Point. Lance and I had spent uncountable hours there throughout our childhood, daydreaming our way out, our way off the island.

Situated on the very eastern coast of Canada, the province of Newfoundland is a marvel of contradictions. On one hand this expansive land mass in the Atlantic is a land of sheer natural beauty and bounty. An independent country until the 1940s, the population of this rocky, wilderness covered gem is made of hardworking stock. Hardy, determined people who fight to stay in their homes.

On the darker, often politically driven, side of Newfoundland are the wild ups and downs of market forces, fishery crises, and an unstable economy. Once a haven for fisherman, the decline in fish stocks and the advent of international water restrictions in the eighties, nineties, and into the new millennium, have continued to suppress the once buoyant nature of a people used to living off the sea.

Englee, like most townsites of Newfoundland, sits on the shore, facing the mighty Atlantic Ocean. It stands on the Eastern most point of the Northern Peninsula at the very tip of Newfoundland. The town itself exists on a shoreline in White Bay. It's a main road that sprawls over a bridge to connect with Englee Island. While the church and most of the stores are located on the main road, the fish plant and about one third of the residences were all built on Englee Island.

Height's Cove is a tall hill on the farthest point of the island covered with a smattering of homes, a cozy little village unto itself, overlooking the sprawling Atlantic; those waters which could give life and take it just as easily. Setting out from the motel, a backpack, a couple of chocolate bars and a camera were all I needed. There was just a slight breeze, but any breeze in the month of June is cold on the Northern Peninsula. I zipped my coat up all the way to my chin and braced myself to become reacquainted with the salt air.

It was a good day for walking. I had spent a comfortable, yet sleepless night. I kept seeing Lance's face. I tried to remember the faces of all the others I had known. Would they recognize me? Would I recognize them? I needed to connect with my roots and nostalgia tore at me from the moment I left the motel. The walk was different from what it had been eighteen years earlier. There was anticipation and uncertainty in every step I took.

Years ago I would have either walked from Heights Cove and the Richards house or my house down in the cove. This time I was almost central. I decided I'd walk to the end of the road and at least look at the Richards house from a distance.

The road no longer passed over the hill that I remembered. Instead it meandered around the steep hill, along the ocean past the now-abandoned sawmill, and straight into town. I walked past the mill, pretended to be taking photos in order to sneak a peek at the house I had loved and now dreaded. I didn't stay long enough for anybody to be suspicious of my intentions, walking to the fish plant instead.

The plant which was bustling with life years earlier looked too big to be lying empty. Except for a few boats and a handful of people, the life had been drained from what had always been the town's main hub of activity.

The wharf was in a state of foundering and I had to pick my way carefully around the building. The door to the boiler room was closed. I stopped and closed my eyes. My uncle had worked there for years. Shovelling coal into a large furnace to provide the electricity made the menial job one of such importance. He had been so proud to demonstrate to me how the controls worked. In my eyes, as a child, he was a skilled worker – a specialist in his field. He too had gone. I stared at the door and tried to pretend he was inside and I was just a child peeking at him as he worked. An old stump at the end of the wharf became a resting place for a moment and I left the nostalgic memories of the boiler room to sit down.

There was something missing. As I sat and took a few deep breaths, I couldn't shake the feeling that there was something important missing from the air. I couldn't quite figure out what it was, but I searched for an answer to the emptiness that churned at me. Children were on their way to school. Unlike the days when I walked like all other students, there were now groups forming at selected areas for the modern convenience of the bus pickup.

I would have loved to go to back to my school days, but I would rather step back to the time when walking to school was normal. *Why do they even need buses in Englee?* I thought as I watched the last of the small children climb the tall steps to board the vehicle waiting for them across the street from the fish plant and my perch. As the gears revved and the big yellow beast belched exhaust it began to climb its way up the main road and out of town.

"Not enough kids..." I muttered to myself as the implications became clear. The town no longer had the population base needed to keep their school open. In its heyday, Englee would have boasted a thousand souls, back when the fishery was bustling and the boats kept the plant running three shifts a day.

Now, with the cod moratorium which blocked Newfoundland fisherman from trawling the cod stocks, the population had once again shrunken to the original size of only five hundred and homes that had sprung up in the days of the fishery now lay empty, boarded up, abandoned as people had left to find a livelihood somewhere else.

I could never tell B.J. what the name Englee meant. I had never known. A brochure in my room at the Park Place Motel had said that Captain James Cook had written it on his map in 1763 as Inglie Harbour. It said that in the late 1600s and early

1700s French fishing crews made annual voyages to the area, arriving in spring and returning home to France in the fall at the end of the fishing voyage. The article went on to say that the French explorer Dupont referred to Englee on his map in 1625 as Port Aigles. Perhaps the eagles had gone the way of the cod. I had never known of any eagles in the area.

When I left Englee eighteen years earlier, the town had every indication of becoming a prosperous community. The resettlement program had caused the population to grow as residents from Canada Bay, Hooping Harbour and other small outports were forced to abandon their homes and resettle in Englee, making it one of the largest and fastest growing towns. What I had returned to was a dying town. As I looked around there was evidence everywhere of despair and hopelessness, as if its life were being snuffed out. The population was shrinking fast as, one by one, they left for a brighter future somewhere else.

The bight, once bustling with motor boats, now lay quiet. Only a couple of battery operated canoes slowly wound their way towards the tickle. I watched as they disappeared beneath the bridge. When they were out of sight I focused on the General Store and what lay beyond. We all knew that the Maritime Archaic Indians had lived in the town as well. Perhaps they were responsible for the name. They had left behind arrowheads, bones, amulets and other artefacts and unlike any of the European visitors, they had left behind a memory that would never be forgotten. I had driven over that area on my arrival. Today I would walk it. I shivered at the thought.

Rising from the stump, I ran a hand over my wig, making sure it was remaining secure in spite of the wind. I looked around the wharf once more before continuing my venture to Locker's Point.

At the bridge I stopped. It was such a small bridge, spanning less than a hundred feet of water, connecting Englee Island to the rest of the town. I looked down at the cove in the distance. I wanted so very much to walk that way, but it would have to wait. I didn't want anybody to see me there. In the distance I could see the house on the hill in the cove. What was once a beautiful cottage was now just another dilapidated house, abandoned like so many others in the area. I didn't want to look too long for fear of being seen. That dilapidated building was the home I had grown up in. I longed to run up the hill, swing open the door and yell just once more, "I'm home." Instead, I focused on crushing the pain and tears that wanted to show me what a vulnerable person was hiding beneath the outer shell. I swallowed back the lump that kept rising in my throat as I stood anchored between the mainland and the island.

As a kid I never ever thought I lived on an island. I remembered the first time I understood that the bridge was our only connection to the mainland. It was the night of the fire.

It's amazing that with all of the buildings built of wood and the crude antiquated way of wood stoves being the only source of heat and kerosene lamps being the sole source of light, that there were few fires, if any.

There was only one fire that I remember, a mystery fire. Then again anything that happened in that area was always a mystery.

I was about ten or twelve when the mystery fire occurred. It was a cold winter night. At first we were safe, just watching the night sky light up in a fiery red display. It was, to us, the most amazing display of fireworks. I also remember someone suddenly knocking on our door and telling me I had to go to the Richards house.

The Richards house was far from the cove, but because my father worked for Mr. Richards I guess I was expected to go there. It was the farthest house from the fire and it looked like the fire was going to "cross the bridge. If the bridge burns we'll be stranded," I had heard. That was the moment I realized I lived on an island in the town. In the midst of the anxiety and excitement I suddenly felt so unimportant. It was as if we were suddenly second-class citizens.

I felt secure arriving at the Richards' house. There were several families of children there, but Lance called me aside and asked his mother's permission to sleep in the living room with me. I remember us lying huddled on the floor together. She brought a blanket and covered us. With our backs to each other we drifted off to sleep. It was probably the first time we slept together.

It's strange how that fire crossed my mind today, but as I remembered it, I also remembered the thoughts that crossed my mind that night, even as a child. What would happen to Lance and to his family now that their general store had burnt down? But within days and for one brief period all unemployed men in town suddenly found employment as Mr. Richards quickly rebuilt. The cause of the fire was never known, but so many strange things happened in that area that nobody even questioned why. Nobody really cared. All that was important was they had back the only place to buy supplies.

I looked towards the fish plant now and tried to forget the fire as I focused on the silence that was so threatening. What was missing suddenly became so obvious. Seagulls! There was an absence of seagulls. Seagulls once had dotted the shoreline like miniature statues. Today there were just rocks. The cry of seagulls had been as natural as fishermen, fish, boats, the lapping of the ocean, of any of the sounds around the plant. The lapping of the ocean was all that remained now, the ocean beating against empty dilapidated wharves.

I turned away from the memories and continued towards the bridge. I looked down but realized there was no gravel to stub my shoes against. Pavement had replaced the gravel. In spite of the road being gravel when I was a child, whoever could afford a bicycle had had one years ago. It had never occurred to us that it was painful to ride on such rugged terrain. We had loved every moment. I had seen cars today, but no bicycles.

Eighteen years ago there were bicycles and dirt roads. Today there were cars and pavement.

To get to my destination, I had no choice but to cross that place where the unnatural lurked. There had been talks about how the French settlers had massacred the Maritime Archaic Indians in the later 1700s. Bones, arrowheads, and amulets had been found both in Fillier's cove and near Heights Cove and throughout the strip of land in between. I looked down wondering if any artefacts were found anymore.

Everybody had known that this was the site of an ancient Indian burial ground. But because it had happened before the town was settled, nobody thought that the spirits would linger into our generation. And still today nobody pays attention to the warning signs to stay away. It's too late now. The town will have to live with the consequences of intruding where it should not.

Didn't anybody ever stop to think what really went on here? Didn't anybody realize that this was all because of what had happened before this town was settled? This town centre had been built directly on the Indian burial ground and the only way from Englee Island to the main town was by the bridge that drove directly through that sacred ground. It was embedded in the town in a place where nobody was ever safe. There were rumours but because nobody had actually lived to see it take place, nobody really believed and placed it all on idle superstitions.

I shivered as I passed the General Store, just the way I had shivered years before. Every time I walked past that building, every time I reached the end of the bridge, I hesitated as my sixth sense told me not to venture beyond.

It was there that evil lurked. It seemed everybody who lived or worked in that area had something happen to them. Mr. Richards didn't believe that the mysterious fire had anything to do with the circulating rumours of a burial ground. He said nothing had ever happened to his family. It had; he just didn't know it.

It was in a house close by that Mr. Jones had committed suicide. Mr. Richards' accountant went insane. Arthur Jenkins, the son of one of the clerks, drowned there. The Talbot family moved out of their house because of 'strange occurrences' in their home.

Several people had died at the batty catters. I shivered at the thought of how close to home they all were and what had caused them to even venture in the dangerous area. I remembered a woman being found frozen to death in that same area after a blinding snowstorm. I thought of the old couple that lived in that last house in Lane's Cove, who were found by a school teacher one morning as he walked past the area; the couple who were seen nightly talking a walk around town. That night they had never made it home, but were found dead just past the bridge, their hands still holding each others.

Jack-o-lanterns were said to float past the pier and disappear as they glided underneath the bridge. Two boys catching Tom Cods on the rocky shore were suddenly swept away on a calm day. I remember Patricia Kempt, a young girl from my class, who fell through the ice while copying—jumping from ice pan to ice pan, tempting fate—in spring. Her body was never found.

In the local paper I had read about Nancy Coish, who came home from university for spring break a year earlier, had walked out of the store, past the men standing just like today in the shadow of the building, and walked down to the batty catters and out into the ocean, quickly to be swept away.

It was the one place I wished to race past. But today I had to stop. I had to ignore the voices that were in my head. I had to ignore their eyes on me. I had to push aside the screams that rose in my throat. It was here that eighteen years ago I saw him kill a man. I had been caught in the evil that had lurked. I should have chosen to hurry past as I had always done. I should not have let the spirits lead me to witness what I had seen.

I stopped before I reached the buildings. Today it wasn't just the place that sent shivers down my spine. It was the memory of what had happened here and of what had been my reason for leaving behind my father and the man I loved.

I was older now. I mustered up the courage; the courage that had been lacking years before. Two men were standing by the store and watched as I stopped. I stared at them before taking the road that went behind the building to the dock. I had to go there. I had to see if it really existed, make sure my memories were right. I stopped on the dock. Nobody was in sight just as there had been nobody the night it happened.

I felt their eyes on me. Just the way I had felt their eyes on me every time I passed this point. Today I heard the whispers, haunting voices on the wind telling me I was not welcome.

I took a deep breath and looked around once more before leaving. Perhaps someday this point will be a memorial to the past and a warning issued to keep the living safe.

Beyond the point, everyone I passed on the road either spoke or nodded. I was happy that the friendliness still existed, along with curiosity.

There were so many changes, though, so many new homes and even churches; far too many churches for the small population. It looked like God had been franchised in the town. There were also many vacant buildings, too many vacant buildings, which were easily distinguished by the boarded windows or the knee-high grass. I stopped and looked up at the hill where the schools stood. My entire pre-university schooling had been in these three buildings which today were boarded up and empty, the grey paint melting into the greyness of the town. I took a deep breath and for a moment a tear threatened to trickle. I glanced at my watch. What was a ten minute walk had become a two-hour stroll and I still wasn't at my destination.

I looked around at the homes I could see and wondered

which one was Lance's. I couldn't imagine which was his. Perhaps he didn't even live in the town. I wondered if he was married and if he had children. With every step I took there were as many questions as there were memories.

Our special place had always been Locker's Point, the direction where I was now headed. I wondered if he ever went there anymore, in fact if anybody did.

The breeze seemed to stop as I went around the park. Except for one woman and a small child, the park was empty. I wanted to run across the field and swing high on the swings once more. The woman stared at me and for a moment I felt a sense of loss. There was only me and I wanted to rush to the swings, to be a child again free of the pangs of loss and loneliness. Instead I chose to walk quietly past. Perhaps one day.

The breeze picked up again when I finally reached the end of the road. I walked to the shoreline and stopped to look at a cat sunning himself on a rock. Without lifting his head he watched my every move across from where he lay. His orange coat shone red in the sunlight and I was quickly taken back many years ago when four lynxes had kept Lance and me prisoners in our high school. I don't know why the cat brought back the memory, but it surfaced as real as it had been many years ago.

The teacher had asked me if I would clean the chalkboards and place the history notes on all the desks. Everyone had gone except Lance who waited with me. When it was time to leave, we were shocked to find four lynxes sitting outside the building as if awaiting our exit.

They probably wouldn't have done any more harm than the cat today would have done, but our imaginations gave them ferocious, dangerous appetites and we were forced to remain alone at the school until the animals gave up on their prey and drifted away.

I smiled as I watched the cat. There had been no danger years ago. It had been only the excitement and imagination of two teenagers and an excuse to be alone again, especially my excuse to be the damsel in distress and of Lance's excuse to be my knight in shining armour.

To get to Locker's Point we always had to climb over wild terrain, follow a path that rambled upwards along the shoreline. Today I was unprepared for what greeted me as I reached the end of the road. Instead of having to climb the sometimes dangerous rocks to reach the point, a paved walkway with a railing meandered along the shoreline and gently upwards.

It reminded me of the place B. J. and I had escaped to on the coast of Maine, a place that had become my home away from home. My escape of eighteen years earlier had been somehow transformed into the escape I had come to call home in Maine. I shook my head to shake away the vision of that coastline and the Marginal Way in Ogunquit. While mine was just a memory, this one was a memory realized. I ran my hand over the bronzed sign that stood at the entrance to the pathway. "Locker's Point."

I breathed a sigh of contentment, followed the pathway, appreciating every step now secure in the paved walkway above the rock formation and as I reached the top I was even more surprised. Englee had changed, at least on Locker's Point.

It was a beautiful modern but narrow paved walkway that ran all along the point and to the far end of the cove. A railing ran across the top of the point where it was most dangerous. There were three anchored wooden park benches on the Point. I ran my hand over the one closest to me. The brass plate on the back of the bench read, "Locker's Point."

What had once been beautiful had become breathtaking. Over the years I had heard of the work projects the towns created. I wondered if all of the work projects had such care and planning that evidently had gone into this one. From the railing I looked down on the cliffs. The nostalgia of my home in Maine tore at me. It was a place where I could reach out and breathe the fresh air away from the city. I had told B. J. how the place had reminded me of my hometown and in his generous way he purchased a house on a cliff overlooking the sea so that I could have my own connection to the island I had left behind. He and I spent weekends there, but even if he couldn't be with me, I made my own retreats. I had to. I had needed my own Locker's Point in order to survive. My heart fluttered anxiously; I had come home.

It was obvious tourism was becoming an ever increasing industry in the province. All along the highway from Deer Lake there were signs. This place had as much to offer or more, yet it was as though its existence was only for the benefit of the inhabitants who were still struggling with their dream. Why hang on to a dream of a bustling fishing community that depended on the fish which would probably never come back the way it had been? Why not build a new dream? The pathway to Locker's Point was one attraction but it needed more. My mind raced suddenly at the thought that maybe I could help. Already the town had a beautiful park to entice tourists.

I turned and walked to the far end of the point. It was always the end of Englee, the final end of the road, the place where Locker's Point ended, the place where we were always denied access. I blinked rapidly, trying to focus on where I was. It was the end of the town. The ocean beat ferociously against the rocks. In summer this was the end. To try to get beyond the point was pushing fate. In winter, the batty catters offered a death defying challenge that few, if any, were willing to take. The spray from the ocean, combined with frigid temperatures created walls of sheer ice rising from the shoreline. It was as if Mother Nature had written 'Do not venture beyond," and nobody did. It lay virgin.

Or so I thought. As I sank into the bench I realized that someone had crossed the line. Someone had gone beyond the batty catters. Across from Locker's Point there was now a property that was obviously inaccessible from the Point. There was no access to be seen. Between the Point and the house stood the killer rocks where ice in the winter forced one to turn around and jagged slippery rocks in the summer taunted even the most adventurous souls. Still stunned, I stared at the killer rocks in disbelief.

I tried to concentrate on the house that had captured my attention and that stood beyond reach. On the manicured ground above the rugged shoreline, a ranch-style fence surrounded the perfect home in the perfect location. It looked as if it belonged to another place, perhaps even another time, but not here.

The shingled country home B. J. and I owned in Maine quickly came to mind as I stared at the house. The two houses were completely different, yet they both had wrap-around porches that looked majestic and secure.

My home in Maine gave me the nostalgia of Locker's Point. This architect had gone beyond the Point and brought the nostalgia home. Through the trees I could see what appeared to be a smaller building and between both was a railing with steps that led down to the wall of rocks – boulders – that defined the property.

If I were to choose any house in any place and any time, it would have been that house, right there and then, facing the Atlantic Ocean. *Wonder if the owner would consider selling...* I mused with a smile, knowing even as the thought formed, that there wasn't a chance in hell. Anyone who owned that house would keep it for life. For generations.

I looked down to where the land had no choice but make a boundary and imagined the ice flows coming in the winter. There could be no other name for the property than Batty Catters. As a child, when I had read stories about the estates in England with their names of Stoneridge Manor, Manfreya, Le Sabot or The Four Winds, I had dreamed of having an estate like the heroines in the stories, but my estate had been right here and it had the name of Batty Catters. My friends had laughed at me. "Better stick to your books, Kenny, because it's the closest you'll ever come to marrying the rich prince and living in your manor. Batty Catters? What kind of a name is that for an estate? If that's the case we all have estates 'cause the batty catters runs from one end of the town to the other. Batty Catters!" I can still hear their laughter.

Perhaps the name is a Newfie word, but it has meaning and in my dreams it was as romantic as Le Sabot or Manfreya. I stared at the property and once again I was dreaming. It was so real, but it wasn't mine. I wondered what name if any the owner had chosen. I knew it never would be Batty Catters. That name was mine and this was my dream. This was my coming home. I had pictured a home, a beautiful cottage house in the country, but this was obviously a tourist escape. I shook my head to shake off the daydreams and the mirage and walked back to stand by the railing once more.

My eyes followed the entrance to the harbour and Barr'd

Island directly across. The ocean beckoned with the gentle lull and its briny air. The air was all I imagined when I inhaled. Eighteen years ago, with Lance's strong arms wrapped around me, we looked out across the ocean and planned our future.

It wasn't the brine that brought tears to my eyes this time. It was the feeling of his arms around me and the comfort and security of years that I had never dreamed of losing.

I shook off the feeling. I had to. One more glance towards the house to see if it would magically disappear. It didn't. My dreams were being played out in front of me; the rugged coast of Maine, my cottage on the ocean. I felt like Fate was playing a joke on me. Lance and I had planned our Batty Catters on Locker's Point. Standing before me was the dream I had had, with no access. I knew it wasn't real. It couldn't possibly be.

Nothing seemed real anymore. The tiny town I had grown up in had changed. Street signs had been erected. I was glad at least that they had retained some recognition of prominent families that had once lived in the area. Dorset Drive meant nothing to anybody. Fillier's Cove, Lane's Cove, Compton's Cove, and Gillard's Place echoed history. Height's Cove had always been Height's Cove. Memorial Drive, which now replaced Barrack's Hill, belonged to some other town, not Englee. To me it was still Barrack's Hill. I just hoped I wouldn't make the mistake of calling it that. I was one of the few who remembered it as such.

Chapter Three

"Look at'cha," Ester tisked as I walked into the dining room of the Park Place Motel. "Windblown and rosy cheeked. You look like you've climbed a mountain, my dear!" She rushed towards me and began fussing to take my coat.

"Feels like I have, too," I said as I allowed her to remove the garment and hang it on the rack beside the door.

"Now, come in and sit yourself down. I'll have a fresh pot o' tea at your table in a tick," she smiled warmly as she led me to the nearest seat. It was nearing lunchtime and the bulk of the tables were full with regulars drinking tea. The fingers of the old men twitched for the need of a cigarette. In the clean air of the room, they chewed stir sticks and tapped the tabletops lightly, longing for the days before the smoking ban.

I watched as Ester came out of the kitchen with a steaming pot of tea. Her blond hair piled high on her head in the shape of a cone didn't dare to move as her ample hips swung back and forth. Her cherry red lips smiled broadly as she set the pot on my table and I found myself, once again, staring at the spectacle that was Mrs. Reg Richards.

"Here you are," she said as she laid out the milk and sugar. "How about a bowl of soup? Chowder today," she said with a flick of her painted acrylic nail towards the menu board.

"Maybe in a bit," I said with a smile as I cupped my hands

around the teapot. "The tea's fine for now."

"Oh," was her only response as she lingered a bit too long and glanced at the empty seat across from me. Subtlety was obviously not Ester's strong suit.

"Would you care to join me, Mrs. Richards?" I said quickly. Ester was seated before the words had fully formed.

"Don't mind if I do, and call me Ester," she said as she smoothed the front of her tight T-shirt.

"Ester, why aren't there any seagulls here? I thought all fishing communities had seagulls." I couldn't tell her how I remembered waking to their cries in the morning or the familiar sight of them hovering around the fish plant. I couldn't tell her about the seagull with the broken wing that my father had found and how Lance and I had taken care of it until it could fly again. When it could fly, it didn't want to leave. Now all of the seagulls seemed to have vanished.

"They do, me dear. But we're not a fishing community anymore now. When I sees those birds comin' I get tempted to pull out Reg's rifle. They're nothing but a nuisance now. T'eres no fish for them, so they gets into all the garbage. Just as brazen as crows. They were good one time. You'd wake up in the mornin' and hear the cries and t'was a welcoming sight." She shook her head. "No, maid, even the seagulls have gone."

Realizing we were going to be there a while, I reached up and unwrapped the scarf from around my neck. As I turned in my seat to hang the pashmina over the back of my chair, I heard Ester exclaim, "Oh," under her breath.

There was no other word than 'panic' for what suddenly hit me. My face might be changed and my hair might have been hidden, but there was one decision I had hastily made years ago that could now unmask me completely. My life seemed to flash before my eyes and that moment which had scared my body forever was as vivid as the day it was created.

"The Wizard's Den is being shut down because of community pressure," someone had commented at school.

"I can't imagine getting rich on that business in this part of the country. Who's going to go there anyway?"

"I did." One of the boys from my class rolled up his sleeve. "See, I got an anchor."

"My parents would kill me if I ever got one." I looked at the boy who spoke. He was stating what we all felt.

"An anchor? Why an anchor? No imagination, Jack?"

Everyone laughed.

"Because I spend all of my time in a boat. That's why."

"Then why not a boat?" Everyone laughed again.

"I understand," I said as I watched his face change from pride to embarrassment. "If I were to get one it would be something symbolic, something that was special to me."

"Girls don't get tattoos. Did you ever hear of a girl with a tattoo?"

"Is there a law against it?" I asked.

"It's just not a girl thing."

"Then maybe I'll get one and create a precedent."

"What's Lance going to say about that?"

"Maybe I'll get one, too," Lance said as he crept up behind me.

"Think daddy's going to let you?"

"Maybe I'll surprise him, too." He turned to me. "Ready?"

It was just hours later when Lance and I entered the tattoo parlour. "Can I help you kids?"

"We've come for tattoos," Lance said.

"Your girlfriend can wait here."

"But she's getting one, too."

There was silence. There's always silence when the unexpected happens. The tattoo parlour had been open for only a few months, but it was obvious from the look on the owner's face that I was his first female customer. "Are you sure? " He quickly added, "Are you old enough?"

"We're eighteen," we lied, surprised when he didn't question us. Then again, I guess he was going out of business so there was no reason to care.

An hour had not even passed when Lance and I emerged from the tattoo parlour. Both of our shoulders had a bandage. The next day at school we showed the shocked class the three stars of Orion tattooed on the back of our shoulders just below the hairline. Both my father and Mr. Richards were angry, but it was too late. We knew in time it would be forgotten, but for a few days we were the talk of the town.

As Ester stared, my hand instinctively covered the stars and I spun back around. "Not too many women around here with tattoos," she said.

I fussed with my wig, wishing it was just a touch longer. "I guess it was a phase at some point. Would you like a cup of this tea?" I tried to change the subject, but it wasn't working.

"Reg has a tattoo. He was with a gang when he was a teenager and they all got tattoos. Certainly not stars. I didn't know him then, but I heard he used to run with a tough crowd. And it seems to me that Lance, Reg's brother, has one, too. On his shoulder..." She stopped and stared at me as if she were searching her memory bank. "I'm pretty sure it's stars." She shook her head. "I can't remember exactly."

"Oh," I said quickly. "His brother?"

"Hmmm? Oh, yes, younger. Younger brother by a few years, Lance. But, let me tell you, there's no love lost there." She arched a tweezed brow for emphasis.

"Really?" I struggled to keep my tone light as I leaned closer to the table. "That's a shame, brothers not getting along. Have they always been like that?"

"Oh, as far as I know. I met Reg, oh, let's see, about seventeen years ago. As you can probably tell from my accent, I'm not from Newfoundland. Born and raised in Nova Scotia," she said, though to my now citified ear, she sounded like any other Newfie to me. Without waiting for a response, she prattled on, "Halifax, to be exact. That's where I met Reg. He was in town for a stint and swept me off my feet. Before I knew it, I was smack dab here in Newfoundland, with a brand new family, and a ring on my finger."

"A whirlwind romance? How lovely," I managed to say while Ester took a rare breath.

"Yes," she responded as she straightened her spine. "Lovely, that's what it was. I was a bit of a shock to his family when I arrived, but they're good enough people. Got status 'round here, that's for sure."

"Really? How so?"

"What Reg's father doesn't own around here, Reg does. Actually, Reg owns the crab plant in Roddickton and fish plants down the coast. He's away most of the time. Got managers, though. Couldn't do it all by himself."

"What about his brother? Couldn't he help?"

"Lance!" She practically laughed. "No, thems two fight like alley cats at midnight. Mr. Richards always helps Reg. Lance, too. That is, if he needed help. Thing is, Lance would never ask either of them for help. Never needed it. He's quite the man. Wait till you meet him. Reg and Lance are as different as night and day. He sure is easy on the eyes."

"Mmm, yes he is," I said as my mind wandered back to the highway the previous night. My eyes refocused on a somewhat stunned Ester. "I mean, yes, he is handsome. I met him, his brother, quite accidently, last night. He was kind enough to give me directions," I fumbled and tried desperately not to blush.

"Well, that was nice of him. I would've hated to have you miss stopping here with us. Are you just here for a vacation, then, Mrs. Toms?" she asked, sensing it was her turn to get some information.

"A bit of business, a bit of fresh air," I said genuinely.

"Business? I like the sound of that in Englee, Mrs. Toms. There's precious little business in these parts these days and folks are wasting away. Just wasting away."

"I noticed there seemed to be new handrails up at the Point on my walk this morning. Was that a government work project?" I asked as I poured another cup of tea and added a dash of milk. Around us, the room maintained its own hum as the regulars conversed amongst themselves. They knew they'd get the dirt on me from Ester later on, so there was no need to eavesdrop. The plump waitress circled the room methodically, refilling glasses and answering questions. I could see Ester keeping an eye on her throughout our conversation. She might not be worldly, but in her world there obviously wasn't a detail she missed.

"Yes," Ester said with a short nod. "Every season the government shows up with a project to keep people's hours up." In order to receive unemployment benefits from the government, workers were required to prove they'd been employed for at least a portion of the year. Once those base hours were fulfilled, the worker could then collect payment for the rest of the year. Since the cod fishing moratorium, collecting hours and unemployment insurance from the government had become a way of life for the bulk of the population. It was the only way they could survive, but it stripped away their pride as a community.

"What about bringing in industry?" I asked cautiously. Seeing the decay of the town was pulling at my heartstrings. "Has anyone tried to bring in more industry, real jobs?"

Ester chuckled. "Who? The town council tries. They try to get businesses here, but being this far from anywhere and with the fish all gone, there's not much they can do..."

The cell phone in my pocket rang, interrupting Ester. I pulled it out and examined the number. "Sorry, Ester, I have to take this..."

"You go right ahead, Mrs. Toms," she said as she stood and pushed the chair back into the table.

"Sean," I said into the phone, trying to keep my voice low so as not to disturb the other patrons. "What's up?"

"Kay, oh good, I'm sorry to interrupt your vacation..."

"I'd hardly call it that," I said lightly as I looked around the dining room. "What's going on?"

"Well, there's a problem at the main factory. It seems that there's been a glitch in the shipping department..." Suddenly, I couldn't hear a word my faithful assistant was saying as the door opened and Reg walked in. Behind him stood his father, Mr. Richards.

Mr. Richards looked older, greyer, mellower somehow: the thick grey hair, the neatly trimmed moustache, the twinkle in blue eyes that had never lost their sparkle. I saw the attractive aging actor that the public craves to see while his leading lady of yesteryear struggles for that comeback that never quite makes it. Mr. Richards was beautiful, even to me who vowed never to forget what a mean character lay beneath the beauty. I had always loved him as a father until he had hurt me in a way I had never thought possible. Just when I needed him he had sent me away.

Staring at him now as I did, I could easily have been persuaded that the beautiful exterior wasn't a cover for anything but kindness and goodness of the man I had once known.

"...and the client is furious. Just furious." Sean's voice said through the cell phone.

"Huh? Sorry, Sean. What do you need me to do?"

"Well, I thought if you could call him and smooth things over a bit, that'd really help. You know how much Mike loves to hear your voice."

Reg and Mr. Richards stood at the counter talking to Ester. Mr. Richards' gaze wandered and landed squarely on me. My hand shook. I looked down at the table and tried to focus on Sean. "Sure, of course, I'll give him a call. Just email me, outlining what happened and our recovery plan. I'll make sure the contract is saved." Mr. Richards touched Reg's arm, whispered something. "Just leave it with me. It's still early in the day in California, I'll be able to get a hold of Mike well before the close of business on his end." Mr. Richards walked tentatively towards me. "Okay, Sean? Thanks for calling and don't worry. I'll sort it out."

As Mr. Richards arrived at my table, I disconnected the call and laid the phone in front of me. I resisted the urge to smooth my wig and looked him squarely in the eye.

"Pardon me," he said as he removed the grey hat from his head. "I don't mean to intrude, but I just had to introduce myself." He looked earnest and eager, which shocked me more than his mere presence.

"Oh, not a problem at all. This is a friendly little town isn't it?" I hoped my voice wasn't shaking as much as my hands folded in my lap were.

"Jack Richards," he said, with slight bow of his head.

"Kay Toms," I said in return.

"Oh, I know. I know exactly who you are, Mrs. Toms." My heart threatened to stop beating. My eyes darted from Mr. Richards to Reg, who still stood at the counter watching our exchange intently. "It's my absolute pleasure to meet you. I was just reading an article in *Fortek* magazine about the expansion you've done with your company. Marvellous. Marvellous." His smile beamed brightly and his eyes lit up.

"Well, thank you, I'm glad you enjoyed the article. I had almost forgotten about the darn thing." I hated publicity, usually avoided it at all costs, but it was sometimes necessary for the good of the business.

"It was wonderful. Very well researched, I thought. And a lovely photo of you, to be sure. The business side of it was very interesting. I'd love to sit down and have a chat with you while you're in town, Mrs. Toms."

"Oh, well, that's very kind, Mr. Richards," I said as I tried desperately to think of a way out of the conversation.

"Tonight!" he exclaimed. I stared at him blankly, unsure of my options. "Yes, tonight. Join us for dinner this evening; 5:30 at the house. It's the last house in town. Can't miss it." He looked so excited, so pleased with the idea. I couldn't think of a polite reason not to accept. Behind him Reg glared at me, as though sizing up his competition. Maybe I would attend; it seemed like the last thing in the world Reg wanted.

"I'll see you there," I said and accepted the handshake Mr. Richards offered. As he walked away I matched Reg's icy stare and gave him a little nod. He nearly jumped, looking agitated as he rattled his keys and stomped to the door. This was going to be an interesting evening.

Chapter Four

A stocky woman in a flowery dress and a white apron answered the door. I immediately thought of my grandmother. It was the white apron I guess. My grandmother always wore a white apron. I stared at her, wondering if she had any idea who I was. Janine hadn't changed much.

"Mr. Richards is expecting me," I said.

"I know who you are. He's waitin' for ya."

I stepped inside. The house had changed over the years. I looked around the vestibule where I stood. Wall to wall mirrored closets replaced the open cut-outs where my coat hung when I was last there. I slipped off the trench coat and passed it to the woman who stood waiting. The last coat I had hung there was a five-dollar raincoat from the local hardware store. There had been no designer name. I didn't know at the time there were such things. Times had changed. I had changed.

"Well, are you comin?"

"Sorry," I apologized. "I was just admiring."

Was it admiration, really? Perhaps it was more surprise, envy, jealousy. Why should I feel any of this for this man? I didn't envy the life he had. Perhaps the feeling was anger. I was angry that he lived a comfortable life and my father's had been one of struggles for survival before being snuffed out too soon for me to help him financially.

I was also angry that he had a family. He still had a wife and two sons. I had nobody. He had taken the man I would have married. He had sent me away. He wasn't responsible for my father's death, but I had lost him also. I knew what Reg had done. I didn't know if Mr. Richards had been involved. I just knew that I was scared and that I was alone.

I followed the housekeeper to the living room. My heart was suddenly pounding. What if he were there? What if Lance recognized me this time? Would he expose my true identity? I trusted him once, but could I trust him again? Perhaps he too had changed. The brief encounter on the highway had revealed little about him.

One person I would never trust was his brother. I remembered him as a pimpled-faced stud, and I mean stud in a way that he was like a prize stallion kept for producing foals. I wonder how many he had produced over the years. He scared me. Lance knew how I felt about his brother but he just didn't know all of it. I wasn't ready to tell him yet.

He was there. The pimples had gone but the scars lingered. I shivered when I saw him. For one brief moment, I was standing behind the general store, watching the knife plunge into the man's body, then he lifted his eyes to me and I felt a fear I had never known before. He was the last person I saw before I left years ago.

Both men rose when I entered.

"Mrs. Toms, welcome. Don't think you met my son today.

This is Reg."

I had no choice but to touch the hand that scared me. I was suddenly taken back years earlier and I saw him look at me, the knife still in his hand; the blood still on the blade. Inside I was shaking.

His light brown eyes searched mine before taking a slow inventory of my body. I could easily imagine he saw me standing in something more scant than the sophisticated, tailored pant suit I wore.

"A pleasure indeed." It was a firm handshake, nothing more.

"Could I get you something to drink, Mrs. Toms?" He was polite.

"Just a Perrier, please." I sat down in the green wing-backed chair by the fireplace and watched Reg pour and deliver a chilled glass. I had spent the past few years in business meetings where there was often millions of dollars on the line, but I had never experienced such a feeling of anxiety. I tried desperately to stop my hand from shaking as I brought the Perrier to my rapidly parching lips. Reg seemed oblivious to my inner angst as he took a seat across from me and sipped his own drink—a double scotch on the rocks, neat.

"Mr. Richards," I said boldly, trying to divert my own attention from Reg. "You look like the man who's holding the entire Northern Peninsula together..."

Mr. Richards chuckled heartily and tipped his glass in my direction. "A keen eye you have there, Mrs. Toms. A keen eye.

To be fair, though, everyone who has stayed in Englee has had a hand in fighting for our collective survival. These are not easy times, but they're not the hardest we've seen either. We'll struggle through."

"Struggle through? Is that all you want to do? Just survive. Just get by? Isn't there a way to turn..." Reg's harsh laughter interrupted me. I turned my head, without lowering my chin, to meet his scowl. "Have I said something funny?"

"A bit, yeah. I always finds it funny when a mainlander shows up on the island thinking they know anything about this place or our way of life. Think you have all the answers, do ya? Gonna swoop in and save us poor unfortunate souls?"

"Reg!" Mr. Richards snapped as he slammed his glass down on the rich mahogany table by his side. "Mrs. Toms is our guest."

Though I held my facial expression solid, inside my blood was beginning to boil with rage. Call me a mainlander, will he? Think I don't know a thing or two about Englee? I wanted to scream. Instead, however, through barely clenched teeth, I managed to say, "I meant no offense. Just trying to get a feel for the town."

"'Cuse me," Janine said as she lumbered into the room. "Dinner's ready."

"We're still waiting for the others to arrive, Janine, can't you see that?" Reg said as the last of his scotch slid down his throat.

Janine straightened her broad shoulders and squared herself

towards the senior Mr. Richards. "Sir, you said dinner at five thirty. That's the time now."

"Yes, yes, of course, Janine. Thank you," Mr. Richards said as he stood. Before offering his hand to me, he threw a stern look at Reg. "Mrs. Toms, please, let's get to the table and see what our irreplaceable housekeeper has prepared for us this evening." Janine's stance softened at the compliment. In one fluid motion she turned on her sensible heel and snatched Reg's empty glass from the table before walking back towards the kitchen.

"Thank you," I said as I took the arm offered by Mr. Richards and began to walk with him to the dining room. I still didn't trust him, not one little bit, but given my current choice of dealing with either him or his son, I'd take the latter. "Is there a Mrs. Richards?" I asked casually, even though I knew there was. She had been like a mother to me and I grew anxious awaiting her arrival in the room.

"She died a few years back," Mr. Richards said flatly, as though it was a practiced response. The shine in his eyes, however, couldn't be hidden. All my life, he had loved his wife truly and deeply.

"I'm so sorry..." I stuttered while trying to swallow the sizable lump in my throat as we entered the dining room. It was definitely not the typical house on the Island. As I entered the formal dining room I forgot for a moment that this was just a coastal village where everyone's livelihood depended on the ocean. The work was seasonal and nobody had money, nobody but Mr. Richards.

The table was set for six people. I stood and waited. Mr. Richards rushed to pull out a chair and seat me. He was at one end. Reg was at the other. I was to the right of Mr. Richards. The other three seats were empty.

"I must apologize for our absent guests," said Mr. Richards. "Reg's wife is coming in from the motel. She should be here in a minute, along with Bob Pearson, Reg's manager."

He broke off as laughter erupted in the hallway and two of the missing guests appeared.

Both men stood. I was impressed.

"Come on in, Ester, Bob," said Mr. Richards. "Ester, you know Mrs. Kay Toms. This here is Reg's missus."

"I do know Mrs. Toms indeed. Best guest we've had in years," Ester said warmly with a deep wink in my direction.

"Why, thank you," I answered. I was glad she didn't mention the tattoo.

"And this here is Bob Pearson. Bob runs the crab factory for Reg."

"Nice to meet you, Mr. Pearson." We shook hands.

"Call me Bob, Mrs. Toms."

I smiled as we all sat down and Ester's natural chatter began to carry the conversation. At the far end of the table, Reg seemed to barely listen to his wife as she prattled on about her most recent visit to her mother, the weather, and then the crab plant. Finally, at the mention of business, Reg seemed to become interested. I wondered if he even liked his spouse. They were as different as night and day. Nobody paid any attention to the empty seat. I was left to wonder who the sixth guest was supposed to have been.

Contrary to Janine's coarse manner, the table was set in impeccable style. I wondered if she'd had any formal training over the years, or if like so many others, she just pulled out an etiquette kit and arranged her table accordingly.

We had just finished the carrot soup and were being served smoked salmon when a very excited Labrador retriever came bouncing in and happily ran from one chair to the other, sniffing each knee he could find.

"Get that dog outta here, Janine," Mr. Richards called.

The housekeeper came rushing in. "I'm sorry, sir." She reached out to grab the collar, but the tall man in the leather jacket grabbed him first. "Come on, Butch." He gave him a tap on his behind. "Out!"

The dog left, still wagging his tail and the man limped towards the table.

My heart fluttered. *Please don't give me away. Please don't give me away,* I prayed, hoping my telepathy could be detected by him.

"Wondered what was keeping you," said Mr. Richards.

"Mrs. Toms, this is my other boy, Lance. Corporal Lance Richards."

He stood beside the empty seat across from me and stared.

I extended my hand. "Corporal." I stared at him. "Corporal," I repeated.

"Well, it's either that or doctor," his father said with a grin.

He shot a glance at his father. "I'm neither, Dad."

"Sure you are, son," Mr. Richards said with immense pride.

"Corporal," I said in a whisper.

He took my hand and held it. He didn't speak. We just stood, he holding my hand and staring into my eyes. I was seeing the man I once knew, but he was still trying to find me behind the disguise.

Everyone was silent. Mr. Richards froze with his mouth open and the fork just inches away.

Reg's knife hung in midair above his plate of salmon. Ester had reached out for her glass and her hand had remained there. I could see it without my eyes ever leaving his. They waited. I waited.

"Is that Ms. Toms or Mrs. Toms?" he asked. I stared at him, my heart pounding. He finally released my hand.

I sat back and everyone breathed again. "There isn't a Mr. Toms anymore. My husband died a few years ago." I continued to look at him.

"I'm so sorry, my dear lady," Mr. Richards said softly as he patted my left hand. I looked to him and saw the meaning in his eyes—the shared comfort of those left behind. Suddenly, an impish grin appeared on his lips and I could have sworn his eye twinkled. "You know, there's no Mrs. Richards in Lance's life, either. Isn't that right, son?"

All eyes turned to Lance. He grunted lightly and picked up his fork, avoiding his father's clumsy attempts at matchmaking. Reg rose abruptly from the table and stomped to the sideboard to pour another scotch. As the cubes clinked in his glass, he turned and stared at his brother.

I knew Mr. Richards was just being playful, but I could also sense anger in Lance's eyes. I felt the same way. I was angry that while the rich Kay Toms was okay for his son, the woman underneath wasn't.

"I read that article in last month's *Fortek*. Did you read that, Lance?" Mr. Richards continued eating. I couldn't tell if he was oblivious to the tensions he had created in the room or was simply just used to the apparent animosity between his sons. "Remarkable what this little lady has done with her company—expanding all over the world, manufacturing entire lines of clothing, gifts, even food products, isn't that right?"

"Yes, we've definitely seen the company grow. My late husband started decades ago with importing cloth for North American clothing companies. By the time he passed away, we had our own research and development department working on a myriad of different levels within the clothing industry. I've always had a bit of an eye for design, so I began looking to the home decor industry and developed a whole line of items, everything from bedding and linens to candles and curtains." I looked down the table, all eyes on me. "The food side has been our latest development, but I don't want to bore all of you." I finished with a slight nervous chuckle, hoping the topic of conversation would change.

Lance kept his head down, but his eyes looked up across the table at me. "You've got quite an empire, Mrs. Toms." I could have sworn there was a glimmer of recognition in his glance; as though he could see traces of the real me under the wig and plastic surgery.

"Some people think so. What about you, Mr. Richards?"

"Lance, Mrs. Toms," said his father. "Call him Lance."

"What about you, Lance?" I asked again. "Are you a partner in the Richards businesses also?"

Everybody chuckled.

"I've obviously asked the wrong question," I said, feeling my face blush.

Ester jumped in, "Lance here won't have any part of the Richards' operations. Does his own thing, so he does."

"And what would that be?" I asked.

"He's our shrimp farmer," said Reg with the faintest mocking tone in his voice.

"Shrimp farmer?" I looked at Lance. He lifted his head and looked at me. "What about the corporal or doctor?"

For a moment there was silence. I don't know what I thought. I tried to picture a fisherman, but Lance didn't fit the picture of a fisherman and I couldn't understand what part any of the titles played.

"Actually, Mrs. Toms, he goes by the title of doctor, these days…"

I felt my eyebrows shoot up. "Interesting."

"He's referring to those little letters you get after you spend years studying," Lance said.

"Ah, a PhD," I said. "Doctor of what?"

"Went to university and went all the way. No stopping him." His dad chewed, then put down his fork. I could see his love for Lance as he spoke.

"Dad!" Lance dropped his head.

"Well, I've got to tell Mrs. Kay Toms about you, son. It's my fatherly right to brag a bit, especially to a guest of such high calibre." He turned to me. "That boy had determination."

"And now you're a shrimp farmer?"

"Can we focus on something other than me?" Lance said with annoyance.

"But this is interesting. Tell me more, Mr. Richards, unless you want to, Lance."

His eyes met mine and for a moment I could see amusement. "Dad's doing a fine job."

"Ever have L.B.C. Shrimp, Mrs. Toms? I'm sure they must have L.B.C. Shrimp on the mainland," Mr. Richards asked in a drawl as he looked at me with twinkling eyes and he continued eating.

"Why, yes, of course they do." I looked from Lance's face to Reg's face to their father then back to Lance. I didn't quite understand.

"He owns a fish farm," said Reg, becoming annoyed with the conversation.

"Oh, so you're both in the same business?" I asked, knowing perfectly well they were not. If Reg was going to treat me like a stupid Mainlander, I might as well give him some ammunition.

"No, not the same business at all," he said through clenched teeth. "You see, while I work the sea hard for my living, Lance here just sits back and waits for his shrimp to copulate."

"Work the sea?" Lance scoffed. Bob Pearson barely suppressed a smile as he stared intently at his plate. "When was the last time you set foot on a boat, my son? Or broke a bloody sweat for that matter?"

"Now, boys," Mr. Richards said sternly. "That's enough. We've a guest, the least you can do is behave well."

"Sorry, Dad," they each said automatically.

I ignored the behaviour. "A shrimp farm here? I thought farming for shrimp was only possible in warm climates." I stared at Lance but it was Mr. Richards who answered.

"Never thought I'd see this in my lifetime. Global warming's turned the world upside down. In this case it's a good thing. Yes, Mrs. Toms, A shrimp farm, right here on the Northern Peninsula."

"How? Why shrimp?"

"Lance teamed up with a Japanese guy he met," Mr. Richards continued. "Seems both of them had always been interested in marine biology. This guy already had a degree in the field and was working with his dad. They owned shrimp farms all over the globe and they asked Lance to join them. First one he was involved in was in Florida," said his father, ignoring the question. "I went to see the operation. Really impressive. Actually they had manmade ponds and greenhouses miles away from the ocean. The whole setup really impressed me. You don't really need ocean water. Computers do everything these days. They keep the salinity monitored. Also the water is re-circulated by waste treatment systems so there is no environmental runoff. The water treatment takes out the waste so you get more shrimp per square meter. It runs all year round. The guy's family had a string of shrimp farms. They started in Florida. Got six in the States."

"So you work in the States?"

"Not anymore, Mrs. Toms. He sold his shares in the farm."

"Mrs. Toms is not interested in this, Dad. Do you mind?" Lance's nostrils flared.

For a moment there was silence, then Ester looked at me and grinned. "Oh, Mr. Richards go ahead and tell her. I'm sure he's read all about her in the magazines, so she may as well know about him too. Right, Mrs. Toms?"

"I am interested. Yes." I tried to hold back the grin that pushed to takeover her face.

"Good," Mr. Richards continued. "He came back and took over the marine research centre in Roddickton. That place is so impressive. Just as impressive as the shrimp farm operation. He's got everything he ever wanted." Mr. Richards' eyes lit up as he spoke about Lance. I knew he was proud of his son's accomplishments. I just didn't know how Lance felt about his dad. Reg kept his eyes on his plate and continued to shovel food into his mouth, his shoulders hunched around his ears.

"Lance has always been passionate about what he does," his father said.

"I'm glad." I smiled at him.

Everybody exchanged glances. They were happy that I was interested in Lance. They didn't know that I really was pleased the same Lance existed. "You always wanted to be a marine biologist."

Everyone looked at me and I realized I had made a statement so I quickly rephrased it. "I mean, it's obvious from the work you do."

"Oh, yes," Mr. Richards said, "ever since he and Ken..." Lance's fork hit his plate loudly. I looked across the table to see a flash in his dark eyes. At the other end, Reg seemed to smirk. "Since he was just a boy," their father finished lamely.

"What about you, Mrs. Toms?" Ester asked, trying to divert the conversation. "Have you always wanted to be an executive?"

"Oh, no, not really. Circumstances beyond my control changed my life forever."

"Were you always rich?" Ester asked, then, catching the scolding look in her husband's eye, began retreating." I'm sorry, perhaps that's the wrong thing to ask."

I smiled at her. "No, Ester. All I had was a dream and determination, and oh yes, I had faith," I added. "I had help along the way though. I had someone who believed in me."

I looked at Lance and his eyes were on me. The room was silent for a moment. A door slammed and a young girl's voice called out. "Butch! Come here, boy."

"It's Asia!" A glow crossed Mr. Richards' face. "It's my granddaughter, Mrs. Toms. It's my granddaughter."

"Asia! What a beautiful name." My heartbeat quickened and I glanced at Lance.

"And she's a beautiful girl," Mr. Richards said. It was obvious he adored her.

I looked to the door as the young girl walked in. She was tall, slim and wearing trendy wide-legged jeans, a midriff red top and a baseball cap. "Hi, Grandpa!" She obviously adored him also. She walked to the table and kissed his cheek.

"You too, Dad," she said as she went to kiss Reg.

She nodded in Ester's direction. "Hi, Ester. How are things at the motel?"

"Good," she replied. "You gonna' help in the restaurant again soon? That place is packed when you're working there."

"Sure thing, Ester."

I guess I raised my eyebrows.

"It's Reg's daughter," Ester said in a somewhat hushed tone, as though conveying a great secret.

I smiled. I could see the pride in their eyes as they looked at her. I remembered my dad having the same pride whenever I was introduced to anyone. I watched her as she walked to Lance. She put her arms around his neck and his arm went around her waist as she stood by him. "I got accepted, Uncle Lance. Thank you so much." She bent and kissed his cheek.

"Accepted?" asked Mr. Richards. "Accepted for what?" He looked to Reg.

Reg raised his eyebrows and shrugged.

"What have you and your uncle been up to now, Asia? Lance?" asked Mr. Richards.

She looked at him and twitched her nose. "I'm going to spend a month at the Acadia Institute of Oceanography in Maine. Uncle Lance took me there last year, remember? He knows some of the people on staff there." Her face was filled with love as she and her uncle exchanged glances.

"Well, good for you girl," Mr. Richards said. He turned to me. "She loves her uncle's work. It looks like she's following in his footsteps. Just don't join the army, girl."

"Joined at the hip, these two," said Ester as she wiped the corners of her mouth.

"Yeah," Reg said as he swallowed the last of his latest drink. "A real pair." Lance seemed to almost wince. "Why is it, my child, that I've not heard anything about this before?"

"Dad, I didn't know if I would even get in," Asia said sweetly. It was obvious she had some experience in dealing with her father's moods. "I didn't think it was worth mentioning, it was such a long shot."

"But your uncle made it happen, did he? Always there, aren't you, Uncle Lance?"

Asia released her arm from around Lance's shoulder and walked to her father's side. "Please, Daddy, I just have to go to the Centre. It's an opportunity of a lifetime," she pouted, donning her best puppy dog eyes. Lance seemed to hold his breath, and his tongue, while Reg stood and poured another drink, leaving his daughter's question hanging in the air.

"Excuse our manners here, Mrs. Toms," Mr. Richards said as he waved Asia over to our side of the table. "This here is my granddaughter, Asia. Asia meet Mrs. Kay Toms."

"The lady from the magazine?" she asked as she took my hand and looked at me with her big hazel eyes. "I know that name because Grandpa read me an article about you."

"Mind your manners, young girl. Pull off that cap, Asia," said her grandfather.

"Sorry," she said as her hand went up and she removed the cap. She shook out her hair and my heart nearly stopped.

I could feel every bit of blood draining from my face. I was grateful I was sitting at that moment. I could hear blood rushing in my head and I fought to keep from fainting.

"How do you do, Mrs. Toms? It's so nice to meet you." I continued to hold her small, warm hand in mine. I smiled at the tall girl with the long red curly hair and I knew I was looking at myself eighteen years earlier.

Chapter Five

I couldn't speak. I looked across at Lance whose face was chiselled stone, his eyes glued to the table in front of him. Reg, back in his own chair, watched my interaction with Asia intently. Finally, after what must have been an awkward moment for the entire party, Ester chimed in and broke my focus. "Gorgeous, isn't it?" she said to me.

"Sorry?" I said, dropping the girl's hand as though it had caught fire. I turned to look at Ester.

"Her hair," she said with a gentle smile. "I've been trying to get her to let me style it for years," her hand went up to smooth the glossy bouffant crowning her own head. "She won't hear of it though. Just shoos me away every time, always has."

"What can I say?" Asia said with a flourish. "I've always liked the natural look." She ran a hand through her unruly curls and threw them over her shoulder. She smiled warmly at her step-mother, "The polished look is great on you, Ester, but it's just not me." Ester's face blushed slightly under her makeup as she waved a pleased hand in Asia's direction. The girl obviously knew how to handle Ester.

Eying her father, she made her way back to his end of the table as he finished the last of his supper and pushed his chair back roughly. "Now, about this program," Asia said as she reached his side.

"Asia, now's not the time," Reg responded firmly. "We'll talk about it when we get home."

"Oh, come on, Reg," Lance blurted. "You can see how much it means to the girl. Just let her go."

"I'm her father, Lance. I have a right to investigate this place, make sure it's safe, and decide for myself what my daughter does and where she goes."

Lance twisted the napkin in his lap fiercely and his face began to turn a bright shade of red. "You miserly little…"

"Little what, Lance? Little what?" Reg leaned forward. He eyed his brother dangerously, his tongue wetting his thin lips as though he was enjoying watching his frustration. Lance said nothing, fuming. "That's what I thought, nothing to say."

"Daddy, please," Asia begged.

"We'll talk about it when we get home." With his final word, he stood abruptly. "Ester, let's go. Asia, get your coat."

"Now, Reg," Mr. Richards pleaded. "There's no need to run off. Stay, have some dessert…"

"No, thanks, Dad. We had a lovely time." He threw a glare at Lance and took Asia's arm. Lance cringed and shook his head.

"Don't be an ass."

"I'm not. It's just time to go. It seems my daughter and I have a lot to discuss this evening." I wanted to throw myself across the doorway, barricade Asia from leaving. My head spun. I couldn't think of what to say or do next. She was leaving. I watched as her lithe form walked out of the room, waving to her uncle and grandfather behind her.

Lance slumped in his chair, looking defeated. Mr. Richards sat beside him, his unfinished dinner still on the table and his jaw slack.

"Thank you, Mr. Richards, for a delicious supper," Bob Pearson, who'd been silent the entire time, said quietly. "I'll be on my way now."

"Sorry, Bob," Mr. Richards said, coming back to his senses. "Family drama…"

"Oh, no need to explain Reg's behaviour to me, sir," Bob said in his thick Newfoundland accent. "See him every day, I do. I knows his moods." He smiled kindly at the old man. "Lance, always good to see ya, b'y. Always good." He shook Lance's hand across the table. "And Mrs. Toms, a pleasure, it was. Not often I gets the chance to share a table with such a lovely lady as yourself." I looked at Bob's round face and nodded my appreciation.

"Thank you, Bob, the pleasure was all mine," I said. "Maybe we'll get a chance to talk a little business the next time we meet. I'd love to hear about the crab plant."

"Anytime," he said and made his exit. The room stood quiet.

"Well," I began to say.

"I'm sorry, Mrs. Toms, for things to have ended so abruptly," Mr. Richards said. He looked as though the weight of the world was upon his shoulders. "My sons just don't see eye to eye at times and Reg has a bit of a temper."

"That's an understatement," Lance muttered.

"Now, don't you start, Lance! I'm embarrassed enough by your brother this evening. Such a short fuse…" his voice trailed off as though he didn't know what else to say. I was a little lost for words myself.

"Please don't be embarrassed. It was actually nice, in a way, to be with a real family for the evening," I said sheepishly. "Not all of us have the privilege of family squabbles."

He reached over and patted my hand gently. Emotion flooded me as I remembered his fatherly attention in my youth. So caring, so kind, so involved. Yet, he had been the one to send me away in the end. I couldn't reconcile the hurt, gentle soul sitting by my side and the man who had recklessly changed the course of my life and taken my daughter from me. Taken Lance's child from me.

The walls were closing in on me and I didn't want to be there any longer. I didn't want to be in the town at all. Coming face to face with my child had never entered my mind when I had set out on what was meant to bring closure to my past. Instead of closure I had reopened painful memories that now made closure impossible.

"I should go," I said finally as I fought to control my emotions.

"Lance will drive you," Mr. Richards offered as we all stood. "Won't you, son?"

"No, that's…"

"Nonsense, Mrs. Toms, he doesn't mind," he looked sharply at Lance.

"No, not at all," he confirmed, knowing his father was desperate to save face. "Let's get your coat."

"Thank you for dinner, it was, well, interesting," I said with a smile, which Mr. Richards returned. "I'll see you again soon."

Chapter Six

"Come on, Butch," called Lance. The dog followed us to the Jeep and jumped in the back seat, his tongue lolling with the excitement of a ride to somewhere.

I climbed into the passenger seat and watched Lance make his way around the hood and to the driver's side. He paused before lifting the handle and there was a blessed moment of silence, for both of us. I drew in a deep breath and tried to stop my mind from swirling. Once more, I wondered about his limp.

"Straight to your motel?" Lance asked as he started the engine.

I looked out the window to the dying light of the day and sighed.

"You know," he said, "it's still pretty early and the sun's just setting. Should we drive to the waterfront and watch it?"

I turned my head and stared at him for a moment. His features were different, yet exactly the same; this man before me had the ability to take my breath away just as swiftly and completely as the boy of his youth had. "That would be great," I said finally. "Let's go taste the brine."

"Taste the brine?" his dark eyebrow arched high upon his forehead. "Talking like that already and you've only been here a day. By the end of the week, you'll sound like Bob Pearson!"

"Oh," I laughed at the thought, "I don't think you have to worry about that. A brogue like his is something you're born with, I'm sure."

As he pulled out of the driveway, I watched the town disappear and realized we were headed towards Locker's Point. I settled in my seat and leaned my head back. Before reaching the point he turned off on a gravel road which was barely visible from the main road. I hadn't noticed it on my previous walk to the point. As the Jeep swayed on the bumpy road, my eyes closed for just a minute.

"Here we are," Lance announced as he parked. "Did we wear you out that much?" he snickered as he climbed out and opened the door wide for Butch to escape.

"Where are..." I started to ask, then looked around. We were parked in front of the house on the other side of Locker's Point. We were at Batty Catters. "But, wait, is this your house?" I asked, astonished.

"Yep," he said as I climbed out and joined him to take in the view. "Built this a few years ago. Took some doing to get around the Catters," he looked at the stunned expression on my face and decided I had no idea what he was talking about. "Catters, batty catters. See, in the winter, the spray from the ocean builds up right along here," my eyes followed the point of his finger, "and does a heck of a job building a natural barrier. It's really something to see. It may not mean anything to you, but I've named it Batty Catters."

"Batty Catters. I like the name." I shrugged, pretending it meant nothing and started to walk to the water's edge. "It's so beautiful, with the sun setting over the sea. Gorgeous, really, you couldn't have picked a better spot."

"Thanks, it was a dream I just couldn't let go." He reached down and picked up a flat stone to fiddle with. "I'm sorry about all that with Reg." The stone flew from his hand into the water.

"Oh, no need to apologize. Family happens, I get that. Although, I must say, the dynamics in yours are a bit more puzzling than the average household."

"Yeah, Reg and I don't really see eye to eye, especially when it comes to Asia." He picked up two stones this time and handed one to me. "I sometimes think he's trying to rein her in, quash her spirit. I just get so mad. I want her to have everything in life, do it all, see it all. Does that make sense?"

"Yes, it makes perfect sense," I said as my stone flew into the horizon. "She's a lot like you." I wondered how much he'd tell me.

"No," he said as he wiped his hands on his jeans. "She's exactly like her mother."

My heart pounded. I didn't think I'd be able to take one more breath.

"Her mother?" I managed to say. "You mean…"

"Her biological mother, not Ester, obviously. Her mom was one of a kind."

"One of a kind."

"Just like Asia. Reg sees that. I think that's what he sees when he tries to hold her back. It's as though he knows Asia will leave one day, once she's all grown up, and he's fighting against the tide. He also knows it gets under my skin." Lance grimaced deeply. "Sorry, you don't need to know all this."

"No, no, it's fine. Your family interests me. But, why would Reg hold his daughter back just to get at you?"

"I learnt long ago not to delve too deeply into Reg's motivations, Mrs. Toms. My mind simply doesn't work the way his does."

"Huh," I muttered as I walked back up to the lawn. So, Reg was comfortable using Asia as a weapon against his brother. And Asia obviously had no idea about her true parentage. Never in my wildest dreams did I think this would be the outcome of my actions so many years ago. This wasn't supposed to happen. Reg wasn't supposed to be in my daughter's life; especially not playing the role of her father while Lance stood helplessly on the sidelines.

"Cup of tea?" Lance offered as he caught up with me. "Might as well warm you before I take you home."

I arched a brow and smirked. "Warm me up, huh?"

Lance's perfectly chiselled cheeks bloomed with the merest of blushes as he looked to the ground. "Well, you know what I meant..."

"Yes," I said, trying to settle his nerves. "Yes, I do and I'd love a cup of tea, thank you. It has been quite a night."

I stopped in the grand foyer of his house, my mouth slightly agape. It was stunning. From the gorgeous hardwood floors to the astounding vaulted ceiling, every detail was perfect. The bank of cathedral style windows across the immaculately furnished living room brought the view of the ocean indoors, as though you could reach out and touch the water.

As Lance disappeared into the kitchen, I wandered through, touching the rich fabrics and textiles and peering at pictures of Asia on the mantel. Standing on the beach with her head thrown back in laughter, she was the most miraculous thing I had ever seen. My hand smoothed over my wig as I looked at her flowing locks, knowing full well that they were identical to mine.

"So, Mrs. Toms, how are you enjoying your stay in our fair town?" Lance asked as we settled into the couch with our steaming cups.

"It's been interesting," I said with a smile. "I'm surprised at the lack of industry, to be honest. It seems like there's something missing here, you know?"

"Yeah, I know. Ever since I came back, I've tried to wrap my head around what's gone wrong. The problems are so systemic."

"Came back?"

"Um, yeah," he said as the corners of his mouth curled. "Sorry, I guess I'm not used to talking to new people. I've known everyone in this town, and the surrounding towns, my whole life. They know my whole story by heart."

"I like a good story," I said, hoping to gain a better insight into his life and Asia's.

"Well, like any good story, it starts with a girl," he seemed to settle further into the couch. I held my breath. "There was a girl I thought I was going to marry. We were young and in love, desperate for each other."

"What happened?" I asked cautiously.

"She ran off," he answered, looking me straight in the eye. "Just up and left one day. I didn't cope very well. Not well at all. Though I had planned on going to university that fall, I just had no more interest and didn't quite know what to do with myself. So, I joined the Army. I left here that August. I didn't give a damn about marine biology or anything else. I would have stayed there but I guess that wasn't meant to be either." He rubbed his right thigh absently. "It was five years before I came home for the first time. When I arrived back, everything had changed in the family. Reg had Asia and Ester—I was suddenly an Uncle." His voice trailed off as his gaze wandered.

"That must have been strange," I offered.

"Oh, you don't know the half of it," he said with a sad chuckle. "I wasn't home for very long before I realized that I needed to do something more with my life. That's when I started university, and began my career."

"Yet, you chose to come back here, again?"

"No matter how much Reg annoys me and the family dramas

get on my nerves, Englee will always be home."

"Hmmm, that's lovely," I said. "But, honestly, can this town survive? The jobs are fewer and fewer each year, from what I hear, and the people are just hanging on."

"That was my other reason for coming back again. I wanted to build something here, bring a bit of stability to the area with jobs. When I took over the Research Centre, I knew I could employ quite a few people, but it's not enough. Without the fish plant right here in Englee, there's just not enough to go around."

"Who owns the plant now?"

"Reg," he scoffed. "Of course, it's Reg. He has spent his entire adulthood acquiring any business my father didn't already own. He owns the crab plant in Roddickton, the three fish plants on the western side of the island, as well as grocery stores and gas stations. He's partners in the cable company and owns the bus line that operates from Englee."

"Wow, impressive," I said in all honesty. "But, I don't get it. If he owns the fish plant here, why isn't it in operation? Are the others that he owns on the island up and running?"

"It's all political."

"I don't understand the reasoning. He gives the work to other towns. Why let them prosper and his hometown suffer?"

Lance shook his head, his emotions showing. "Reg can be as vindictive as he is greedy. He has tried to create a monopoly up and down the coast."

"Why not here?" I asked.

"It started here, or tried to. My father had sold the plant to an outside buyer just before the cod moratorium started. He got a great price for it. Reg was upset about that, but settled down once my father gave in and financially backed him, to help him get started. He got the motel. It just wasn't important enough for him. He could see a market opening up for crab and shrimp, so he bought back the old plant. Paid next to nothing for it. He offered to reopen the plant, buy the crab and shrimp, but at a lower cost. The fishermen were upset and said they'd take it down the coast. They did."

"And?"

"Reg had already bought the plant where they took it. He bought one after the other. Finally he owned all three plants down the coast. The fishermen had no choice but to accept the price he offered. He stripped all he could from the plant here to use in the others and he let this one die.

"My father offered to do something. He tried to get a permit, but he was turned down. Everyone here complained— the frustrated citizens watched their jobs pass them by for jobs down the coast. Reg finally came out and offered the plant as a holding station. The fish can be brought to Englee, then trucked to his plants for processing. He still has the ice making equipment running there. That's about all the old plant does have. He says he can't get a license from the province to start operating the Englee plant again, so he had no option."

"And can he get a license?"

"He doesn't want one. If he got a license for Englee, then the other plants production would drop because the license they offer here is not specialized. It's general. If you look into the three towns involved, you'll see Boardwalk Industries owns the grocery stores, the hardware stores, and at least one gas station in each town."

"Boardwalk Industries?"

"You know, Monopoly, the game? Reg never won when we were kids. I guess he figured whoever got Boardwalk was the winner."

"Is that why the motel is called Park Place?"

"It is and every property he owns has a name from the game."

"Did you ever try to do anything?"

Lance stared at me. "I did what I thought was best for the area. I got the research station going. Eventually though, because of the experience I had already, I spent more time on shrimp farming and less on research. I'm still a part of the team but I got heavily involved in the shrimp farming and started my own business. It was one of the first in the province. Both the research centre and the farm employ lots of people." He took a deep breath. "Then again, Reg employs a lot of people. Difference is he wants to control, to own things. The towns where he has plants do okay. He keeps them employed and their money goes back to his holdings. After all, they have to buy groceries and they need gas and transportation.

"So, you see, Reg has the monopoly. It's like owning the property whether or not you put hotels on them. You still own it. Everybody pays you at some point, some more than others."

We both sat staring at each other for a moment, with the implications of Reg's empire hanging in the air. A shiver ran up my spine. Lance laughed, "I'm sorry, I've made my brother sound like the devil incarnate, haven't I? He's not all bad—I'm convinced that under all his hatred and greed, there's a kernel of goodness somewhere. There has to be."

"Maybe," I said absently as my mind drifted back to Asia. "Maybe there is, but in my experience, cold hearted businessmen like him are usually cold to the core."

"Well," Lance said as he stood up and stretched his injured leg, "if I knew how to fix him I would."

"Hmmm," I said as I walked behind him to the door. I turned my back and held out an arm as he helped me with my coat. His hands lingered on my shoulders once the garment was in place. I felt myself leaning backward, tempted to curl into his broad chest. He inhaled deeply and I could have sworn the world had disappeared. His hands rubbed my shoulders lightly as he tried to snap himself out of it and I felt his thumb on the back of my neck. My wig! I jumped forward, almost tripping over the dog and leaving Lance standing there a bit stunned. I couldn't risk him noticing that I wore a wig.

"Sorry, I, I..." he stammered as he grabbed the keys to his

Jeep.

"No, that's fine, fine," I said, trying to ease the awkward tension that had suddenly filled the room.

"I'll drive you back to the motel, Mrs. Toms."

"Kay. Please, Lance, call me Kay," I said with a light touch to his arm. All I really wanted, though, was to hear him say my real name, just once more. Kennedy. Kenny, in his deep tenor voice.

"Kay," he said as he opened the door.

Chapter Seven

I woke the next morning with a vision of Reg's self-satisfied smirk still dancing in my head. As I rose from the motel room bed, showered, and dressed, it stayed with me. Should I just leave? I wondered as I walked into the restaurant looking to ease the tight knot in my stomach with a meal. Should I get in the car and drive out of town, never to look back? I was trapped. Trapped by my disguise, trapped by the choices I had made and trapped by the power Reg now, unwittingly, held in my life by his parentage of my daughter.

"G'morning," Ester said brightly as I took a seat at a table near the window. "Coffee?" She waggled the nearly full pot in her hand and smiled.

"Yes, please," I said, flipping the cup in front of me over to accept the steaming beverage.

"Here you go, nice and fresh," she smiled eagerly as I looked at her. "Now, about that business last night..."

"No, really, Ester, it's fine. It's family." I waved my hand, dismissing any attempts she might make at excusing her husband's behaviour.

"It is indeed. And when it's the Richards family, it's always heated. Sometimes I just don't know what to say." I felt sorry for her; she had obviously been thrown into the Richards' lives without knowing what she was getting into. From what I had seen of her so far, she was just managing to make the best of the situation.

"Now, you sit right here and enjoy your java for a minute and Asia will be right over to take your order."

My eyes darted around the room, looking for the girl. I hadn't noticed her when I walked in. My pulse raced as the kitchen door swung open and Asia stepped out carrying a full tray of plates. She spotted me and smiled, then went efficiently about the business of delivering her orders.

"Mrs. Toms, good morning," she beamed as she approached my table. "How are you?" She had Lance's eyes. I hadn't noticed the night before, in the swirl of activity and emotions. Her father's eyes.

"Good, Asia, I'm good," I sputtered.

"What can I get you?"

"Eggs, two of them please, and some whole wheat toast, and fruit," I said, utterly unable to look away from her face.

"Fruit? Well, we should have an orange in the kitchen somewhere," she giggled. "We don't get asked for fruit around here very often."

"Oh, right," I said sheepishly. I had forgotten that fruit was always in limited supply on the Northern Pennisula where they tended to stick to a more traditional diet of meat and potatoes, forsaking the other food groups.

Within ten minutes, Asia delivered my plate of fresh eggs, thick cut toast lathered in butter, and a neat pile of tinned orange slices. I ate slowly, watching the other patrons as they finished their meals and made their way out the door to continue with their days. Eventually, the morning rush ebbed, and Asia made her way over once again, still carrying a coffeepot.

"Do you have a minute to sit?" I asked boldly. I knew I shouldn't. I knew I should leave well enough alone, but I couldn't.

"Sure," she said as she flipped a cup over for herself and topped mine up. "Ester won't mind." Across the room, Ester looked to her stepdaughter and winked deeply.

"Do you work here often?" I asked.

"Once or twice a week," she explained. "Dad says it's good for me to work, earn my own spending money."

"Can't disagree with him there," I said through clenched teeth.

"And I don't mind it. I like talking to the regulars and getting all the gossip firsthand," she smiled devilishly.

"Oh, so what's the hot topic today, then?"

"You," she said bluntly.

"Hmm, anything specific about me?"

"Oh no, it's everything about you. What you're doing here, how long you're staying, that you had dinner at Grandpa's house last night—that has people thinking you might have business here in Englee, you see—and that you went to Uncle Lance's house after dinner. That one has people thinking..."

"Oh, I think I know what it has people thinking," I

interrupted with a smile to match her own. "I just went to see the house. That's all."

"Don't you just love it? I wish I could live at Batty Catters. It's incredible. I stay there with Uncle Lance every chance I get. Isn't it great?"

"Oh yes, Asia. Yes, it is. So you're close with your uncle then?" I prodded.

"Don't say anything to Ester or my dad, but when I was a little girl, I used to wish that he was my father, so I could live with him all the time..."

I almost choked on my coffee.

"...But, short of that, I know I'm lucky to have him as my uncle. He's always here to help me, or take me places. Sometimes we go to the States together and he takes me shopping for clothes. I love fashion, and there's not much of that in Englee, let me tell you."

"Now, that's a passion in life I can truly understand," I confided. "I love shopping."

Her dark eyes looked longingly at the deep purple cashmere sweater I was wearing. "I go shopping with my friends, but it's not the same. Most of the clothes people around here buy comes from the Sears catalogue." She breathed deeply. "Thank God for Sears."

I grinned.

She shrugged. "Really, Mrs. Toms, there's nothing here to buy. Even when there is, I just look. I can't buy something for me when my friends have no money. When I come back from a trip with Uncle Lance to St. John's or south, I know they won't know how much my new clothes cost, so I feel a little better about showing them off. Like the way you dress—classy, not flashy, elegant, I would say. Nobody here would know the cost. I bet people in Montreal or Toronto would know. I bet you could buy seven or eight pairs of jeans for what you paid for just the pair you have on right now. Nobody knows that though. To them you're just like them. To them it's just jeans."

"I know what you mean, Asia, I usually shop alone, just so I can enjoy it, guilt free."

"Huh, you're the first woman I've ever met who has truly understood that," she said, then took a long sip of her coffee.

"What about Ester?" I asked as my eyes took in Ester's outrageous outfit from head to toe.

"Oh, no, I make sure to throw out all the tags and receipts before I get home. My dad would kill Uncle Lance if he knew how much he spoiled me. He doesn't see the point of fashion. Heck, he even has Ester on an allowance. I'd be surprised if he let her spend more than a few hundred dollars a year on herself." She shook her head and I watched as a thick curl escaped the tight bun at the nape of her neck and fell forward. "Well, it was really nice talking to you, Mrs. Toms. I should get back to work."

I slid a twenty dollar bill onto the table before I put on my yellow raincoat, which matched my rubber boots, and stepped outside. The clouds had socked in and the drizzle of the early hours had given way to a full blown downpour.

My umbrella was an oversized black golf umbrella, which hid the bright colours of my other outerwear nicely. The wind was light and I was pleased with not having to suffer the humiliation of having the umbrella turn inside out.

A few cars passed me and either they thought I was dressed for it or they scored points for splashing pedestrians because none slowed down, and all of them sent a shower my way.

I hesitated at the bridge before choosing to stay on the island and walk what once was my way home—the road to Lane's Cove.

The only signs of life I encountered for quite some distance were a couple of forgotten-looking wet dogs. Even they seemed to be questioning my sanity for walking in such weather.

I stopped for a moment and stared at Harry Lloyd's house. Like so many houses in town, the boarded windows were a giveaway to the abandonment.

I stood in front of Harry's house and stared at it. The structure looked strong. I remembered every detail of the inside: the kitchen, the living room, the three bedrooms upstairs, the sun room facing the ocean. I had been there many times. It's funny how I had been friends with both Jenny and Rita, but when I looked at the house today I thought of Harry and not his sisters. Perhaps it was because he had been autistic and he was so special to us. Everyone seemed to be there to protect him. I wondered what had become of Harry and his sisters. I wondered who protected him now.

As I stood there, I turned my head towards the house on the hill. It looked even more desolate than the rest. In between Harry's house and the house on the hill were two abandoned houses, roofs sagging and windows empty, littered with debris from the old days, the days of the fishery. I tilted the umbrella to let the rain fall on my face. I needed an excuse for the tears that were falling. Nobody would question the wetness today.

There were just a few houses from Harry's house to what once was mine. I looked up and felt so many emotions. I felt sorry for the house on the hill. I felt sorry for the neighbours stranded between eyesores. Not only had the house been neglected, but the road as well. The gravel had worn down over the years. Small trenches had appeared and today the rain changed the trenches to a creek as the water ran down the hill and across the road. I was thankful however for the large property that surrounded what once was my home. I was happy and thankful that the town had not infringed. I wondered who, if anyone, had paid the taxes or if the town had taken it over.

For a moment, I closed the umbrella and let the rain fall on me. I felt so vulnerable that I needed to be one with the elements. My hair was protected by the raincoat hood. The tears slowly fell on the outside as the new me, the Kay Toms protected the Kennedy Warren who was crying on the inside.

I closed my eyes and saw the concerned look on my father's face that last night we were together, as I lied when I said I'd be okay. He had no idea of the fear I felt. And I had no idea of how my life would have changed forever. I opened my eyes and stared at the house where I had always felt so secure and happy. I wished my father were alive today. I wished both he and my mother could be alive to see that I made it in spite of the difficulties. I wanted them to know what I had become and that I had all they had ever dreamed for me.

A car passed me and I continued on. Charlie Cole's house seemed suddenly so close to mine. I had never noticed it before as it was around the bend but separated by only four houses. A figure moved in the window. I wondered if it was Charlie.

As I rounded the point, I walked past the last house on the island. The tide was low and I stood and looked at Barr'd Island just a few meters from me. I could see the beginning of the massive staircase that wound its way to the top of the uninhabited rock.

It looked like the rain was about to stop, so I decided to climb the wooden steps to the top. It was steep. I stopped at each landing and looked around. After what seemed an eternity, I reached the highest point of the Island where I had an unobstructed view of the town and the sea. I felt very tall as I stood there and looked down. A boy ran with his dog along the shoreline, skipping stones that the dog thought were solely for his amusement.

I tried to concentrate on the Island and not on the pain that had created it. I walked through the forest now manicured into an island park, safe from the wind and sheltered by thickened tangles of overgrown branches. Trees clung together, dimmed and softened by the mist.

I followed the trail until it led me back to the beginning and walked slowly down the steps again. It was a typical Newfoundland day. The rain had stopped, but the hint of mist still lingered across the water. There was a touch of warmth in the soft breeze.

I stood at the shoreline, watched the waves rise and fall and stared across the ocean. I knew that if I were to see what lay at the end of that endless waterway, it would be England, or so we always said. There was nothing between that very spot and Europe. It looked so far away, yet it was so close. The gap between where I stood and the land across the ocean was smaller than the gap that separated the new me that stood at the ocean's edge and the old me that had stood here eighteen years earlier. A deep-throated roar of thunder came out of the mist and the heavens opened once more and I quickly hurried along the road towards the motel.

I glanced back at the car that passed me and watched as it turned around at the end of the road. As it came close, it stopped and the window was lowered. "Are you okay?"

I walked towards the car. Mr. Richards leaned across. "Are you okay, Mrs. Toms? Get in," he said before I could answer.

I lowered the umbrella. "I'm okay really."

"Get in," he said again.

I slid in beside him. "Thanks. How did you know it was me?"

He smiled and it reminded me of Lance. "There's definitely nobody here that dresses that colourful, Mrs. Toms. Especially in the rain."

"Thanks. I just wanted a walk."

"It couldn't wait?"

I shook my head. "I was trying to get a better idea of the town and I thought I'd start with this side. I saw two boarded-up houses."

He pointed as we drove past. "Only two? There are more than two, Mrs. Toms, but yeah, nobody's lived in either of these for years."

"Who pays the taxes or do they belong to the town?"

"Don't know about the Decker house or the one down the street from it, but I've paid the taxes on the house on the hill for years."

I was shocked. My voice almost failed me. "Why?"

"I guess I felt obligated. The guy who owned the house worked for me. And she lived there."

"She?"

"The girl Lance cared for. I could never make it right with Lance and me after she left, so I paid the taxes just so that nothing would happen to the house. I keep hoping for a miracle, I guess."

"Does he know you paid the taxes?"

"I'm sure he does, but I never told him."

I wanted so much to continue the conversation, but I had to know more about the properties. "Do you think I could buy the properties?"

"What are you going to do with these rundown buildings?" He slowed down as we came close to the motel then drove past. "How about a cup of warm tea?"

"I'd love one."

"Janine! Could you bring us some hot tea?" Mr. Richards took my jacket from me as we entered and shook off the water. I followed him to the living room. Butch came rushing to meet us, his tail wagging.

My heart beat fast. "Butch! Is ...?"

Mr. Richards smiled. "Lance? No, he's at work today. He always leaves the dog here when he's away." His eyes searched mine.

I sat down across from him. The dog lay on the floor beside me.

"So, what do you want with these two old properties, Mrs. Toms? We got lots more in town if you want them, too. But, why?"

"I don't know yet. I just know I want to own something here," I said with a weak smile. "This town could turn around, you know."

He shook his head. "Mrs. Toms, turning this place into something is not as easy as running one of your companies. You can't walk in here and buy up the whole town and decide what works and what doesn't."

"I haven't said I would do anything of the sort, Mr. Richards. However, I don't see the harm in making a small move. Buying those houses means nothing to me financially. I'd spend more on a two week vacation," I said as I stirred my tea absently. "If I can't be bothered to do something, even something as small as buy a property and take it off the town's hands, then how can anyone expect this town to turn around? Investment changes communities."

"And you're going to be the one to invest, are you?" he asked, still sceptical of my motives.

I wished I could have told him the truth. "Might as well. There hasn't been new money in this town in generations. Why not mine? There's just something about this place. Something about this town that just makes me want to do something..."

"Well, perhaps you came along at the right time, Mrs. Toms. Englee could use a little something. More than I can give at my age." He frowned deeply.

"Are you planning to retire soon?" I asked.

"I can't quit," he said. "If I quit, where would people get their supplies? Right now, Mrs. Toms, I'm caught between the devil and the deep blue sea." His gaze drifted to the portrait of his late wife that hung above the mantel. "That being the case though, I'm not closed to new ideas. I've looked out for Englee my entire adult life and want nothing more than to go into retirement, finally, knowing that the people are taken care of. They need work, Mrs. Toms, plain and simple. Since the fish plant shut down..."

"You mean since your son shut the plant down, strangling this town," I interjected forcibly.

Mr. Richards cleared his throat loudly. "Yes, since Reg shut the doors, the people here have suffered greatly. I wish I could go back, keep the plant myself. I should have stopped him, but I had no idea he would do that to his own people." He looked deeply sad as he set his teacup down on the table and rubbed a hand across his wrinkled brow.

"Well, what's done is done," I said. I didn't want to feel sorry for him. I didn't want to see the pain in his blue eyes as he spoke of Reg's underhanded tactics. I wanted him to be the cold-hearted son-of-a-bitch of my memories. Yet, I couldn't deny his genuine anguish over the town. I couldn't deny that there was a chance I had more in common with Mr. Richards than I had ever thought possible. "Let's start with those two houses on Lane's Cove. It's a start."

Chapter Eight

"Sean, call me as soon as you get this message," I said into my cell phone as I walked to the General Store. It was just past one in the afternoon and the street around me was nearly empty, aside from the group of men loitering in front of the abandoned fish plant.

As I walked through the front door of the store, the chimes rang clearly. Behind the counter stood Melissa Young, who I remembered from high school to be a sweet and kind girl. She had changed over the years, but I could still see her warm nature shining on her heart-shaped face, even with the added thirty pounds and lines from troubling times.

"Hi," she said brightly as I walked forward. "How are ya, today, then?"

"Oh, I'm fine, thank you," I said, trying to tuck away the thoughts that were swirling in my mind about the state of the town. I went to the back of the store, selected a few items, then made my way slowly back to the counter. "That should do it for now," I said, though my gaze lingered over a package of Purity candies near the till.

"Oh, go on, a little sweet can't hurt you," Melissa said with a wink. I shrugged and picked up the package. My dad used to carry those candies in his pocket. I smiled. "Are you enjoying your stay then?" she asked.

"Um, oh yes," I said, knowing there was a certain amount of chitchat required on any visit to the store. "I am. Englee's a great little town, isn't it?"

"I guess it is, if you look at it in the right light," she answered.

"Have you worked here long?" I asked. In school Melissa had wanted to be a chef, a proper chef. I remembered it clearly. She had given a lengthy report on the amount of schooling required and the costs involved. The boys at the back of the room had laughed openly, telling her she'd never leave Englee. It broke my heart a little to see they had been right.

"I'm just part-time, when they need me," she said. "If there aren't enough hours here, I'll take on a work project when I can. I've got two boys at home and my husband hasn't seen steady work since the fish plant went."

"Work projects?"

"Oh, yes, don't know where we'd be without them some years. See, the government hires us to do small jobs, like building the new stairway on the island. Those give the workers enough hours so they can qualify for unemployment for a few months once the work is done. It gets us through."

I pictured Melissa Young, clinging to the bald mountainside with one hand, while in the other she carried planks to be used for the steps that wound their way up and around the island and through the forest at the top. I knew Melissa was just an example; nearly the whole town was surviving the way she was. Hoping year after year that the government would throw them some work, scraps to keep them going.

"Thank you," I said as I collected the bag of goods from her hand. I opened the package of candies, popped one in my mouth and offered another to her. She smiled as she took the treat.

My phone rang as I walked to the door. "Sean," I said as I turned back and gave Melissa a wave. "I have a few things I need you to do for me."

"Anything, bosslady," Sean's perky voice replied. "Your wish is my command!"

"Alright, first, I'll need you to contact Mr. Richards and the Town of Englee office here in Newfoundland. I'll email you the contact information in a few minutes..." My concentration wavered as I walked past the plant and saw Reg. He was confronting the men I had seen loitering earlier, reading them the riot act for being on his property.

"Get out of here," he yelled. "Right now, go on."

"We're not doin' no harm, Mr. Richards, just resting a bit and catching..." one of them tried to say as he fidgeted with his ball cap.

"Resting?" Reg laughed manically. "From what? Get the hell off my property and get a job!"

I watched in stunned silence as the men slunk away. I remembered each of their faces. They had all worked at the plant with my father, back in the day. Reg turned and gave me a half-hearted smile as he walked to his truck.

"Um, hello, Earth to Kay, Kay are you there?" Sean asked with his usual lightness.

"That's it," I said. My mind had been made up. "Sean, I'm most definitely here and I'm not going anywhere. Get the Town on the line. There are two properties I want to buy immediately. Now. I want the deeds in my hand by the end of the day, if at all possible." My voice held steady, though my rage was boiling inside. Reg had bullied this town—my town—for long enough. He was about to meet the real Kay Toms. The Kay Toms of boardroom legend, who'd taken her husband's company and spun it into a global multinational without losing a single night's sleep. "Then, set up a meeting later today with Raj from product development and start researching tax incentives in this jurisdiction."

"Right, right, and got it," Sean said lightly, though I knew him well enough to know that he had scribbled down every word. Sean had been my executive and personal assistant for nearly five years, seeing me through the ups and downs of business and the loss of my husband. He might have been flamboyant, but he had never failed me, not once. "Anything else, Kay? Can I book you a massage somewhere? Get you into the local spa? You sound a bit stressed."

"Spa?" I laughed out loud. "Oh, lord, Sean, you've really never been to Englee, have you?"

"Can't say that I've ever seen the sights, no," he said with a chuckle. I knew he'd be sitting at his desk in my office on the top floor of the Tomtex building, with the whole of the Boston skyline glimmering through the three hundred and sixty degree view.

"Well, get your galoshes ready, I just might need you here."

His laughter stopped short. "Oh, oh God, really?" I could picture the look of terror on his pretty face and it made me smile.

I spent the rest of the afternoon holed up in my motel room, thinking, planning and talking to my head of product development at the Boston office. Raj Patel was the hardest working man I had ever known. He'd taken on the task of expanding our product lines year after year, never backing down from a challenge. After an hour on the phone with him, I knew he'd get me the plan I needed for Englee. More than anything, this town needed a chance.

A semblance of a plan began to take shape in my mind. Englee needed a multi-pronged approach. On one side, they needed industry. Jobs. Real jobs with real hours, and real benefits. On the other side, Englee needed new blood, tourism. It wouldn't be an easy task to get people motivated. I knew it wouldn't be easy. Living on government handouts for so long had crushed any hope they had once held. They would also be sceptical of me. How could they ever believe that a stranger with no connection to the town would suddenly be interested in their plight?

I knew they were hard workers. They had to be. Just surviving in a place where fighting the elements was a continuous struggle was proof enough of one's willingness to work hard. They were as rugged as the land itself – a geographic necessity in order to survive.

The lean years, however, had made their fight for existence the sole focus of their lives. A few days of work each year, given to them by work projects created solely for the purpose of giving the qualifications to receive the unemployment insurance. That had become the "legitimate reward of work"; giving them justifiable employment to prove they were not merely seeking handouts. It was not their fault that their homeland had been stripped of its resources. It was a bureaucratic misunderstanding and social status that denied their own voices of what was best for them. Because of some idiotic rantings of self-proclaimed experts on the nature of things in Newfoundland, the citizens whose lives depended on their environment had been reduced to a slave society.

I pondered all I knew, or all I believed, and I knew that my help would not be accepted as readily as I could give it. Nobody knew I had grown up among them. Nobody knew that although I had lived my adult life in a more influential world, that I still chose to call the town my home.

I wanted to share with each and every one the good fortune that I had been blessed with. I could not, however, give handouts and crush the tiny bit of dignity that remained. I had to plan my moves, but better still I had to get people involved.

I knew the tourists would come to the area, whether or not there were craft stores or coffee shops. If they were coming, however, it was to the economical advantage of the townspeople to offer their local talents.

Tourism became the big promotion after the moratorium. Some adventurous people never returned to tell just what an adventure it was in Northern Newfoundland. Blinded by the hospitality of the people they never considered the dangers that existed. The wild rustic windswept barrens on treacherous mountains were anything but hospitable.

Tourists went where natives themselves refused to go. Because a small isolated town of people was friendly and charming did not mean the mountains sheltering the town extended the same welcome. Search parties were often called on to locate missing hikers, especially in the killer barrens in the Harbour Deep area.

However, Englee needed tourism. It also needed an information centre showing the dangers in hiking alone on the Peninsula. Because such dangers existed, there was a market for guides. That would be employment for middle aged men. Young men did not have the experience to go alone on the country. It was a skill that was taught by elders as if being a part of a tribe. Tourism schools could not teach how to navigate the vast untamed wilderness that surrounded the town.

I had ideas. I had too many ideas.

As I continued to pace around the small motel room well into the evening hours, there was a knock on my door. Startled out of my thoughts, I stepped forward to reach for the doorknob. My other hand went to smooth my hair and realized it was touching my natural locks.

"Just a moment," I said to whoever was waiting. *Damn, I'll never get my wig on in time!* My eyes flew frantically around the room, finally landing on a towel I had left on the bed earlier. I grabbed it, flipped my head upside down, wrapped the large bath towel around it turban-style, and rushed to the door.

"Hello," Lance said, standing on the other side of the threshold.

"Hi," I said, trying to sound nonchalant.

"Sorry, is this a bad time?" he asked as his dark eyes took in the towel balancing on top of my head. He was dressed much as he had been the night before, casually attired in jeans and a deep blue long sleeved T-shirt, with his black leather jacket open. It took all my strength to stop perusing his torso.

"Uh, no, no, not at all," I said, opening the door wider and sweeping my arm to invite him in. "Just washing my hair..."

"Oh, that old excuse," he smirked. As he entered the room it seemed to shrink to the size of a shoebox. Suddenly, there didn't seem to be enough room, or air, for both of us. I shook my head fiercely, trying to snap out of the illusion, and felt the towel waggle dangerously. Raising a hand I steadied it and my nerves.

"To what do I owe the pleasure?" I asked. He walked to the small table where I had been working.

"You have been one busy bee, Mrs. Toms," he said as he looked over my scribbling. "You're not very good at vacationing, are you?"

I could feel my cheeks blushing. "What makes you think that?" I said as I shuffled some of the papers. He placed his large hand over mine gently and turned to face me.

"Relax, please, for just a moment," he said softly.

"See, now," I cleared my throat, "I think we've just established that I'm not very good at that."

"Obviously," he said, then removed his hand slowly. I wanted it back. "Now, I had a very interesting call this afternoon, Mrs. Toms."

"Please, Kay, remember?"

"Right, Kay. I received a call this afternoon from a man named Raj Patel, in Boston." My stomach muscles clenched. "Now, of course, you know Mr. Patel quite well, don't you?"

I dared to look into his dark stare and found my knees threatening to buckle. "Hmmm. Patel? Patel?" I scratched my head through the towel. "That does ring a bell..."

"Kay, what are you up to?" he asked bluntly. "There I am, minding my own business, when he calls and asks about the quantity of shrimp my centre would be able to produce every seven days, our delivery schedules, shipping rates, our credit terms. All the while, he wouldn't actually say why he needed all the information."

"Oh, he wouldn't?" I asked, trying to sound as innocent as possible.

"No, he wouldn't. Then, on my way here, I bump into the mayor and she tells me that, miracle of all miracles, two of the abandoned properties on the hill sold today. Out of the blue. An out of town buyer just called up and wired the money, no questions asked. It's a nice little sum for the town coffers. Busy day, I said, and she prattles on, telling me about another call requesting information on zoning and town statutes. What am I to make of all this, Kay?"

I walked to the far corner of the room and sat in one of the wing-backed chairs. Lance followed and sat in the other. We faced each other and he leaned forward, with his elbows on his knees. I took a long breath.

"No secrets in a small town, huh?" I said, trying to collect my thoughts. I had no idea how he would receive my plan. "Right, well, here's the thing. I've been in Englee for only a few days..."

"Three. Three days, Kay."

"Yes, just three days. And all around me, I see people who need help. They're dying in this town, Lance. Without proper work, without more motivation, they'll just idle away their lives."

He stayed silent.

"Yet, I see so much potential. There are a thousand things

that could be done. And there are opportunities here ripe for the taking."

"Opportunities for you or for the town?" he leaned a touch closer.

"Both," I said firmly. "There are plenty of opportunities for both. I'm a businesswoman, that's what I do. I look for opportunities and exploit them. That doesn't mean that I bleed them, or the people involved, dry. It means that if I can develop an idea and bring it to market, I can provide jobs and income for a lot of people."

I waited, not wanting to go too far.

"Jobs," he said ponderously. "What kind of jobs? And what does this have to do with my business?"

"Well, I think my plan, which I'm still trying to work out fully, could bring more work to your centre, as well as provide long lasting jobs right here in Englee." I could see the suspicion written all over his stoic face. "Hear me out?" I asked as I reached forward and touched his arm. "Just hear me out, okay?"

"Alright," he sighed. "I can do that."

"You have a fantastic, state-of-the-art shrimp production facility, right?"

"Yes, besides our aggressive marine research, the Roddickton Research Centre houses my own shrimp farming facility. It's the largest of its kind in Eastern Canada, possibly in North America. We ship flash-frozen shrimp to suppliers and retailers across the continent." He straightened a bit with obvious pride.

"Impressive," I said, nodding my head cautiously so as to not disturb my flimsy disguise. "So, you have an established supply chain of high quality shrimp. I have a line of ready-to-eat food products that we launched at Tomtex last year. The line has taken off and we've been looking to expand." I waited a moment to see if he would connect the dots himself.

"So, you want to use my shrimp in some of your products?" he asked finally.

"Well, yes, but more than that, I want to develop an entire line of shrimp dishes to accompany our existing products."

"How does that help Englee exactly? I mean, don't get me wrong, I'd be thrilled for the increase in my own business, but I'm still missing something here."

"Well, the way I see it, Tomtex could just buy your shrimp and ship them to our existing plants for manufacturing or we could keep the whole line local."

"Local? You mean..."

"I mean, why not have a production center here, right in Englee?"

A long, low whistle escaped his pursed lips. "That's big bucks, Kay. Really big."

"Yes, yes it would be, but I think it's doable. With an initial investment in developing the site and getting things started, a production facility here in Englee could be quite profitable in time. Shipping from here down the eastern seaboard of the US would be a breeze, Europe even easier. And there are plenty of workers available, that's for sure."

"There are, but they won't work for nothing, Kay." He rubbed a hand over his face, still processing everything I had told him. "They won't. Don't you start this by thinking these people will work for slave wages. They won't lift a finger for less than they're making on unemployment, I guarantee."

"Of course they won't," I said as I stood up. "I wouldn't think of asking them to work for anything less. There will be good jobs, real jobs. From construction and maintenance of the facility to working the line and administration, there will be opportunities. Tomtex has an excellent human rights and employee rights record. We pay our people well and expect good work from them in return. Here," I walked to the table and took a business card out of my briefcase. "Look into it. Do your research, talk to my people. You have Raj's contact information, but call Len, my head of human resources, and talk to him, too." I scribbled Len's number on the back of the card and handed it to Lance as he stood from his chair. "I know it might seem like I'm rushing into all this, and maybe I am, but this town needs forward momentum. I wouldn't expect you, or the other people who live here, to go into any business deal with their eyes closed. You're the next step, Lance."

"Sorry?" he asked as he looked up from the card.

"Tomtex will need to know that you're willing to supply us, year round, with a consistent product. If you agree, in principal, to the terms my legal department will set up, we'll then move

forward with establishing the line and the site here in Englee."
I looked at him hopefully. "You're the most important step."

"No pressure, huh?" The corner of his mouth curled. "None
at all. Just sign on the dotted line and the whole town will be
saved..."

"Basically, yes," I said with a smile. "That simple. All you
have to do is grow your own business and I'll take care of the
rest."

"Now, why do I get the impression it's just not going to be
quite that simple with you, Kay?" he said playfully.

"Whatever do you mean, Mr. Richards?" I said with a flutter
of my eyelashes. He chuckled as he made his way to the door.

"So, you'll just up and build a whole new multimillion dollar
facility?" he said, holding the doorknob and turning back to
look at me.

"Something like that," I said evasively. "Do your homework,
Lance. Make sure you want to do business with Tomtex and
would be happy with the terms. I'll have my legal team forward
a draft agreement to you first thing tomorrow morning, then
we'll go from there."

"Thank you, Kay," he said, reaching a hand out to touch
my shoulder.

"You're welcome," I replied as I felt the warmth of his hand
seep through my shirt. "Do me a favour though and keep this
under your hat for the time being, just until we know for sure
that the project will move forward?"

"Interesting choice of words," he said as he reached up and twirled a curl that had escaped from under my towel around his index finger. I felt the slight tug on the strand and could have sworn my heart would stop.

My mouth hung slightly agape as he turned without another word and left.

Chapter Nine

After a long, relatively sleepless night worrying over whether or not I had blown my cover completely, I spent the next morning on conference calls with my legal team, Sean, Raj Patel, and Tomtex's human resources department. I had to bank on the fact that Lance, even if he had figured out my true identity, would put the welfare of the town ahead of his own feelings. I needed to move quickly.

"First things first, Jennifer," I said as I looked at the image of my top lawyer on the screen of my laptop. Video conferencing was a miracle of modern technology, one I was ever grateful for. "Reg Richards."

"Right," Jennifer said as she straightened her heavy framed, very fashionable, glasses. "The owner of the old fish plant. Is he going to be a problem?"

"Reg Richards is always a problem. He's a mean SOB and a rather keen businessman. If he knows it's Tomtex trying to buy the property, he'll stall and drag this whole process out, just to up his price. I need you to acquire the plant through a dummy corporation, one he can't trace back to me. And I need you to make the deal, fast. There are rumours around town that he's been trying to unload the property for years, but refuses to sell to anyone who might start a rival fishing operation. The dummy corp needs to look like a land development operation.

One that will tear down the plant and build housing. He'll love that, the idea of seeing the plant ripped to shreds in front of the people of Englee," I said as the image of Reg's glee made my skin crawl.

"Wow, sounds like a class act," Jennifer said with disgust. "The dummy corporation won't be a problem at all. I'll make sure he can't see the line back to Tomtex. I'll also make sure we make him a deal he can't refuse. I'll get this done." I liked Jennifer, always had. B.J. had hired her years before his death and she always delivered, whether it was handling litigation or cobbling together acquisitions.

"Our timing's perfect. Reg's wife, Ester, mentioned earlier this morning that Reg has gone out of town on business for a few days. He'll be at the office he keeps in St. John's trying to negotiate an extension on his licenses with the provincial government. I'll email you the contact information and you can send the offer to him there. Make the price good, but don't make him all that much richer. The man has more than enough already."

"Great, I should be able to seal the whole deal before the close of business on Friday."

"Perfect," I said with a feeling of relief. It felt good to know that my team was behind me. "Now, Lance."

"Lance?" Jennifer asked with a slightly raised eyebrow.

"Lance Richards," I said, shifting in my seat. "I'll need you to get a draft agreement to him regarding supplying Tomtex with shrimp for production. The terms will be negotiable, but they also need to leave room for a profit on our end. Have someone in your department get the documents to him today, please."

"Right," Jennifer said as she continued to take notes. "Lance Richards. Is everyone in that town related? I just spoke with a Jack Richards yesterday about the residential properties."

"No, that's almost the whole family right there," I said with a smile. "Almost. Remember, these three men need to be dealt with completely separate from one another. Don't cross any lines between them. Lance is an ally to us in this plan, Jack might be, and Reg could bring the whole damn thing crashing down. They might be related, but there's nothing similar about them."

"I've got it. Now, don't you worry about all of this. I'll handle the details and get all the balls rolling. I'll be in touch as soon as I've made some progress." She looked directly in the webcam. "And try to get a bit of rest, would you? You are supposed to be on vacation, remember?"

"People keep reminding me of that, but it doesn't seem to be working," I said and signed off. As much as my body wanted a rest, I couldn't stop my mind from working. There was so much more to be done.

After a quick check in the mirror, I put on my walking jacket, a three-quarter length trench coat in charcoal grey, and stepped outside. The air was warm and light as the sunshine washed over my face. I stood for a moment, with my head thrown back and soaked it all in.

"G'mornin'" a voice said to my left. I opened my eyes and saw Charlie standing on the sidewalk through the sunspots in my vision. He shuffled his feet from side to side and stared at his boots.

"Good morning, Charlie," I said warmly. "How are you today, then?"

"Not complainin', not complainin' me. Weather's broke nice and I've got a whole day a work, missus." He almost made eye contact then, but shied at the last moment and looked back to the ground. He was exactly as I remembered him. My dad had always been kind to Charlie, giving him work on his boat when he could, and making sure Charlie's family stayed afloat. It seemed now that my dad was gone that Charlie was reliant on Reg for such kindnesses. I had no doubt that Reg would take all he could from Charlie and never give him all that he deserved back. "Whatcha at yourself?" Charlie asked. It took my mind a moment to process and translate the question.

"What am I doing today?" I restated. "Oh, a bit of this, a bit of that. Thought I'd go for a walk first, clear my head."

"Off you go, t'en, don't ya mind meself," he mumbled and shuffled away towards the fish plant. In the back of my mind, I tried to remember the last time I had seen Charlie before I ran away.

My thoughts were interrupted again as Mr. Richards' car pulled into the parking lot in front of me. He waved enthusiastically to get my attention as he parked. "Mrs. Toms," he said as he climbed out of the Cadillac. "Mrs. Toms, do you have a moment?"

"I do, Mr. Richards, if you're up for a bit of a walk. I feel the need for a bit of air this morning," I answered as I secured the tie of my coat around my waist.

"Lovely, lovely," he replied, placing his hat on his head, and walking to my side. "Where to?" he asked.

"First, a quick stop at the General Store for something to sip on, then up the hill, I think," I said as we made our way to the main street.

We chatted about the weather on our way to the store and were both delighted to see Melissa standing behind the counter once again. She interrupted the conversation she was having with two other young mothers the moment she saw us.

"G'morning, Mr. Richards, sir, Mrs. Toms," she said brightly. I stopped at a cooler and grabbed two bottles of water, then made my way to stand by Mr. Richards at the counter.

"Oh, what are these?" I asked as I looked over a selection of fresh muffins in a basket beside her.

"Fresh just this morning, wild blueberry," Melissa replied as she held out the basket. "Just a dollar each."

"Oh, none of that Melissa. This is on the house," Mr. Richards said with a wink. I selected a muffin and took a small taste from the top. It was delicious, melting in my mouth and bursting with flavour.

"You're a genius," I said before taking a large bite.

"Oh, there's nothing to it," Melissa said, trying to wave away the compliment.

"Don't you listen to that," one of the young mothers at the end of the counter said. "She's an amazing cook and baker, this one. Can make a cake that will fill your dreams!"

"Oh, Rita, stop," Melissa fussed.

"Seems to me, Melissa, that you have a real talent. Have you ever thought about going into business for yourself?" I asked as the taste of her creation still lingered in my mouth.

"Now, Mrs. Toms, I'm sure you're not out to steal my employees out from under me, now are you?" Mr. Richards said as he took a muffin for himself. "Oh, my," he purred after the first taste.

"See, they're delightful, aren't they?" I nudged him with my elbow. "Confess, Mr. Richards, young Melissa's talents are wasted behind your counter."

"I must say, you might just have a point," he chuckled and once again I saw the sparkle in his kind eyes. I wanted to believe he was a kind man. I wanted him to be the father figure of my childhood and nothing more.

"Let's continue on our walk, shall we?" I said as I ushered him out the door and onto the main road.

"To the cove, then? Shall we take a walk through your new properties?" he asked as we set out.

I handed him a bottle of water and took a sip of my own.

I hadn't thought about the properties all day. "I guess they are mine, aren't they?"

"Lock, stock and barrel, as they say," he grinned and offered me his arm. We were both quiet as we approached Lane's Cove and stopped in front of the first house I had purchased. It was in decent condition, but was desperate for some attention. Mr. Richards turned his head and must have seen the look of consternation written all over my face. "I believe it's what they call a fixer-upper," he said with a smile.

"You're telling me." I removed my hand from the crook of his arm and stepped forward onto the lawn. It had been freshly mowed. The mayor must have wanted to make an impression on the new owner, I thought.

I stepped back from the house and stood on the road, where I could take in the sight of both properties. It was a start. My sights, however, wandered to the house on the hill. Home. Forever home.

"There's one more property I'd like to purchase, Mr. Richards," I said after only a moment's thought.

"Is there?" His blue eyes twinkled. His grey hair curled at the corner of his ears. I studied his features and imagined that Lance would age to be the attractive senior his father now was. In spite of what I knew, it was difficult to dislike the pleasant gentleman.

"The house on the hill."

He coughed.

I studied his face. "You said you paid the taxes."

His smile disappeared. "I know which house." He suddenly looked older, sadder, as he turned towards the house in question and took a deep breath.

"Who owns the house, Mr. Richards?" I felt he was holding back.

He turned around, hesitated, and adjusted his hat. "Asia." He took a deep breath and suddenly stood tall, his confidence returned. "Asia," he repeated.

I wasn't prepared for his answer.

"There was no will," he continued. "But Mr. Warren's house would have gone to his daughter if she'd have come back. She didn't return, so technically it belongs to Asia. The daughter was Asia's mother."

My knees weakened. I felt so guilty for hiding my true identity. The feeling of betrayal, of distrust, of conniving, the feeling of evil that I had convinced myself Mr. Richards possessed stared at me and I realized I had become what I was accusing him of being. I couldn't speak. I was losing my battle with sanity. He interpreted my silence as questioning his reply.

"Asia is the daughter of Kennedy Warren and Lance. I assumed you had figured that out at dinner, the way you were looking at Asia and Lance so intently."

I still couldn't speak. Mostly from the shock of him talking so openly about what I had assumed was a great family secret.

"Well, Asia's mother never returned so until she does the

house belongs to Asia. My granddaughter doesn't know any of this—about her true parentage, or the house. I pay the taxes and keep an eye on it for her. When the time is right, I'll tell her."

"What if she comes back?"

He grunted. "Why should she? She deceived my son and gave up her child. She'd have a lot of explaining to do as to why she ran away."

My head was spinning. He had no idea who I was. He was speaking about the real me as though I was a ghost. I wanted the subject of me changed, but more than ever, I wanted that house. "Could I rent it from you?"

"No."

"Mr. Richards, I want to help this town. I have plans and will need a more permanent place to stay, my own roof. That house is in a perfect location for the time being."

"It's not liveable. It needs thousands of dollars worth of renovations. Nobody has lived in it for seventeen or eighteen years."

I thought for a moment. "How about if I renovate the house completely in return for living there? Then when Asia is at the age to get the house, you'll be able to give her a beautiful home, not a rundown building. After all, when her grandfather left it to her I'm sure it was a beautiful home."

His body seemed to shrink under the stress that I had somehow put on him.

"So, Mr. Richards, can I live in the house and fix it up?"

He turned and looked at me with that deep gaze, which made me feel as though I might lose my cover if I stared into his eyes too long. "You're probably right, Mrs. Toms. Mr. Warren would have died of shame seeing the state of his place now. He was a good man and would have loved his grandchild, if he'd have had been given the chance to meet her."

"Change has to start somewhere," I said with a scant smile. Hearing him speak of my father was bringing me to the brink of tears.

"I guess you're right. I find you very refreshing Mrs. Toms. Very refreshing indeed. I know you'll do a great job on my granddaughter's house." He extended his hand.

"Now, you've taken over almost the whole cove!" he said with a chuckle. "What's next? I have to tell you, Mrs. Toms, the town is absolutely buzzing with rumours about what you're up to. It's exciting!"

"Well, Mr. Richards, I can't tell you everything," I said as I took his arm and we walked around the first house. "But, there are a few ideas I'd like to run by you, if you don't mind..."

"I'm all ears," he said sharply. "My father always said it doesn't cost a thing to listen."

"Just hold onto that thought, would you, Mr. Richards?" I replied.

"Why do I suddenly get the feeling that I might have that saying all wrong?" He raised his eyebrows so far on his forehead, I could have sworn his hat moved.

Knowing I had to get back to my motel room for another conference call, I parted company with Mr. Richards. We planned to meet the next morning to discuss my ideas.

"Deep breath in," Sean's voice said over the webcam on my laptop. It was good to see his beaming face on my screen; I had only been gone from Boston for less than a week, but I missed him terribly. "Deep breath out..."

"Sean, I don't need a yoga lesson right now," I said a bit too tersely.

At his desk in my office, Sean sat up a little straighter and arched an elegant brow. "Are you sure about that?" he muttered.

I threw my head back and let out a great big sigh. He was right. I was a ball of tension and utterly exhausted.

"Sorry, Sean," I said meekly. "I just don't know what I'm doing. In a matter of days, I've purchased two rundown properties, rented another, made a multimillion dollar supply deal, started the process to buy a decrepit fish plant, taken on the whole Richards' family and possibly adopted the responsibility of reviving an entire town."

"Oh, well, when you put it like that, sure, it sounds like you have a right to be bitchy," he said stoically, trying desperately not to snicker.

"You're right, you're right," I said as I threw an arm over my forehead and closed my eyes. "What am I going to do now,

Sean?"

There was a firm knock on the door. "Hmmm, expecting company?" Sean asked as he took a sip of his latte. I would have sold my soul for a venti chai at that moment.

"Um, no, hold on a second," I said as I stood and walked to the door, leaving my laptop running on the table.

"Oh, hello," I said to Lance as I opened the door. This was getting to be routine. "How are you? Come in."

"Thanks, thanks, um, I can't stay," he said as he walked in just a couple steps. He was dressed in a beautiful deep grey suit with a matching two-tone tie and polished black shoes. I wasn't certain I'd be able to breathe much longer. On the table, Sean's image sat stock still, as though he was nothing more than a screensaver. I knew my assistant well enough to know that he wouldn't have missed eavesdropping and looking at Lance for anything in the world.

"What's the occasion?" I asked as I gently touched his sleeve. The Italian fabric felt like butter.

"Bank," he said with an uncomfortable shrug. "I don't know why, but I always feel naked going to the bank in anything less than a full suit." I swore I heard a whimper coming from my computer.

"Oh, the bank," I said weakly.

"Yeah, I received the papers from Tomtex this morning. I've gone over them, but I want Jones at the bank to give them a once over. Thought maybe you and I could get together when

I'm done and talk it all over..."

He waited for me to answer as I stood there, locked in his gaze.

"Sorry," I snapped myself back forcibly. "Sure, absolutely."

"We'll have some dinner and talk. My place around 5:30?" He was already turning back towards the door as he looked at his watch. "I gotta run. Jones'll be waiting."

"Yes, of course, go, I'll see you there at 5:30," I said as I walked to the threshold and leaned against the doorjamb. He walked back to his Jeep, limping, and climbed in. I gave him a wave as he pulled out of the parking lot and couldn't help but smile.

Behind me, Sean cleared his throat loudly. "Oh, my God, now I'm starting to see the appeal of that little town! Did you see that man? Um-um, yum!"

"Yeah, I've seen him alright..."

"Like seen him, seen him?" Sean ran a flamboyant hand down the length of his torso and leaned forward into the camera.

"Oh, stop, it's a business dinner," I said, trying to keep the heat from blooming in my cheeks.

"Business, right, that's the kind of business I'd like to get into..."

"Oh, Sean! Honestly, sometimes I swear your mind lives in the damn gutter," I said as I took a seat at the table once again. "Right, well, I have work to do, so I'll let you go. Get me an update from Raj about production and email it over before my dinner, okay? I want to be prepared to discuss the details with Lance—uh, Mister Richards. Oh, and remember how you were chirping on a few months ago about micro-lending?"

"Chirping? I do not chirp."

"Yes, you do. I seem to remember that you had written a proposal about it that you were thinking about sending to our charitable foundation, weren't you?"

"Yes, as a matter of fact. I've been working on it in my spare time. You know that if I ever left your office, perish the thought, that I'd want to transition into the philanthropic wing of Tomtex." While the world might have seen Sean as nothing more than a stereotypical, trend-obsessed fashionista, I knew he was so much more. That was why I hired him. Under his shiny façade, lay a deeply compassionate man with lofty goals for enriching lives. He had certainly achieved that goal in mine.

"Fantastic! Send me all the research you have," I said with a snap.

"Ten-four, bosslady," Sean said with a jaunty salute as he clicked off.

I spent the remaining hours of the afternoon reviewing the numerous preliminary reports my staff had hastily compiled. The most interesting came from Jennifer, my lead legal counsel. It was a short email that said: "Contact has been made through the arrangements we previously discussed. Initial response very positive. Expect completion of the deal shortly." Being the legal dragon she was, Jennifer always censored her written correspondence to within an inch of its life.

With that, I shut down my laptop for the day and stepped into a hot shower. As the water ran through my natural hair, my mind wandered to Lance. Had he figured out my true identity? Was this dinner a trap or an actual business discussion? There was only one way to find out.

After dressing in a deep purple, silk Jersey wrap dress and dark leggings, I fixed my wig, dashed on a sparse amount of makeup and made my way outdoors. The early evening air was fresh and warm, a westerly, my dad would have called it. That's what he said whenever a warm breeze favoured the island. I decided to leave the rental car behind and walk to Batty Catters. As I made my way through town, I exchanged friendly waves with the people I passed. They were getting used to me, starting to drop their guard.

I stayed to the side of the road as I neared the old fish plant. I stopped for a moment to look at the old building. Memories of my dad flooded my mind's eye. His laughing smile as he walked the length of the dock, exchanging jibes and jokes with the fisherman as he checked on something or other for Mr. Richards. Or his toothy grin as he moored his boat on the occasions when he still went out to sea for the odd day, happy with his catch. While the accident at Mr. Richards' sawmill had left him with only one arm, he said he still needed to fish once in a while, to keep his skills sharp and his salt levels up. On those days, he'd take a helper with him, anyone he could find who was willing. Some days it would be Charlie, or Lance, or one of the boys from the plant. I think those were his happiest days. He loved being on the water. He'd only ever taken the job at the sawmill to pay the bills when the fishing turned bad. He'd planned on going back to the ocean full-time eventually, but never got the chance.

"Good day, me darlin', for us, not the fish." I could hear the timbre of his voice as he began bantering and bartering with the dock crew, setting his current price with the foreman. He had a way with people, the ability to smile through his hard work that was contagious. God, how I missed him.

I shook my head to clear the memories and turned to continue on my way. Feeling a bit maudlin, I passed the Indian burial ground and shivered violently. Voices whispered. I walked faster. Behind me something clanged loudly to the ground. I jumped and spun around. In the alleyway between the fish plant and the General Store, I saw a shadowed figure lurking. *Reg*, screamed through my mind. I had seen this all before. *No, no, no*...my feet stumbled backwards on the loose gravel of the deteriorated pavement. The figure moved forward. My jaw muscles clenched, preparing to scream—scream the way I should have seventeen years ago on that very spot.

Taking another step forward, the figure bent at the waist to overturn the toppled barrel. As he reached forward, the sunlight touched his woollen cap. Charlie. I raised a hand to cover my mouth as the other pressed into my chest, trying to stop my heart from racing. Having set the barrel to rights, Charlie continued on his way, exiting the alley and walking onto the street, his eyes cast firmly to the ground.

"Oh God," I mumbled and turned away from the plant. Adrenaline surged through my veins. My feet ran as fast as they could towards the Catters; towards Lance. That was the choice I should have made that night so many years ago after seeing the glint of the knife. I should have run to the man I loved, not away.

As I came to his driveway, I slowed and tried to calm my breathing. Smoothing my hair, I turned onto the lane. The sun was still bright and the breeze still warm. As I approached the house, Butch lumbered off the porch to casually greet me. It seemed I had interrupted his nap. Without so much as a bark, he walked to my side. We rounded the side of the house, but I stopped short as I heard voices. Around the front of the house, I could hear Lance. He was straining to hold his temper as his brother responded.

I had no idea what Reg was doing back in town and had no desire to see him, especially after the scare I had just given myself.

"What are you trying to say, Reg?"

"Exactly what I've just told you, asshole," he voice slithered. "I'm on the verge of a deal that will change this town forever. And I'm going to get stinking rich doing it!"

"What deal?"

"Like I'd tell you the details."

"Then why are you here? If you don't want me to know about it, why are you here tellin' me?"

"Oh, I want you to know about it, I just don't want you to know *all* about it...yet. It'd ruin the surprise."

"Whatever, do what you want, Reg. I gave up caring long ago." Lance sounded tired.

"Huh, so you won't care when I make enough dough on this deal to move my family out of town permanently?"

A chair slid across the decking.

"You selfish fucking pig!"

"Oh, that's right, yelling at me is the way to go here." Reg's voice dripped with sarcasm and power. "I'll rip her out of this town so fast, your head'll spin..."

"She'll come back. She'll be off to university soon anyway. Then you won't be able to keep track of her every move. She'll be free to visit whenever she wants."

"We'll see about that. Seeing as we're all moving, I suspect it'd be nice to relocate in whatever town she decides to go to school. Hell, we might as well have her live at home while she's studying...you know, keep family together..."

"Sorry," I said as I took an impulsive step around the corner. Someone had to shut Reg up. "Am I interrupting?"

Both brothers turned in unison.

"Mrs. Toms," Lance said, quickly moving forward. "You're

here."

"Sorry I'm a bit late, I decided to walk. It's such a lovely evening, isn't it?" I directed my question towards Reg.

"Hm, yes, well, I should be on my way," he muttered as he adjusted the blue ball cap he wore. He tilted it slightly in my direction as he hurried past. "G'evening."

"And to you, Mister Richards," I said, my voice dripping with sweetness. "Send Ester and Asia my best."

Lance looked at me queerly as we heard the slam of Reg's truck door and his engine start.

"What? Haven't you ever heard of killing them with kindness?" I asked with a flutter of my lashes.

Lance laughed out loud. "Yeah, but it'll take a lot more than nice words to take my brother out. Mean son-of-a-bitch."

"You're probably right, but it's a theory worth testing, wouldn't you say?"

We climbed onto the front porch and Lance disappeared inside for refreshments. I took a seat in one of the four chairs and took a moment to collect myself.

"Beer?" I looked up as he stopped by my elbow. He held a bottle in each hand.

"Perfect," I sighed and gratefully accept the brew he held towards me. As he sat in the next chair, I took a deep swig and let my shoulders roll back. "Oh, that's good." I closed my eyes for a moment and took a deep breath.

"So, a beer drinker at heart, huh?"

I turned my head slightly and opened one eye to look at him. "I was thinking about Katrina."

"Katrina?"

"My best friend and..." I swallowed hard. I could still see her face. "She would have been my step-daughter."

He looked confused.

"We were just out of university and there was a terrible car accident. I survived, barely, but Katrina didn't. During my long recovery in hospital and all the surgeries, her father and I consoled each other. B.J. got me through it all and we formed a relationship from it."

"Your husband's daughter? Oh, I had no idea." He fidgeted with the bottle in his hand, picking at the label. "I mean, I knew your husband was older than you, but I didn't realize..."

"It's not something either of us publicized," I said with a shrug.

"Did you love him?"

Both my eyes were open now. I shifted in my chair and saw the earnestness of his question written all over his face. "Yes, very much." A slight frown creased his cheeks. "We loved each other as friends. He was so good to me. I was all he had. He was all I had."

"So, it wasn't what you'd call a romantic marriage?"

I shook my head. "No, not really. There was no passion. When his first wife died, I believe his love—his physical passion—died with her. We had sex, but it wasn't making love.

It was probably just the human instinct; we were married and that was part of it."

He smiled shyly.

"Lord, I don't know why I'm telling you all this..." I muttered.

"No, no, don't be embarrassed, Kay," he said as he reached over to pat my hand. "It's okay to talk. I like that you trust me. So, all those years together and nobody knew you weren't the perfect couple?"

I shook my head again. "If they did, they didn't say. In public it didn't show. It was easy to hold hands. It was easy to reach up and kiss his cheek or for him to bend and kiss mine. It was easy to walk up behind him where he sat and to gently massage his shoulders. It was easy to walk arm in arm down the street. It's easy to fool people, don't you think?"

My question surprised him. I could tell by the way his eyebrows arched. "How would I know?"

"Because I've seen you with your daughter." My breath caught as his jaw went slack.

"So, you know. You know about Asia?" he asked quietly.

"I suspected and your father confirmed it," I said, matching his tone. The subject was obviously taboo. It scared the hell out of me.

"Oh," he took another swig of his beer, trying to sort through his thoughts.

"It's the way you look at her. Like she's your whole reason for being, your whole world. I was married to a father of an only daughter, the apple of his eye, for years. I know that look. B.J. would get it every time he looked at Katrina's photo, every time her name was mentioned."

"Asia...is...my...daughter," he stuttered. "That's not something I usually get to say out loud. It runs through my head every single day, but never gets spoken."

"I'm sorry," I said, feeling the words in every cell of my body. I wished I could go back, back to that night, to the choices I made and do it all differently. I had fled for fear of my life, but hadn't taken into account that Lance would pay for that decision with his own. He looked me straight in the eye, unblinking.

"It's okay," he said. "We've made it work, as best as we could. She doesn't know the truth. By the time I came back to Englee, she was a full grown child. I just couldn't bring myself to shatter her world, rip her family apart. So, I opted for the role of the doting uncle. We have a close bond, one that's maybe even stronger than what she has with Reg. I have her in my life and that's all that matters."

I sat silent. What was there to say?

"You know that," he said, looking at his outstretched feet. "You know as well as I do that compromises are necessary in life."

"Sorry?" I asked, a bit rattled. Was this the moment of truth?

"Your marriage," he said lightly. "You made a choice to accept the comfort of your marriage, a compromise. You said

B.J. nursed you back to health—were your injuries severe?"

I was grateful for the change in conversational direction. Back to safer ground. "Yeah, they were pretty bad." My hand instinctively brushed my cheek. "It took many surgeries to put me back together again." He watched my hand retreat. "But, you'd know a little something about that yourself," I deflected, looking at his leg.

He rubbed his thigh absently. "Yeah, I do. Bosnia."

We looked at each other, each with our own war-wounds.

"It was a roadside attack. Nasty. Thought I'd lose the leg at first, but they managed to save it. Save me..." his voice trailed off as his gaze wandered to the horizon. "Sorry, that's another topic I usually don't talk about out loud. Why are you collecting my secrets, Kay?"

I smiled deeply. "I didn't mean to, it just sorta keeps happening."

"Well," he said as he set down his beer and hoisted himself out of his chair. "I suggest that I start cooking, before you get any more dirt on me."

I stood and met his smile. "Fantastic. I'm starving. Tell me you have a steak to go with this beer and I'll be a happy woman."

"Getting tired of fish already?" he smirked as I followed him through the patio door to the kitchen.

"Oh, just a bit," I said.

"Well, from what I hear, you'll be with us a while yet, so

you had better get used to it." He opened the fridge and pulled out two beautiful rib-eyes. "But, not tonight."

"Praise be! Those look wonderful, thank you."

"I'll tell you what, I'll grill these up and you can tell me all about my brother's latest business deal..."

"Well, I shouldn't..."

"It's the only way you're getting steak tonight," he said, showcasing the cut that would be mine.

"Huh, tough negotiator," I said. "Alright, fire up the barbeque and I'll tell you everything I know."

And I did. As he worked his magic on the grill, I told him all about my plan to buy the fish plant from Reg. He agreed that it was smart to hide behind a dummy corporation for the deal and pleased that Reg looked like he was going to sign.

"But, what did your lawyer tell him this corporation would be doing with the plant? He wouldn't sell to anyone who might compete with his other plants."

"No, he wouldn't," I said as I cut into the perfectly prepared steak. "But, he was more than happy to hear that the company was in the business of land development. He was downright gleeful at the thought that we'd be coming in to tear down the old plant and build a housing development."

"Asshole," Lance said, slamming down his knife. "He'd rather see this town rot than..."

"I know, I know," I said gently. "I know who I'm dealing with here, Lance. He's a sadistic bastard, and a greedy one. He'll sell quickly, but I don't imagine he'll be too happy when he figures out the buyer is me or about the plans I have to refurbish the old site for production of our new line of products."

"Then why are you smiling?"

"Because, I love to see the bad guy lose," I said, trying to contain myself.

Lance threw his head back and laughed. "All these years, everyone in this town has complained about Reg, but no one has dared to take him on. You've got guts, Kay, I'll give you that."

"It's not so much about winning against Reg, really," I confessed. "It's about moving him off to the side, so the town has a chance to regain its footing, grow. He's standing in the way of progress, out of pure spite and pettiness."

"Well," Lance said, raising his bottle of beer, "here's to progress!"

We spent the rest of the evening reviewing the agreement between Lance's Centre and Tomtex. Now that he knew exactly what my plans were, he was one hundred percent onboard. The terms of the initial contract were reasonable for both parties, so there was nothing standing in the way. After polishing off the pie he had served a la mode, he ducked into his home office, returning with a signed letter of intent regarding the agreement. If Tomtex got the production facility up and running, he'd guarantee a consistent supply of shrimp. He also agreed to a friendly inspection by Raj, our head of development and a few other executive types the following week.

As the hour had grown late, he drove me back to the motel. We shook hands in the parking lot, in front of his Jeep, lingering much longer than was necessary. I looked into his deep brown eyes and could have melted on the spot. I felt my body move closer to his. Felt him lean equally into me. His free hand floated to my face, tracing the line of my jaw ever so softly. I closed my eyes, wishing this could be real.

"Kay," he said softly. "There's too much at stake, I should go."

I opened my eyes reluctantly and searched his face.

"If I stay, what will happen? The whole town is depending on you to pull them out of the trap their lives have become."

"What does you staying have to do with any of that?" I asked, genuinely confused.

"They need *Kay Toms*," he said. "If I stay, she might not." With that, he dropped my hand, turned on his heel, and climbed into the Jeep. I stood there, stunned, as he drove away. *Oh, God...*

Chapter Ten

"How would you like to be my partner in helping get this town back on its feet?" I asked Mr. Richards the next morning. We were sitting in his living room sipping coffee. All of my plans were starting to come together. Reg had signed off on the sale of the plant just an hour before and the funds were already being prepared for transfer into his accounts. Jennifer had written an ironclad contract. He couldn't back out now if he wanted to.

Next on my list was breathing some life back into the town. The production facility would bring jobs, but the community itself needed to move forward also. I could have done it without Mr. Richards, but I wanted him to give back. He knew what I wanted. I just wanted him to be a part of it with me. I needed him. Perhaps I was searching for his approval.

"I never thought I'd ever meet B.J. Toms, let alone be asked to be a partner. It looks like you've made nothing but the right decisions so far, so I'm willing to listen."

"The Federal and Provincial governments can only come up with so many work projects. The rest has got to come from private enterprise." I told him. "I realize that geographically this is not a 365 day tourist area. We can, however, aim for seasonal activity to promote. Winter has skiing, skating, skidooing. Summer, of course, is the high but in between there's moose season, iceberg watching, seal watching, ice fishing. And did you know that the Japanese come in droves to Yellowknife to see the Northern Lights?"

"Northern Lights?"

"There's a belief that you will conceive if you make love under the Northern Lights."

"Guess that's why there are such large families in Newfoundland," Mr. Richards said with a chuckle.

"But just think. We could advertise the Northern Lights and dogsled rides. If Yellowknife can do it, why can't we?"

"Young lady, why not?"

I jumped up and hugged him, then handed him a list I had compiled.

"I've been thinking about some of the attractions needed here. Here are some of the ideas that have crossed my mind." I passed the paper to him.

I watched his face as he read:

Offer berry-picking tours

Cross-country trails in winter

Craft stores

Offer areas for flying kites

Make a museum

"You can cross the museum off your list," he said.

"Really?"

He looked up. "The yellow house on the other side. It's the Barnes House. Believe it was owned by one of the original families in Englee; a Fillier who married a Barnes. It was built in 1937."

"How did I miss that one?"

"Well, it is set back from the road. Guess they need to make it more obvious that it is a museum." He looked down at the list and continued.

Offer guides for moose hunting/deer hunting or whatever game attracts sportsmen

Offer sea safaris

He looked up. "And what is a sea safari?"

"Don't say whale watching. It's too plain. Whale watching is offered everywhere. Call it sea safari, advertise taking pictures of marine life. It sounds more interesting, don't you think?"

He smiled. "We'll see...*Open up the Tickles.*" He looked up. "Sounds good. How'd you know about the Tickles?"

I guess I blushed. I hadn't thought about that one. "I've heard about the Tickles. I thought about whitewater rafting tours there. Surely there's some kind of whitewater around here. Aren't the Tickles suitable?"

"The Tickles are rapids, but I'm not sure. We could look into it." He shook his head and smiled. "Draw up what you've got in mind. We need more than this." He passed the paper back to me. "This would never make it into the *Fortek* Magazine."

"So you'll help?"

"I don't want to go down in history as the man who wouldn't help B. J. Toms. But, what are you suggesting here? That I fund each and every one of these projects?"

"Well, sort of. But, not really," I said, pausing to take another sip of my cooling coffee. "Have you ever heard of micro-lending?"

He stared at me for a moment, blinking his blue eyes. "Yes, I've heard of it in the Third World. That's where small amounts of money are lent to people who have a plan for a small business. The loans are interest free, am I right?"

"That's right," I nodded. "Interest free with a generous repayment plan that allows the small businesses to get up and running. In India, these micro-loans have allowed people, mostly women, to start their own businesses, support their own families and employ their neighbours. They wouldn't qualify normally for a traditional loan, but they're good people who are willing to work for success. And the success rate is impressive. Really impressive. Over ninety percent of the original loans are paid back in full and those businesses are profitable within less than a year. It's incredible, really."

"So, this is what you plan to do here? Micro-loans?"

"Well, I think it'll be a bit more complicated than that, but that's the general idea." I waited hopefully.

"Hmm, I'll have to do a bit of research and think about it, Mrs. Toms," he said finally.

"Please, are you going to call me Mrs. Toms forever?" I asked with a smile.

"Well, that depends," he retorted. "Will I ever hear you call me Jack?"

"Let's see," I said as I stood and extended my hand. "Will you think about it, Jack?"

"I will, Kay," he said, accepting my hand with a firm shake.

"Great! I'll leave some information for you here," I picked up a file and handed it to him. "And, I have a specialist on the subject coming into town next week. We could all sit down and talk over the details. I'm not asking you to do this on your own, Jack. I'm just asking for your help. If we move forward, I'll be putting up the bulk of the funding. I'd just ask that you contribute what you can financially and lend your name to the project. The people of Englee trust you."

"Thank you, Kay, that's nice to hear," he said as he walked me to the front door. "I'll read over your materials and we'll set a time to meet with this expert..."

"Sean, Sean Chen," I offered.

"In the meantime, are you still planning on moving to the house on the hill?" he asked.

"Absolutely," I said as I donned my coat and stepped out the door. "I'm meeting with a contractor today. Melissa Young's husband, Tom. I hear he's good?"

"Tom Young, oh, yes. Good man, honest. I think you'll be happy with him."

"Would you like to join us this afternoon? It's your house, I'd like your input into the renovations, Jack." His first name still felt strange on my tongue.

"Yes, yes, that would be fine. I'd like the chance to talk with Tom and learn what your ideas are for the house. Will he be putting a crew together?"

"I suspect so. I'll find out this afternoon. I was thinking I'd suggest that he take on Charlie..."

"Oh!" Jack exclaimed.

"No? Bad idea?"

"No, no, I think Charlie means well, but just be careful there. He's a bit, well, unpredictable, is all. Plus, he's Reg's man, you know."

"Yes, he is." That was why I had originally wanted to hire him. To give him a chance to step away from Reg Richards. "Thank you, Mr...Jack. For everything."

I breathed a sigh of relief as I walked down the driveway. I had made another beginning.

I could feel a friendship starting to build between Jack and me. It was a friendship that tugged at me in a most unusual way. I wanted to trust him, but I didn't want to trust him. History held me back. I wanted to hate him because of that history but I couldn't. It was a friendship on the outside and a struggle with emotions on the inside. His feelings towards me looked so honest and real, just the way they had been to Kenny Warren. Because of what he had done before I wondered if they were indeed real and honest. Perhaps they were as phony as my whole being.

In any case, he was the one I needed. In the game of trust and distrust, he won in both areas. Today it was trust.

"Sean," I said into my cell phone. "Big plans next week?"

"Just the usual," Sean replied. He sounded distracted, papers shuffling. "Why?"

"Well, cancel whatever you had on the go. I need you here." I waited for the silence on the other end of the line to dissipate.

"There? Where? Englee, Newfoundland? Canada?" he sounded shocked and utterly appalled all at the same time. "But, what? Why?"

"Well, look at it like a trial run," I said, trying to keep the smile out of my voice.

"Trial run at what? I can't fish, you know," he said, confused.

"At your promotion," I exclaimed. I had always known I wouldn't be able to keep Sean as an assistant forever, but would be heartbroken to lose him.

"My promotion? You, you mean, the research, OMG, did you love it?" I could picture the beaming smile on his face.

"I did love it, enough that I think you might be able to use it right here in Englee. I'll explain when you get here. Raj and a few others are coming out next Friday, but I'd like you here sooner, Thursday. Book your flight and rent a car on your expense card..."

"Can't I bring the helicopter?" he pouted jokingly.

"Do, just a car. You'll need to blend in a bit. I'm not entirely sure Englee's ready for you, Sean."

"Blend, me? Oh honey, unless it's a margarita, I have no idea how!" he laughed nervously. "Oh, you're serious. Oh, right, blend. I'll do my best bosslady! I'll email you my itinerary as soon as I'm booked. And, Kay?"

"Yes, Sean?"

"Thank you." His voice rang with sincerity.

"You're welcome," I said. "And, Sean? Watch out for moose on the way into town, alright?"

"Oh God..."

On my way back to the motel, I stopped by the General Store to find Melissa Young. She was busy cleaning the floors as I entered.

"Good day, Mrs. Toms," she said as she hastily set the mop aside. "What can I do for you?"

"Well, I'm just on my way to see your husband this afternoon," I said.

"Yes, ma'am, and thank you so much. I can't tell you what it would mean to us for Tom to get the work." She looked nervous, as though she was interviewing for the job herself.

"If he's as good a contractor as everyone says he is, I'll be more than happy to have him do the work. Now, setting that aside for the moment, I was wondering if you'd have some time to meet with me next Friday morning."

She stared at me for a moment, her pretty face frozen as though caught in the headlights. "Meet with you?"

"Yes, I have a few things I'd like to discuss with you. Can we meet for breakfast Friday, say 8:30 at your house? I'd love a bit of home cooking, if that's not asking too much."

"Ah, sure, sure, I'd be happy to cook, but, Mrs. Toms, what could you possibly have to talk to me about?"

"Don't worry, Melissa, it's nothing bad, just a chat. I'll be bringing a friend along, too. See you then."

She waved limply as I exited the store, still unsure what to think. I had probably set her up for a week of worry, but I needed to make sure Sean and I got the chance to talk with her, before I set my ideas in full motion.

I took a deep breath as I made my way down the street. The air was muggy, thick, with the smell of the sea. I was lost in thought as I rounded the corner and almost ran headlong into Asia. Half a step behind her was Reg.

"Sorry, Asia," I said as I stepped back and regained my balance.

"Oh, Mrs. Toms, that's fine," Asia smiled brightly. Her long red curls shone, even in the gloomy light of the day.

"Still with us, I see," Reg said gruffly. "Thought you'd be longin' for the city by now."

"Oh, no," I said as sweetly as I could. "I think I'm falling in love with this town."

"Huh, this town or my brother?" he mocked.

"The town, Reg, Englee is enchanting." My hand itched to slap his smug face.

"Well, money in my pocket," he smirked.

"Excuse me?"

Asia shuffled her feet as her cheeks turned bright red. "Dad!"

"You, staying at the motel," he said, puffing out his chest. "I likes a long-term lodger, does the accounts good."

"Oh, yes, well I've enjoyed your wife's hospitality," I said with emphasis. "I don't know how much longer I'll be there, though."

"Really?" he looked surprised, yet satisfied.

"Hmmm, really," I replied shortly. Turning to Asia I asked, "You know, Asia, we really should go shopping together, like we discussed. Maybe sometime next week, I'd love the company."

Her face lit up. "Awesome!"

"No, no goddamned way," Reg said, taking the girl's arm somewhat roughly. "I'm not sending you out with a virtual stranger to blow a bunch of money...."

"Oh, I'm sorry," I said meekly. "I thought I heard you say at your brother's last night that you had hit the jackpot. I assumed that meant the family could afford a few luxuries..."

"Oh, I got money, lady. You think you're the only one with cash around here?"

"What jackpot?" Asia asked. "Dad? Did you win the 6/49?"

"Not that kind of jackpot, Asia. I was going to tell you and Ester at dinner tonight." He looked flustered, as though he had been caught in a lie. "Just signed the papers this morning. I've sold the fish plant."

"You sold the plant? To who? Does that mean it'll be up and running again soon?"

I looked at Reg intently, enjoying how much his daughter, my daughter, could make him squirm.

"No, not exactly, land developers, they are. Not planning on keeping the plant." He couldn't help but smile.

"What, they'll tear it down? But what about the town? What about jobs? Everyone around here has stayed, hoping it will reopen someday. They need the plant. How could you do this?"

"It was an offer I couldn't refuse," he said. "Now, if you please, I'd rather not air our dirties in front of Mrs. Toms, and the whole world. Let's go."

"No," Asia said, standing defiant. "I don't want to go. I want you to explain how you could do this to this town, to our friends!"

"That's enough, Asia. Start walking. Now." With that, he took her by the hand and pulled. As she brushed past me, I stepped in front of her momentarily.

"You know where to find me," I whispered to her. As they continued on their way, I couldn't help but feel hopeful. Asia had more than enough backbone to take on her father. Reg was in for a long day of fighting.

"And see that t'ere," Tom Young said as he pointed to a water spot on the ceiling. T'ere'll be water damage comin' t'rough the roof." Mister Richards and I had already spent nearly an hour going through the house on the hill room by room. The problems were large, expensive, but fixable.

"Right, Tom," Jack said as he nodded and frowned at the cracked windowpane in the living room. "Well, if Missus Toms is up for it still..."

"I am," I said quickly. "All of it. And I want it done right, this house needs to be restored, not torn down, Tom. Are we clear?"

"Yes, missus, yes indeed," Tom said, nodding enthusiastically.

"Take a day or two and put a quote together for me. We'll meet again next week and go over the details," I said. "You'll be in charge of the whole project—hiring, overseeing the trades, all of it. I won't be far, but I'll trust you to take care and come in on time."

"Of course, Missus. T'ere won't be any shortage of workers." He smiled warmly. I could picture him easily by Melissa's side. He had a face just as kind as his wife's. A big man, Tom towered over Mister Richards, yet his gentle nature showed through.

"Oh, I know that," I said. "By the time I got back to the motel this afternoon, there were ten 'applications' under my door. Word doesn't take long to spread around here, does it?"

"Sure doesn't at that, Kay," Jack said with a chuckle.

"Whole place is abuzz today, what with you hiring and Reg selling the plant," Tom said casually.

Mister Richards stopped dead in his tracks. "He what?" His

face went slack as he quickly flipped through the possibilities of what such a move by his son could mean.

"Sorry, Mister Richards, didn't mean to gossip," Tom said. "I'll just be on my way." Not wanting to risk his new job, Tom fled the house quickly.

"Sold the plant, well. Seems I owe my son a visit," Jack said as he slid his hat back on. "This wouldn't have anything to do with you, *Missus Toms*, would it?"

I simply stood there and fluttered my eyelashes a bit. "Me?"

Jack laughed heartily. "Honest to goodness, Kay, I don't know what you're up to yet, but I'll get to the bottom of it, come hell or high water." With a light pat on my shoulder, he made his exit.

I stood at the window that overlooked the harbour and gazed out. I saw Charlie working on his dock. I watched him mending a net. He looked up and saw me and I waved. He waved back. I needed to make the connection.

The evening was growing cold and lonely. The quietness was deafening. There I was, home, yet so far from it. There were no voices calling to me from the kitchen and the aroma of my mother's freshly made bread was in memory only. I stood in the room that had been so familiar to me. The main pieces of furniture remained, but little else. The photo of my mother that had hung on the wall was gone, the souvenirs and trinkets of their lives must have been packed long ago.

Through the window I could see the treetops outside and

I listened to the chirping of the birds. In the waning light, the birch leaves looked a pale pink against the darkening sky, their slender silver trunks swaying gracefully like dancers.

I had come home. I brushed aside a tear that threatened to fall. I had come home in one sense. In another I could never come home again.

Except for the chirping of the birds and the ticking of the clock on the armoire, I was alone in the silent house. No mother. No father. Not even the daughter who should be asleep in the next room. Not even the husband whose gentle breathing should be heard and whose warm body should be next to mine. I was home but I was alone.

I glanced towards the clock. The day had been long. I didn't want to leave, yet I knew I couldn't stay at the house. It was cold, damp, the electricity had been cut years before and the only water was as cold as the Arctic.

While I had accomplished a lot in a week, there was still so much more I wanted. The business side was easy—deals could always be made, compromises made. It was my personal desires that seemed impossible. I wanted Lance. I wanted my home. I wanted both the dependence and the independence. I was becoming confused as Kenny Warren tried to surface in the space now occupied by Kay Toms. I needed Lance. I thought he had all the answers.

Chapter Eleven

Yet, Lance was busy. It was my own fault. In the week that followed he was flooded with work at the Centre, trying to get ready for Tomtex's upcoming inspection. While he toiled away, making sure the whole operation was shipshape, I spent the days working from my makeshift office at the Park Place and taking numerous trips each day to oversee the construction at the house on the hill. Tom was already making good progress. He and his crew of two men and one woman had gutted everything they needed to and cleaned the space out. There were plumbers and electricians coming and going daily. It was a hive of activity—one that brought out nearly half the town to watch at some point each day. This was the most excitement Englee had seen in years, apparently. Rumour had it that there was a fair sized betting pool on the final outdoor paint colour. The odds were favouring yellow.

As I made my way back and forth each day, I stopped and chatted with the locals, getting to know them once again, ever so slowly. Most were still cautious, but there were signs that they were starting to get used to me. In many ways, I envied them. They were so relaxed, almost content in their accepted lifestyle. I was stressed beyond reasoning. I had taken on a task, which nobody had asked me to do and which nobody had any idea I was doing. It was all my doing – the pressure to help them achieve their goals. Perhaps I was wrong. They were happy not having. Perhaps I was bringing them an unhappiness they didn't deserve and hadn't asked for. Perhaps it would not be the utopia I had envisioned. Moments, hours, of self-doubt plagued me, but I was too far in to stop now.

Reg was growing cockier and more openly hostile by the day. With the sale finalized and the cash in his pocket, he strutted around town. When our paths crossed, he dropped all pretence he had once held about enjoying my company. Apparently he believed that the elevation in his bank account had brought him up to my level. If only he knew how many more zeros he would need for that to be remotely true. I tried not to laugh openly as he looked down his nose at me and made jokes about my impending status as a 'townie.' I knew I had to bide my time. He'd find out soon enough who he had sold to and what I would be doing with the plant. I couldn't wait.

Thursday morning, I jumped out of bed with a smile. Sean would be arriving in a few short hours and I couldn't wait to see him. It felt as though my exile was coming to an end. My people were finally arriving, to help my people. It was such a strange notion—my two worlds colliding in living Technicolor.

"Is the room all ready?" I asked Ester as I walked into the lobby of the motel. She was her bedazzled self, standing behind the counter proudly in her newest velour track suit. Reg must have cracked open his wallet.

"Oh, yes, ready and waiting," she said with a warm smile. "You must be excited to see your friend."

"Well, Sean's actually my employee, but he feels like a friend," I said, feeling a bit sheepish.

"Then he's a friend indeed," Ester chuckled. "Is he bringing his wife?"

I almost choked. "Um, no, no, Sean's not married," I said through the most ladylike cough I could muster. "I think he's seeing...someone...but I'm not entirely sure."

Ester wiggled her plucked eyebrows and couldn't hide the mischievous glimmer in her eye. "Maybe he has his eye on you..."

"Oh, lord, no," I blurted. "I'm not his type." There was no point in explaining it to her and, besides, it wasn't my place to discuss Sean's sexuality with people he didn't know. They'd all figure it out, I was sure. My assistant was many things, but closeted was not one of them.

After saying goodbye to Ester, I made a quick run to the house to talk to Tom. He had a number of fixture samples for me to look at and choose from, then needed to discuss the roof. By the time we were done, I had only minutes to race back to the motel to meet Sean. I had promised him breakfast the moment he arrived.

As I came around to the front of the motel, I saw a brand new rental car in the parking lot and had to hold myself back from running to the door. Sean's lean form crawled out of the driver's side and paused as he took in his surroundings. Over his perfectly tailored pants and light blue buttoned down shirt he pulled on a Ralph Lauren jacket. As he turned in my direction, he slid his sunglasses on to finish the look. No one in the world could have guessed that he had just traveled by plane and then by car for hours on end. He looked like he had just stepped onto the catwalk.

"Aren't you a sight for sore eyes," I said as I stepped up and hugged him fiercely.

"Oh my God, it's so good to see you, Kay," he said, his voice wavering slightly. "But, seriously, where the hell am I?" He pulled back and looked at me over the rim of his glasses.

"Welcome to the Rock," I said, flinging my arms wide. "Sean, you are standing on land first discovered by the Vikings centuries before Columbus was even a twinkle in his father's eye, the land of fishing and fisheries, the land, my son, as the locals say, that is about to give you the biggest break of your life." I inhaled deeply. Sean's eyes wandered down the nearly abandoned streets and back to me once again.

"Right, but seriously, drab," he winked and took my arm. "Now, before anything else, let's get some caffeine in my system. I'm running stressfully low. Where's the Starbucks?" he looked earnestly from left to right.

"Well..." I said as I lead him towards the restaurant. "They do things a little differently around here."

He stepped boldly through the door and stopped dead in his tracks. I didn't know who was more shocked at his arrival—Sean or the tables full of regulars. Not only was Sean young, impeccably dressed, and obviously flamboyant, he was probably the first Asian who had set foot in town since the Woo family had closed their restaurant in Roddickton after the moratorium. Sean was half Chinese, half Thai, with a little bit of English thrown in somewhere along the genetic line. He stood just a couple inches shy of six feet tall with a bone structure that every model in Milan would sell their souls for. He was what one could only call stunning. In the Park Place restaurant, jaws hung slightly agape as the regulars took in all that he was, spoons came to a standstill, and the air itself seemed to quiet.

I took Sean's elbow and pushed him towards an empty table by the window. "Oh my God, Kay! It's Deliverance! What have you done?" he tried to control the volume of his voice as his dark, deeply set eyes continued to scan the faces, and clothes, of the locals.

"Oh, Sean, please," I said leaning forward over the table. "Englee's not that bad. They're just not used to new people."

"New people, gay people, little bit Chinese people," he said frantically as he set his sunglasses down and pointed to his eyes. "Lord help me."

"Sean, Sean, please relax, it's going to be alright, I promise. You'll see." I patted his hand as Asia came over with a fresh pot of coffee. "Ah, see, a friendly face!" I declared. "Sean Chen,

Asia. Asia Richards, this is my friend Sean."

Asia's smile beamed, while Sean's mouth worked silently. "Funny, Kay. Super funny. Hilarious!" Both Asia and I looked at each other and shrugged, baffled.

"Hello," Asia said, extending her free hand. "Nice to meet you, Mister Chen."

He looked at her hand, then started giggling. "Oh, oh, no, sorry, that's your real name? Asia? I thought Kay was making a joke!"

"Oh, God, I'm sorry, Sean!" I blurted. No wonder he looked so confused. It hadn't even dawned on me.

"Yes, Asia is my real name," she explained as she turned over our cups and started pouring. "That's not...ummm...well... oh, how do I...ummmm..." she stammered as she realized why he had been taken so aback. All the colour drained from her face, leaving a canvas of freckles.

"Offensive?" Sean offered. "A white girl named Asia, no. We're totally used to that sort of thing these days. Just promise me you do not now, nor will you ever, get a tattoo of a Chinese symbol anywhere on that cute little body of yours," he looked her straight in the eye and took her hand dramatically. "Swear it, Asia. Swear it to me on all that is Prada and holy."

Asia let out the breath she had been holding in fear that she had been racially insensitive. A smile spread across her beautiful face as her rosy cheeks returned to their natural glow.

"I swear!" she saluted. The customers at nearby tables were

watching the exchange sceptically.

"Swear? Swear on what?" Sean said, closing his eyes for effect and biting his lower lip.

"On all that is Prada and holy," Asia said, giggling, yet trying to keep a straight face.

"Excellent!" Sean clapped.

"Now, can we get on with breakfast?" I asked. I couldn't help but smile at his cocky grin. "So much drama and you've only been here two minutes!"

"Oh, just you wait and see, Kay, I'm going to take this town by storm!" he declared as he scooped a menu from behind the sugar jar. "Hmm, do they have anything low carb?"

"Ah, yes, you'll be mayor here in no time," I chuckled.

"No, seriously, she actually slept with him," Sean said as he pushed back his chair after we finished eating. We had spent an hour over eggs gossiping and catching up. It seemed that life back in Boston had just kept rolling on without me.

"Come on," I said as we stood. "Let's get you checked in, then a quick tour of the sights. We have a meeting with Mr. Richards, Jack, later this afternoon and he's invited us for dinner. You'll have time to rest for a bit before we see him." I slid enough cash on the table to cover the bill and a generous tip for Asia, who had fallen in love with Sean over the course of the meal. She giggled every time she swooped by our table and had a rather in depth conversation with him about his outfit. At one point she even thanked me for bringing Sean to Englee, as though he was a gift just for her. I couldn't help but smile. I knew exactly what she was feeling; that there really were people out there in the world that held the same views as her. She had seen them on television, seen them on the streets of the cities she occasionally visited, but the idea that someone like Sean could be right there in her hometown was a revelation.

"Mrs. Toms, if you're heading that way, could you remind Ester that I've got to leave in about twenty minutes?" Asia asked as we made our way out the door.

"Sure, Asia, and we'll see you later, okay? Sean's going to be here for a few days..." Her smile widened dramatically.

"Thank you," she said as she twirled back to the kitchen.

"You're so welcome," I said as I watched her go. I could feel Sean's eyes on me, taking it all in.

"Beautiful girl," he said as we walked through the parking lot.

"Um? Oh, yes, she is," I couldn't stop the feeling of pride that swelled in my chest.

"I have to say, she reminds me of someone, just a bit," he said slyly.

I stretched my neck and looked straight ahead. Sean knew me better than anyone in the world. While he didn't know all of my secrets, he knew enough to make me nervous occasionally.

"Sean," I said, slowing the pace of our short walk dramatically.

"The people here, they don't know that I have a connection to this town. They don't know my family connection..." Sean knew I had originally come to the island to see my parents' graves. He didn't know that I had grown up in Englee or my real name. He did, however, know my real hair colour.

"Mrs. Kay Toms," he said, turning his head to look at me directly. "All of your secrets, business and personal, are yours to keep. They will never, and I mean never, cross these lips!"

"Thank you, Sean. There's so much I want to accomplish here, for this town. Anything personal would just get in the way."

Just then a slightly muddy Jeep pulled into the parking lot and stopped right in front of us. Lance stepped out, in all his glory, his hair shining in the sun, the muscles of his arms rippling under the fitted grey T-shirt he wore with slightly faded jeans. Sean's mouth dropped at the sight of him in person— the video conferencing camera on my laptop obviously hadn't done Lance justice.

"O...M...G..." Sean said under his breath.

"Kay, hi," Lance said as he walked over. "I'm glad I caught you."

"I should be so lucky," Sean muttered, then quickly smiled up at Lance.

"Lance Richards, it's my honour and privilege to introduce Mr. Sean Chen, my friend, assistant and soon to be vice-director of Tomtex's philanthropic arm. Sean Chen, Mr. Lance Richards, owner of The Roddickton Marine Centre." The two shook hands.

"Ah, the new supplier," Sean said. "You've had our product development team working overtime, Mr. Richards."

"Please, call me Lance and I can promise you they've had me working even harder." He smiled and I watched Sean melt a little. "Actually, that's what I wanted to talk to you about, Kay, the itinerary for tomorrow's meeting..."

"Yoo-who!" Ester's voice shrilled as she stepped out of the lobby and right into our conversation. Sean's focus went immediately to the glitz and glitter that was Ester Richards. His eyes slid slowly down her entire outfit, from the top of her hair-sprayed head to the bedazzled design of the toes that peeked out of the stiletto sandals she wore. I quickly raised a hand to push his mouth shut, then turned to Ester who was waving a set of keys in my direction. Lance tried valiantly to hide the smile on his face as he, too, watched Sean's reaction.

I introduced them quickly, trying to hurry their meeting along before Sean starting picking apart Ester's outfit. I was surprised that I felt somewhat protective over Ester; I had grown to really like her over the past few weeks.

"Sorry to interrupt," she said. "But I've got to get to the restaurant, so I've closed up the check-in for a bit. Here's your keys, Mister Chen, room's just down there. Do you need help with your bags? I can call Charlie down from the dock..."

"Ah..." Sean hesitated, only because in the city he would

never be caught dead hauling his own luggage. That's what bellhops were for.

"Don't worry about it, Ester, I'll give him a hand," Lance said.

"Oh, you're a doll!" Ester leaned over and gave him a rough hug. "I'll be back at the office around one, Mr. Chen, if you need anything."

"When do you take a break, Ester?" Lance said with genuine concern. "Tell that brother of mine that you need to hire more help, would ya?"

"Oh, Lance, you know how expensive it would be to hire all the people he'd need to replace me? Ha!" Ester chuckled as she rushed towards the restaurant.

"Lord, isn't that the truth?" Lance said to me and shook his head.

"She's fabulous!" Sean declared, breaking the moment of reflection Lance and I had fallen into. "God, so much glitter, so little time!"

"So, Lance, what was it you needed?" I said, refocusing.

"Oh, there were a set of specs Raj was supposed to send me, but I can't seem to find them, do you..."

"That's because he sent them with me!" Sean said with a light pat on Lance's chest. "They're in my briefcase, here." He stepped to his rental car and popped the trunk.

"Are you moving in permanently?" Lance asked as he peered at the full set of designer luggage Sean had packed.

"No, probably just a week," Sean shrugged, as though the volume of his wardrobe was completely acceptable.

Lance just laughed and started lugging the cases into Sean's room, right next to mine. After quickly freshening up in the powder room, Sean stepped back outside, moisturized and looking marvellous. He handed Lance the papers he required.

"Raj said to let you know that this isn't absolutely necessary for tomorrow's meeting, but if you wanted to go over it, you could."

"Thanks, Sean, I think I'll feel better if I'm fully prepared." Lance flipped through the pages, giving them a quick glance. "Well, I better get back. I'll see you tomorrow..."

"Definitely," Sean said. "Kay's taking me on the grand tour of the town next."

"Ah, the dime tour, you'll love it," Lance smirked as he climbed into his Jeep.

After walking our way through town, I took Sean to see the two houses I had purchased in the cove and the house on the hill. He took notes of the dimensions of the two and started scribbling ideas for possible uses as we picked our way through the neglected structures. I could see inspiration hitting him and knew, right then and there, that I was making the right decision. No matter what Jack's reaction to my proposal would be, I had to make a go of it all.

I dropped Sean back at his room in the early afternoon,

then hurried to my own to jump online with Jennifer. The deal for the fish plant was completely done and dusted. Now I had her working on setting up the micro-lending system that I envisioned for Englee.

We arrived at the Richards' house shortly before five that evening.

"Come in, come in," Janine said as she ushered us into the entrance hall. "That wind's been picking up all day and I'd rather leave it outside the house." She smoothed the front of her wide apron as she inspected Sean's tweed pants and immaculately pressed white dress shirt. She nodded tersely before taking his jacket, then mine. We'd obviously passed for acceptable as she lead us into the sitting room.

"Thank you, Janine," I said as she turned to leave us. She grumbled something and disappeared into the kitchen.

"Ah, you've made it!" Jack exclaimed happily as he extended a hand to Sean. "Welcome, welcome. Jack Richards."

"Mister Richards, a pleasure," Sean said, his voice firmer and slightly deeper than I was used to hearing. He held his spine straight and smiled warmly. "Sean Chen, thank you for meeting with us."

"Anything for Mrs. Toms," Jack said as he kissed my cheek and gave me a deep wink. "Kay, lovely to see you, as always. And Mister Chen, I'm glad to finally meet you. I've heard a lot of good things."

Sean took a deep breath. He was obviously nervous, but

trying not to let it show. He knew that his future depended on our success in Englee and that Mr. Richards could make that happen.

Jack poured us a round of drinks before we settled into our chairs. "As you know, Mr. Richards..."

"Ah, ah, Jack..."

"Right," Sean took a long sip of his gin and tonic. "Jack, Tomtex has a charitable branch that's active around the world in a multitude of projects. In the past, we've focused on donating funds and working with established organizations."

"Yes, I'm aware of the work your company has done and it's impressive, however I want to be crystal clear. Englee does not need a handout. This town doesn't need charity." Jack's voice was as firm as his stare.

"Oh, of course," Sean replied, his voice raising half an octave. "We would never propose handouts. What we, what Kay sees for Englee is a cooperative movement of sorts. You've read my report on micro-lending?"

"Hmm, yes, very interesting."

"Well, that's basically what we'd like to do here for the community. Tomtex would establish a micro-loan program eligible to the residents of Englee and the surrounding community. We'd offer the applicants a chance at loans of fifty thousand dollars or less to develop their business ideas. Those loans would have a grace period of one year, where no repayment would be required. After the first year, the business owners would need to pay back the original loan, interest free, in reasonable installments."

"It's a fascinating idea, son," Jack said as he contemplated his drink. "Brass tacks. How much are we talking about and what would you need from me?"

Sean looked to me. "We'll want to start small," I said. "Ten loans to ten different applicants, if we get that many, in the first year. We'll be learning on our feet, Jack. It might work, it might not. The first year will tell us, without a doubt, if we're on to something positive for the town."

"Ten loans at fifty grand," he mused. "That's a lot of money, Kay."

"Sure is. I'm aware of how much this idea's going to take to get off the ground and I'm willing to take the majority of the risk."

Jack and I eyed each other for a moment. Sean sat nervously, his head swivelling between us like he was watching the tennis match of the century.

"Think of the profit," Sean finally blurted.

"Profit?" Jack scoffed. "I thought this was a charitable endeavour." He eyed Sean as a cat eyes a mouse. He was testing Sean, and therefore testing me.

"Oh, yeah, no, it totally is," Sean stammered. "I didn't mean the direct profit. No, no. The indirect. As these businesses get up and running, they'll need supplies, they'll need operating space, they'll need transportation. Seems to me you have a hand in all of those avenues. And, as the businesses grow and provide long term employment for the town, that'll mean more people, more groceries, more, well, everything."

Jack turned his stare from Sean's nearly shaking form to me. He smiled. The deal was done. Right there. Sean had said exactly what he'd needed to hear—long term growth for the town. "I've made enough money in my lifetime, son. Enough for two lifetimes, really. My interest, as I suspect your boss here knows, is that as my businesses grow, so does Englee. So does Newfoundland."

"Newfoundland," I echoed and tilted my glass. "Slainte."

"Sociable," Jack responded, raising his own. He looked sideways at Sean and raised a brow. "That means drink, lad."

"Oh, right! Sociable," Sean said and took a drink.

"So, those brass tacks," Jack said to me. "Lay it out."

"Ten percent into the pot from you, plus your endorsement and invaluable experience in overseeing the projects." I said plainly.

"So, you'll both set this in motion, then off you go, back to the mainland to leave me running the show?"

"No, not quite," I countered. I knew what he was asking. "I plan on being here for a while yet, though I'm not entirely sure how long. When I do return to Boston, I'll be keeping a close eye on Englee. Sean's job will be to oversee the running of the micro-bank and will be here on-site regularly."

"I will?" Sean said slowly. He looked to Jack and suddenly

sat up straight as a pin. "Of course, yes, I will. Plus, our office in Boston will be behind the project all the way. Right?" he looked at me sheepishly. We had discussed most of the details prior to the meeting, but I too wanted to see how he'd perform under pressure.

"Yes, one hundred percent," I said. "My plan is to have Sean running his own division, one dedicated to the micro-bank, for the whole first year. It's going to work, Jack."

"The government has tried before..."

"Yep, they have. They've handed the money over and walked away. That doesn't work. Our company will be here, present in Englee with resources—legal advice, business planning and development—whatever the business owners need, within reason. We don't want to prop them up forever, while they learn the ropes."

Both men nodded as they each mulled over the implications.

"Like I said, we'll be learning on our feet, but we have the drive to make it happen."

"Well," Jack said as he stood. "Where do we start?"

Sean and I both rose and accepted his handshake. "I'll have Jennifer send you the legal documents right away. It'll be a clean, straightforward agreement, friendly. Then, first thing tomorrow morning, Sean and I are going to start recruiting."

Jack laughed heartily. "God love ya, Kay, you don't let the grass grow, do you?"

"No point, this town has been languishing long enough."

"As have we, let's eat. Janine!" he hollered towards the kitchen door. "We'll be seated now."

"Oh, right, just get on with it then. I'll serve when the food's ready and not a moment sooner," she replied through the door.

Jack clapped Sean on the back. "Foul temperament has Janine, but a brilliant cook. You're in for a treat. Loosen that collar now and follow me, the business is done."

Sean's shoulders rolled back and he exhaled fully for the first time that night. "Fantastic! I'm famished. This business stuff is hard work," he said lightly as he tackled the top button of his shirt.

"Just wait till we actually get started," I said, only half joking.

As we took our seats at the table, I noticed Jack had once again set more places that were needed. "Expecting someone else?" I asked.

"Oh, round here, you never know..." his eyebrows rose. As though planned, we heard the front door swing open and Lance walked in.

"Sorry I'm late, Dad," he said as he cleared the doorway, stopping dead in his tracks at the sight of me and Sean. "Oh, you didn't say you were having company." He looked his father straight in the eye.

"Oh, come now, Kay isn't *company*, she's a friend of the family and has just become my new business partner, of sorts." Jack motioned Lance to the seat beside Sean and directly in front of me.

"Funny, looks like we have something in common then, Dad," Lance said with a brow that rose almost as high as his father's.

"Really?" Jack laughed. "I knew it! I knew you were up to something!" His fist hit the table. "Now maybe you can tell me what you're planning on doing with that fish plant you bought."

"Sorry?" I asked, trying my most innocent voice.

"Please, darlin', you may have fooled Reg with that dummy corp, but you won't get one over on this old man so easily. Land developers in Englee, bah!"

The whole table laughed, including Sean who knew the details of every deal I had ever made. "Well, Jack, sometimes it's necessary to use a cover, a disguise, to get things done."

"You're right there," Jack nodded. "I didn't tell Reg that I suspected you were the buyer. I knew you'd have your reasons. But, now, tell me what your plan is. I can't take the suspense much longer!"

As Janine served the starter course of lobster bisque, I explained my intention for the old plant and Lance's supply chain. Jack was thoroughly impressed.

"So, a real, honest to God business plan and investment! Wonderful!" he patted Sean's hand. "That's exactly what we need. Oh, I wasn't sure I'd ever see that place running again." There were tears forming in his blue eyes.

"Now, Dad, don't get ahead of yourself," Lance said. "We

have a long way to go yet. I've got to pass inspection tomorrow and Kay still has all the details and renovations to the plant. She's not cutting the ribbon tomorrow."

"Oh, a ribbon cutting!" Sean chimed. "So much fun! Can I be there?"

"Slow down, Sean, you've got your own work to do first." I shook a finger at him.

"Of course, but just think about it all, what this place could be by this time next year! A beautiful main street with flowerpots overflowing, tourists shopping, fine dining, oh, and the influences of fashion..." his gaze looked out into the room dramatically, somewhere in the distance.

"That's one hell of an imagination you've got there, son!" Jack said, thanking Janine quietly over his shoulder for delivering the main course to the table. "I don't know that Englee will be a fashion Mecca, but I like where you're going."

"Kay's just full of good ideas for this town," Lance said, raising his glass. "Thank you."

"You're welcome," I said, responding with my own glass. My eyes lingered on his and I suddenly had visions of throwing myself across the table at him.

"Were you like this as a kid?" he asked.

"Like what?"

"Full of ideas, so business minded. It must be genetic. Was it your mother or your father?"

"Neither. I was a tomboy. My mother died when I was only

four. I don't think my father had the entrepreneur spirit in him."
I immediately regretted my spontaneous response.

Suddenly the silence that engulfed us was so uncomfortable
as Lance and I stared at each other.

"This dinner looks wonderful," Sean interrupted the
moment. "Scott and I went down to the fish market in Boston
just a few weeks ago, but nothing we found there looked or
smelled anywhere near this good!"

"Oh, well, dig in, please. Knowing Janine, there's probably
more in the kitchen," Jack said as he watched Lance's eyes
slide off me and back to his own plate. "So, do you and your
brother eat fish often then?" Jack asked Sean in an effort to
distract himself from daydreams of his son's marriage to the
famous Kay Toms.

"Brother?"

"Scott? Is that what you said..."

Sean chuckled and shook his head. "Oh, no, Scott's my
boyfriend," Sean said lightly as he took another bite.

"Oh! Oh, dear, me, I'm sorry," Jack stammered and stuttered.
"Boyfriend, well, that's nice."

Sean saw the look of despair on the older man's face
and felt sorry for him. Jack obviously had no idea what to
say. "Sorry, Mister Richards, if I've shocked you. I've become
accustomed to being open about my life. It's the only way I
know to honour who I am and the people I love. I'm aware,
though, that I tend to live in a bit of a bubble, surrounded by

people who are used to me and the gay community in general. I forget that my orientation can be difficult for some."

Jack looked to Lance for a moment. "I learned long ago, Sean, to accept the choices people make in life and their true nature. Some will lead mediocre lives, settle into tradition happily, and never reach for anything more. Some have spirits that wander, searching the world for the pieces of their lives that complete them. Some run from their families, from who they really are..." His eyes slid to me. "Some try to make it right."

He shook his head, as though clearing it, and turned to face Sean head on. "I can respect a man who knows who he is and lives honestly."

"Thank you, Jack," Sean said warmly. "I've been a bit worried that Englee might not accept me."

"It might not be easy at first," Lance said. "This is a small town and some people will remain closed-minded. However, on the island, a man is generally judged by his deeds—what he does and how hard he works. Show them you're here to work, for them, and they'll welcome you soon enough."

"God, you're beautiful," Sean said as he leaned a touch closer. A burst of laughter escaped Jack as Lance's spine stiffened. "How on earth are you still single?"

"Oh, well, thank you, Sean," Lance's face began to burn a bright red. "Just haven't met the right girl, I guess." He looked to me for a lifeline.

"I fear my son might be going blind, Sean," Jack said, swinging his eyes between me and Lance none-too-subtly.

"Oh, that's so common in straight men," Sean said, nodding his head.

"Janine!" Lance called over his shoulder. "Is there more salmon?"

"You know there is," Janine's voice boomed as she poked her head out from the kitchen door. "I haven't let you hide behind my apron since you were five years old and I'm not about to let you start again!" She smiled wickedly, then slammed the door.

I laughed harder than I had for years at the look of disappointment on Lance's face. "Damn! I thought she'd totally back me up!" he chuckled. "So, how about that weather today?" he tried lamely to change the topic.

"Beautiful. Lovely. Now, back to the question of your bachelorhood," Sean teased. Seeing Lance genuinely squirm in his chair, he decided to take pity on the poor soul and gently turned the topic back to questions about the town and life on the island. "So, what's the town like in the winter?"

I looked to Sean and smiled my thanks. He was making quite an impression on the Richards' men. I had picked the right man for the job.

As the main course came to an end, Janine rolled in a tray of coffee and a plate of assorted sweets. We were ogling the treats when the front door slammed. In a rush of cold air, Reg and his manager, Bob, walked into the dining room. Dressed in jeans and flannel shirts, the two wobbled slightly on their feet. Apparently they had had a few beers with their dinner.

"Oh, well, would you look at this," Reg said with a slight slur as he plunked himself down at an empty place setting at the end of the table. "Looks like we missed dinner, but made it just in time for dessert. Janine! Get me and Bob some plates and a couple a drinks."

"Now, son, we were just finishing a lovely supper. Perhaps you could leave us be and come by tomorrow morning." Jack looked nervously from me to Sean to Lance. Sean was quietly trying to fade into the wallpaper. He knew a bully from a mile away. Lance looked ready for a fight.

"Oh, come on, we'd love to join you for dessert, wouldn't we, Bob?"

Bob looked mortified and started to rise from his seat. "T'ank you, Mister Richards, I'll see you later..."

"Sit down, Bob!" Reg barked. "Janine, where are those drinks?"

Janine stormed out from the kitchen, walked behind Reg and clipped him smartly upside the back of his head. "Hey!" he yelled and smoothed down the hair her hit had tousled.

"You mind your mouth at this table, Reginald Richards!" she snapped as she set a coffee mug in front of him. "Your mother'd roll over in her grave seeing you speak ta your father that way! Now, straighten up, sober up..." she poured the hot

178

coffee in a long stream, "...and behave yourself or I'll show you the road meself."

Reg stared at her for a moment, as though contemplating his options. He finally nodded and took the coffee. "Sorry, Janine, had a few beers."

"Ha, doesn't take a few beers to get you nasty t'ese days, walking around this town like God Almighty himself has kissed the soles of your feet," Janine grumbled as she pushed her way back through the door to the kitchen.

The whole table sat, staring at nothing for a moment as we heard her banging around.

"Feisty!" Sean said quietly in admiration of the woman who had raised three of us at that table. If only he knew. Janine was a strong woman, fierce, and loyal to the Richards' family through and through. She'd disciplined us well when we were young, fairly and swiftly, leaving no question in our minds as to what we'd done wrong. She didn't have a mean bone in her body, although Reg had very nearly forced her to the edge of reason on many occasions.

"That she is," Lance said.

"Tough as nails," Reg concurred. The two of them were obviously stuck in the same memory I was.

"Well, here, Sean, pick a sweet for yourself," Jack said, trying to regain control of the room. "Whatever you like."

"Hmmm, chocolate," Sean said as he selected one of Janine's world class brownies.

The tray was passed around the table, finally falling to me. The tart I had been eying was luckily still there.

"Perfect," I said as I picked it up and prepared to take my first bite. Lance quickly reached across the table, snapping the treat from my hand. "No. You're allergic to bakeapples."

Everyone stopped speaking and stared my way. Lance and I stared at each other dumbfounded. *He definitely knows!* I thought in a moment of sheer terror. I had suspected, but this one action confirmed it. Confirmed all my fears; my cover was blown.

"Never knew anybody allergic to bakeapples except Asia," said Reg, eyeing me suspiciously.

"And a girl t'at was in my brother's class in school," said Bob. "I remember one day at school when she ate some and within minutes her face was so red and swollen. No, you're right, Reg. Not too many people allergic to our Newfoundland berries."

Reg continued to stare at me over his cup of coffee.

"I guess I'll try one of these instead," I said wishing it would change the conversation as I reached out for a chocolate brownie. I hoped nobody could see my hand shaking.

"How'd you know she was allergic to bakeapples, Lance?" Reg asked.

"I offered her some last week when we had dinner. Opened up a jar of Janine's jam to go with the ice cream," Lance said, forcing himself to look his brother straight in the eye. "Broke out in spots, just like a leopard."

I looked to Sean, hoping, praying he would drag the conversation away. Any topic would be better.

"Oh, totally," Sean stammered as he picked up my look of desperation. Reg and Bob both looked to him, as though they had forgotten he was even in the room.

"And you are?" Reg asked.

"Sean, I work for Kay and your father was nice enough to invite me for dinner. Don't know what I would have been doing tonight without his kindness, probably sitting in my motel room reading informational tourist brochures. They sure do give you a lot, don't they? Did you have a stack like this high..." he motioned his hands a foot and a half off the table, "...when you checked in, Kay? It's incredible, really. Who knew there was so much to learn about this place?"

"Oh, yes, so much to learn," I agreed happily. "You know, Reg owns the motel..." I led. Of course Sean knew.

"Really?" he said enthusiastically. "It's darling. Really darling." Reg sat perfectly still, staring at Sean as though an alien had landed at the table. "Did you pick the wallpaper yourself?"

Sean leaned forward and batted his beautiful eyes. Reg looked to Bob, who looked at the table. "What?" he asked incredulously.

"The wallpaper, it's fantastic. Love it! Oh, and the woman who works the front desk..."

"Reg's wife," Lance jumped in, "Ester." He shot Sean a warning glance.

"Yes, that's her, Ester," Sean said without missing a beat. "What a star! She's incredibly efficient, running around there, handling absolutely everything and with the biggest smile. Oh, worth her weight in gold, an employee like that."

"As Lance said, she's not an employee, she's my wife," Reg snarled.

"Oh, well, even better for you," Sean winked.

"Excuse me?"

"Gold mine! Cha-ching!" Sean trilled, throwing in a set of jazz hands for added effect. "All that gusto and you don't even have to pay her. That's the bloody deal of the century for you, my friend!"

Lance almost choked on his coffee as Reg's face turned a shade redder than I ever thought possible. It looked good on him.

"Who the fuck do you..."

"Now, Reg, there'll be none of that," Jack slammed a hand on the table. "Mister Chen is a guest in this house, a guest who was simply trying to pay your wife a compliment."

"Like hell he was. Faggot!" Reg had barely gotten the word out of his mouth when Bob grabbed him by the back of the neck. In one swift move, the normally mild-mannered man had Reg's head pushed a quarter of an inch from the tablecloth. In the next second, he pulled Reg's head back, forcing him to stand, and yanked his arm tightly up his back to land between his own shoulder blades.

"Too far, b'y, too far," Bob said as Reg struggled to get free. Bob had him in a complete bind. "T'at's enough for one night." Without another word, Bob pushed Reg out of the room, down the hall and out the front door, leaving the rest of us standing at the table in utter shock.

"What the hell was that?" Lance asked once the stillness sunk in. "I don't think I've ever seen Bob like that. Heck, I've never seen him move faster than a snail's pace before."

"I reckon he didn't like Reg's attitude anymore than I did," Jack said as he sat back down. "I'm sorry, Sean. So sorry."

Jack looked old once again and once again I felt him tugging at my heartstrings. How could this same sweet, sensitive man be the same cold hearted bastard who'd sent me away all those years ago?

Sean simply waved a forgiving hand in front of his face and took hold of Jack's hand. "It's fine, it's fine, you have nothing to apologize for. Unfortunately, I've been called worse before and probably will again."

"Not in my house," Jack said. "Reg is an arrogant fool. Always has been, but he's getting worse. I'm so sorry."

"Please, Jack, don't be. It's fine."

"Thank you, Sean, for being so gracious," I said. "I don't know that I would be."

"If Bob hadn't taken him out when he did, I would have..."

"Alright, alright, thank the lord it didn't come to that," Jack said, rubbing a tired hand over his face.

"Well, only one thing to do," Sean said lightly.

"What's that?"

"Drink!" he said as he stood and walked to the sideboard for the bottle of sherry. "A little something to settle the nerves."

"Sounds good to me." I could have kissed him. After Sean poured a round, I raised a glass to Jack. "Well, Mister Richards, never a dull dinner party do you throw!"

"With this family," Jack responded, "the chances of ever having one are slim to none!"

Chapter Twelve

I knew we needed to talk. I knew I couldn't avoid the conversation for much longer. The elephant in the room finally had a name and it was Kennedy Warren. Lance knew who I was, that much was clear. I suspected, also, that Jack might be catching on. There was that comment at dinner about making it right...I couldn't deal with that yet, though. First, I had to summon the courage to talk to Lance.

Unfortunately, after dinner he had had to rush off to prepare for my production team's arrival in the morning and Sean had needed an early night before our meeting with Melissa. Our whole day would be filled with business obligations, followed by a dinner that evening hosted by Lance at Batty Catters for Raj and the rest of the inspection squad. Their visit to Englee would be brief, with all five of them leaving the following morning.

"Good morning," Melissa Young said to Sean and I as we arrived at her door sharply at 8:30 the next morning. Sean was dressed more casually than the night before in a pair of designer jeans and a light cashmere sweater. We must have had been on the same wavelength, as I was wearing the same thing, although in different colours.

"Good morning, Melissa," I said as we handed her our coats. The fresh morning air was crisp with potential rain coming in the forecast. I introduced the two and followed Melissa down the short hallway. As we entered the kitchen, we were greeted with the smells of fresh baking and a still-warm oven. Sean and I both melted into the seats she offered at her small table, intoxicated by the aromas.

"Have mercy," Sean said. "It smells like you're my new best friend."

"Oh, thank you, Mister Chen," Melissa said shyly. "I hope you like a big breakfast. I may have made too much." Looking around the room, it was apparent that Melissa was expecting the whole town to drop by later in the day. There were enough muffins, scones, quiches, potatoes, pies and tarts to feed a small army.

"Oh, Doctor Atkins forgive me," Sean said, raising his eyes to the ceiling.

"Coffee to start?" Melissa asked with a nervous chuckle.

"Yes, please," we both said. Then we heard the sweet, sweet sound of milk being steamed. "Could it be?" Sean asked, clasping his hands in excitement. "Espresso!"

"Oh, I can make regular, if you'd prefer," Melissa said, turning away from the small countertop cappuccino machine.

"Don't you dare!" Sean said. "I haven't had a latte in two days. That's a new record for me."

"Oh good," Melissa sighed in relief. "I love being able to use this machine. My brother bought it at an auction a few years ago and thought I might like it. I've fallen in love with it, to be honest. Can't stand tat instant stuff everyone in town makes anymore. I stick to tea when I'm out." She looked slightly chagrined.

"But, where do you get the beans?" I asked as she handed me the first cup.

"Oh, see, me brother, same one, he lives in St. John's these days. Comes up here once a year at Christmas to visit. I has him bring me a supply of green coffee beans from one of the shops there with him."

"You roast your own beans?" Sean asked, looking around the room for the roaster. "Where?"

"Well, if you can keep a secret," Melissa said. Then she pulled a hot air popcorn popper out of a cupboard. "Hot air. Does the trick every time. This old machine roasts enough for a few days worth of good coffee at a time. It took a bit of trial and error, but I finally got it down pat."

Sean took a sip of his latte and rolled his eyes in ecstasy, an expression he repeated again and again throughout the meal, as he tasted each of the delicious creations Melissa set in front of him. I had a feeling Sean would be going back to the city a few pounds heavier. Then again, so would I, probably.

"So, we're thinking of trying something new in Englee," Sean said halfway through the quiche, which was divine. As the meal progressed, he outlined the plan of the micro-bank and how it would work. Melissa listened intently, nodding and asking a few questions.

"Sounds like a wonderful plan," she said finally. "But, Missus Toms, why have you come to me?"

"Well, I think you have an amazing talent, Melissa. A gift with food and I'd like you to be the first applicant in the program."

"Applicant?" Her big eyes blinked.

"Yes, I think this town needs a bakery, coffee shop or fine restaurant, or all three. And I think you're the perfect person to own such a business."

"Me? Own? But, Missus Toms," she started to protest, then paused. "Where? You said the loans were for fifty t'ousand each, right? T'at wouldn't be enough to buy a property and all the equipment needed. One or t'other, but not both. I've dreamt of my own kitchen, commercial like, for as long as I can remember. I know what they cost from looking at the magazines I get delivered a few times a year. It's more. More than what your program could give." She shook her head in defeat.

Sean looked at me with a pout forming on his own lips.

"Well, now, there might be something I could do about that, outside the micro-bank program. You know I bought those two properties in the cove?"

"Sure, whole town knows about those."

"Well, I'd like to keep them as investment properties, fix them up. The first one, you know down the hill a bit, would make a great restaurant space, if it were fixed up."

Her eyes started to sparkle once again. "You mean..."

"I mean, I'd be willing to fix the place up and rent it to you at a fair price."

"I don't know what to say," she said, on the brink of tears.

"Say you'll talk to your husband and think about it," I said, taking her hand. "This is a chance, Melissa. A chance for you to have your dream, while supporting your family and growing the community. Think about it?"

"I will. Oh, thank you, Missus Toms. Thank you so much for the opportunity." She wiped the tears from her eyes and foisted a basket of muffins towards Sean. "Just a bit of a thing, you are. Eat, eat..."

After rolling ourselves out the door of Melissa's tiny house, Sean and I walked the whole length of the town and out to Locker's Point. On the way I showed him the old mill and outlined my thoughts about making it into a park. That was another project to discuss with Jack, we both noted. Then we made our way to a scheduled meeting with the mayor and members of town council. It would be an informal discussion about the micro-bank concept. I had assumed the powers that be would be happy to have such a program, but wanted to make sure before we went any further. As agreed the night before, Mr. Richards was waiting for us when we arrived.

Jack introduced Sean and me to the mayor and I was happy to see it was a woman who held the coveted job. I was equally happy that it was somebody I already knew. Of course, she didn't know me. To her, I was Kay Toms. To me, she was a school chum from a grade ahead of me. We had grown up together but had never been close friends. I had known her brother. He had been in my class throughout school. I needed her to know who I had become.

As so, Gina Wilson, the mayor, answered my questions, told me of the current situation and of the problems the town constantly incurred. She explained her vision of what she and the rest of town council had of the future, but how it had become a dream with no reality in sight.

"Up the river, comes to mind," she said. "We're running on limited resources with a limited population."

"That's true, Gina," Jack said. "But Missus Toms and her young friend here have some great ideas that could move things in a positive direction for Englee."

Sean then repeated the same explanation of the micro-bank that he had told Melissa. The council seemed impressed.

"How could we say no?" Gina said with a big smile.

"Well, I want to be clear on a few things, though," I said. "This will not be a government program. It will be a private, not for profit endeavour through Tomtex. We will decide who and what business plans qualify for the funding we'll provide. Council will have no influence over those decisions." A few of the members grumbled audibly. "However, those business plans will be subject to normal town licensing and approval, along with provincial and federal regulations. In effect, this will be a joint project, but the lines will be very clear. We'll decide who is a good lending risk. You will decide what's a good fit for Englee within the town statutes and regulations."

"Sounds perfectly fair to me," Jack said, peering at the council members.

"Yes," Gina concurred. "You're the money and we're the regulatory body, as always. I have to say, I think this could really work." I could see the excitement in her eyes.

We walked out of the meeting feeling good about the program and how it would proceed. I blew a sigh of relief and smiled up at Mr. Richards. He put his arm around my shoulder and squeezed it gently as Sean trailed slightly behind us. "You know young lady I think it will work this time. Whoever would have thought that Kay Toms would come here to help us rescue our dying town?"

"I guess you never know where you'll find what you need."

"True, true enough. But you and I both know there isn't anything that can be done without money. Without cold hard cash it would be just a dream. Money attracts money. You've got me rearranging my thinking, Kay.

"I can see how you got to be where you are in life. Although I must admit I haven't met many rich people who were so willing to give complete strangers a chance. You're what my mamma would call a real Christian. That part about a rich man not being able to go into the Kingdom of God – well – that certainly doesn't apply to you. You have a better chance than

Pastor Simms has when it comes to getting to heaven."

"Thank you," I managed to say, just barely keeping my voice from shaking.

He withdrew his arm. "But you'll break me, at this rate." He winked and smiled that crooked smile just like Lance always did. I wanted to tell him I loved him, that all of the ugly memories of him had never existed.

"I like you, Mr. Richards," I said instead.

"I like you, too, Mrs. Toms. Now, you'd better get a move on if you're going to make it to Lance's party on time." He patted my hand gently before veering off towards his General Store.

Sean was suddenly by my side, matching my pace as we approached the motel. We'd had a fairly full day already and were expecting an even longer night ahead. "Let's each rest for a bit, then meet up again in an hour and a half to go to the party," I was saying as a car pulled in to park in front of us.

"Hello, there," Mayor Gina said as she opened her door, stepped out, and stood beside it. Her body language made it clear that she wasn't planning on stepping towards us, so I threw Sean a look that sent him indoors and turned to face her. She looked nervous, rattling her car keys in one hand.

"Hello, again," I said.

She waved slightly, beckoning me closer. I took the two steps, putting us in semi-uncomfortable proximity.

"Yes?" I asked in a whisper. She looked relieved that I had

caught on.

"Mrs. Toms, sorry, but I wanted a word, private like," she said in a forced whisper that was probably louder than her natural tone. A spy she was not.

"Yes?"

"Well, it's about the fish plant," she looked at me knowingly. "See, I'm the head of the town planning committee, so I've been working with the, um, the....well, new owner, the company, on the permits for construction and establishment of the new business." She took a deep breath.

"Yes?"

"Well, I don't think it's quite time to bring it to the council's attention, the plans, as they're not done yet."

"Oh, that's good." I had no idea what she was driving at.

"So, you see, I am aware at this point who the new owner is." Her eyes flicked quickly around the near-empty parking lot.

"Oh, I see," I said with a nod.

"I just wanted you to know that I'm committed to working with your people to get all the paperwork sorted as quickly as possible. I can't wait to share the news with the whole town. And, well, I guess I just wanted to thank you. Keeping it to myself has been almost impossible to bear!" She smiled warmly and genuinely, yet still managed to look as though she was going to be arrested at any moment. Her keys rattled.

"I can imagine how difficult that would be," I said, suddenly aware of how badly I wanted a nap. "Thank you for your discretion, Gina. I really appreciate it. We'll be ready to finalize our plans shortly, I'm sure. Then the announcement will be made and the pressure will be off you entirely."

Her eyes slid to the ground momentarily and her smile faltered.

"Oh, we'll need you there with us," I said, extending my hand. "Will you be the one to make that announcement when the time comes?"

She shook my hand thoroughly, almost roughly, as her face beamed. "I'd be delighted!" she whispered hoarsely.

"Good, now, if I could just get that back." I looked to our still shaking hands. "I've really got to go. Thank you, Mayor, for everything."

"Oh, geez, sorry," she dropped my hand like a hot brick. "Right, of course, thank you, Mrs. Toms."

I walked to my door as I heard the tires of her car crunching the loose gravel. As I stepped inside, I was already loosening my coat and flinging my shoes in the corner. I locked the door and grabbed one of the heavy curtains. A nap was all I could think of as I started to draw the shade. Just outside the window, there was a flash of movement. Flicking around the corner of the row of rooms was the sleeve of Charlie's coat. It was only there for a moment, a millisecond, but it was there. Well within earshot of my conversation with the mayor.

The nap I longed for eluded me. Every time my eyes fluttered shut I'd hear Reg's voice, feel his breath sliding down my cheek; the darkness of that alleyway would surround me again and the man screamed...

"Wonderful!" Raj Patel said, standing at my side as we made our way towards the front door of Lance's home. The evening had been just that. After a very successful tour of the Roddickton facility my team was more than happy to recommend moving forward with the new line of products. Raj, dressed very sharply in what I knew was a brand new suit, had made the official announcement over a well deserved toast. Lance's eyes had crinkled at the corners as he smiled widely at the success of the business deal and the meal laid out in front of us.

The visit to the centre and the farm was still reeling in my mind. I had felt such an outsider when Lance introduced me to the staff, including several doctors working on different projects and students all with the same love of the ocean. Years ago this had been my dream, the dream Lance and I had together.

I felt regret that although I admired their work, I knew nothing about it. It had escaped me in the world I had built.

At the centre research was conducted on organisms ranging from bacteria to seals. Lance showed me the touch tanks where visitors could experience a never-ending variety of local marine life. He showed me the Harp and Harbour seals with outdoor viewing platforms. There were teaching laboratories with flowing seawater for hands-on student enrichment programmes and demonstrations. Where once I would have seen and understood the excitement, I now looked at the centre as another tourism promotion.

I followed Lance around the centre as he explained the research into aquaculture, biological and chemical oceanography and of the fundamental principles of behavior, biochemistry and physiology.

I understood nothing about the behavioural ecology of larval, of marine lipid chemistry, of phytoplankton physiological ecology, of antifreeze proteins or fisheries oceanography. I felt a failure at not knowing. I felt relieved when he was called away and one of the doctors continued the tour.

He explained what they were now working on. With the collapse of the cod fishery there was a growing need for aquaculture. Oysters, mussel, scallops and clams are the main shellfish under cultivation in Canada. However, the centre was now working on abalone, goeducks, quahaugs and sea urchins as well as continuing on the cod and salmon research. The dream I had when I had left the island was now foreign to me, all I knew was cod, salmon, herring, squid and caplin. I had no idea what abalone or any of the others were.

I looked around for Lance and Raj. They both had disappeared and I was forced to continue the tour. I had no idea what I was being shown, but I admired the work that Lance had done and the centre. The doctor explained how shellfish farming was regulated. He explained why the demand for seafood products continues to increase. From my own business I was extremely aware of that demand. He explained the biophysical parameters, the types of culture, the potential environmental impact of shellfish farming and the future of the aquaculture industry.

When our tour was interrupted by a student seeking advice, I stood at a loss. My father had died from fishing on the ocean. I wondered what he would have thought of the operation.

"It's all coming together," Raj said as he accepted his overcoat from one of the waiters Lance had hired for the night.

"It is indeed," I said. "Thank you, Raj, for everything you've done in these past few weeks and everything you're going to do as we make this a reality."

"You're very welcome," he replied with a warm smile. "There's profit here, Kay, profit for everyone. What would we do without your ingenious business mind? Perish the thought!" He looked to the heavens and kissed his knuckle. Raj had lived in the United States with his wife and three daughters for nearly twenty years, but his heavy East Indian accent remained almost as fresh as it had been the day he'd arrived.

I chuckled as he embraced my hand. "Travel safely home, Raj, and send my very best wishes to your family. Apologize to Vee for the late nights that are ahead of you."

"No, no, no, no," he shook his head as Lance came to my side. "I am a man blessed with many daughters. Daughters who all expect to go to university! I work happily to afford their futures."

"Bet it doesn't hurt that it gets you out of the house once in a while either," Lance quipped.

"No, sir, it certainly does not," Raj chuckled, touching his index finger to the side of his prominent nose and pointing it to his host. "Four women in one house is more than most mortal men can bear."

With a shared laugh, Lance and I stepped back and bid each member of the team a good night. They filed out the door into the darkness of the late evening well fed and satisfied with a solid day's work. They'd spend the night at the motel in Roddickton and then fly off the island the next morning.

After watching the taillights of their rented SUV mosey down the driveway, I shut the door and leaned against it. I had planned to leave with Sean earlier, but Lance had quietly whispered in my ear to stay. He told Sean he would see me safely back to the motel.

We stood in the foyer for a full minute in the quiet that had enveloped the house, staring at each other. A standoff. Who would say it first? Lance flinched when one of the waiters clanged a dish on the dining room table.

"Why don't you relax in the living room while I pay these guys?" he suggested.

Unsure of my own voice, I simply nodded and made my way to the sofa. As I sunk into the plush cushions, I pulled off my shoes, curled my legs under me and tugged the silk jersey dress I wore over my bare ankles.

After a few minutes, Lance entered from the kitchen with a bottle of red wine and two glasses. "Had a feeling we might need this," he said as he poured. Again we stared. Waited.

"Are the servers gone?" I finally asked.

"Yep," he said, taking a seat in the chair directly in front of me. "It's just us."

"Just us..."

"Well, who goes first?" His dark eyes ducked to his glass of wine.

"Rock, paper, scissors?" I tried lamely to lighten the mood. It didn't work. "I'm sorry."

"Sorry? For what, Kay?" There was an edge to his voice, a warning. He was giving me one chance. One chance to say what needed to be said.

"For coming. For going. For running. For lying. For, for..." I took a deep breath and closed my eyes. "For everything, Lance, everything I've put you through."

"So, I'm right?" His voice was quiet, his head bowed. "I need to hear you say it. I didn't think I did at first, but now I know I do."

"I am..." I reached up and carefully unpinned my wig with my free hand. In one small motion, it slid off the back of my head. "I am Kennedy Warren," I said plainly as I loosened my natural hair. It could leave no doubt in his mind. I felt naked as he took in the sight of my long auburn hair; his eyes twitching frantically from it to my face.

The room stood silent.

"What, oh good god, what am I supposed to do here?" He took a deep gulp of his wine.

"I..."

"No, no, don't," he continued to stare at my hair. "Just don't. I have to figure out where to begin, where to start. Where do I start, K..." he suddenly looked me dead in the eye. A nervous tremor made its way down my spine. "There, I guess. Right there. What do I call you now? Kay? Ken...Kennedy?" He stumbled over my real name, as though it was foreign to his lips.

"It sounds strange to me, too," I broke his stare and looked at the wig lying on my knee. "I haven't been Kennedy in so long, so long, Lance. I can't quite remember what it's like to be her."

"Her? Her?" He stood and began to pace in front of the dying fire. "Her? Like Kennedy Warren is a different person? You are her!"

"Yes," I said meekly. "I am Kennedy Warren."

"What the hell? Why? Why are you here? After all this time, this whole fucking lifetime, why are you here?" he yelled, unable to control the emotions surging through his body any longer. "For the past week that's all I've been able to think of. All I've wanted to ask, but you've made it impossible. Impossible! To ask would be to let the whole goddamned town down. Ruin any chance this place has of coming back to life. Was that the plan? Come back here as the knight in shining armour? Save the town and look like a saint, after all the pain you've caused?"

"No, Lance, no!" I had to explain. I had to tell him the whole story, but he was fuming with rage.

"You leave here, leave me, abandon your own child, then come riding in on a mountain of money, trying to what? Buy it all back?" His glass slammed onto the mantel. "Buy back all the pain you caused? Did you really think that would work? Did you? Think that we were all so pathetic that we'd grovel at your designer shoes and thank you for all the hurt and pain?"

I let him yell, let him rant, until he had said his piece. He deserved the chance to say it all, scream it out. After so many years of biting his tongue and standing stoically by, living by the decisions I had made, he had earned his anger.

"God, what are we supposed to do now?" he finally said, dropping back into his chair and covering his face with his hands.

"I don't know," I said quietly. "I've never known. I had no plan, Lance. All I wanted to do was come back and find closure with all I had left behind—my mother who died when I was a child, mourn a father whose body was never found, and say goodbye to the memory of you. That was it. I thought, foolishly, that I could come back to Englee quietly, make my peace, and leave. I thought I could be unaffected by this place, by the people...by you. I didn't even know you'd still be here. I didn't know if your father was still alive. I didn't know about

Asia." He looked up at me then.

"What do you mean you didn't know about Asia?"

"I didn't know, Lance. I didn't know anything about her. I had no idea Reg adopted her. I still don't understand how he adopted her, it doesn't make any sense."

I could see the tears in his eyes. "I loved Asia from the moment I saw her and she loved me. I knew who she was. My father didn't lie to me. He told me she was my daughter. It was too late. Reg had adopted her when she was just a baby. I couldn't turn her world upside down. I don't think I'm the only one to blame. I can't believe you had my child, without me there, without telling me. I didn't know. You left, were gone, and I didn't know if you even gave birth. I thought maybe you'd had an abortion, maybe you'd lost the child. Imagine my surprise when I come back here, after fighting a war, and find that you had given her up. You had no part of her life and I had to live as her uncle, not her father. Her uncle!"

"I had my child taken from me. When you asked your father if she was your child, did you also ask him about me?"

"I did. He said he didn't know anything about you or the baby or why you left so suddenly. He only knew that Reg had returned with the baby. He didn't know why you had chosen Reg over me."

I felt my life was draining from me.

"What gives you the right to come back and mess with my life? You are as fucked up as I am. I went through two years

202

with a friggin' shrink because you left and of all the shit that happened over there and now you come back here and start messing with my head again."

We sat staring at each other, tears falling down our faces.

"I don't know what happened to you over there, Lance."

"No, dammit and you never will. But just when I think I'm getting my life together, you come back and screw it all up again."

"No, Lance. I didn't. I'm sorry. I had no idea what happened to you..." I could barely see him through the tears that fell. "I'm sorry. I'm sorry."

"Enough," he said firmly. "Enough. Tell me. Tell me what happened the night you left. I deserve the truth, finally."

"We might have been young and unmarried, but we were happy," I said, trying to set the scene for him. I knew I wouldn't get a second chance to tell my side. I had to reach him. "We had plans. We were both going into marine biology, raise our child together, and be happy. We were in love."

"Then why did you go?"

I put up my hand. "Let me finish. I was given an ultimatum."

"What are you talking about? We already had plans with my mom and dad. They loved you. There was no ultimatum."

I shook my head. "I had no choice. I had to go."

"No, the Kenny Warren I loved would not have left me and she definitely would not have left her father alone. No matter what."

He stared at me, waiting.

"I couldn't let anybody hurt you or my father," I blurted out.

"We're talking about you, Kenny. Not about me or your father."

My body started to shake. "He came to see me, Lance. He stuffed an envelope of money in my hands. He also gave me an address of where I was to go. I was told not to go see you at the library, but to be on the bus when it left in the morning. I was told if I didn't go he'd kill you and my father. I couldn't let him do that to either of you."

Lance rubbed his hands through his hair and shook his head in disbelief. "My father would never do that."

"It wasn't your father." My hands shook. "It was your brother."

"Excuse me?" he blinked rapidly.

"Reg. It was Reg," my shoulders slumped as the weight I had been carrying around for years lightened ever so slightly.

"You expect me to believe that Reg threatened my life, your father's life? Reg is a bully, plain and simple. He'd never actually do..."

"I left a book at school that day," I said softly as I pictured it, seventeen years before as though it was yesterday. "It was one we needed for the library. I went back to get it. It was just before supper. On my way home I heard a noise, voices from behind the General Store. I knew the store had closed early that day."

I couldn't look at his swollen eyes as I told the story. Instead, I gazed out the front window into the darkness.

"At first I was going to run. It was just Indian spirits again I thought. Then I decided I wasn't going to be frightened again. So I thought I'd prove a point. I'd walk around that building and see just who was there."

I put a hand over my mouth. The tears fell faster.

"I saw Reg kill a man."

Until that moment I hadn't known a room could be that silent.

"You what?"

"There were three men in the alley. One was holding another by the arms and Reg was standing in front of him. I saw Reg stab the man. I gasped and Reg looked around. He kept his eyes on me as he pulled out the knife and the man's body fell to the ground."

Lance stared at me. Suddenly there were miles between us.

"Lance, I saw your brother kill a man. He came by my house later. He said your dad knew and gave me the money to leave. He said your dad wanted me out of town. Then he threatened to kill you and my father if I didn't leave. He even mentioned the fact that you and my father were going trouting the week after."

Lance slumped back into his chair, his hand covering his mouth. Then he looked across at me and for a moment, he didn't speak.

"You're right. Your dad's body was never found. I cancelled the trouting with your dad because I was upset at your going away. Your dad's body was never found."

"You believe me now?"

"I don't know what to believe anymore. But tell me everything, Kenny. Everything. Everything he said. Everything he did. Let me decide whether I believe you or not."

"They wanted me out of town, he said, him and Jack. I asked him why his father would want me gone. 'Nobody gets in our way,' he said." I forced the lump in my throat down.

"I said to him, 'So your father knows you killed that man?' He said, 'What do you think?' He had me pinned against the wall of my house. I'd run home after seeing what he'd done, after seeing the man die. I don't know how much time passed from when I got to the house and when he arrived. It must have been at least an hour. I couldn't think straight. Dad wasn't home yet. I was alone when he knocked on the door. He pulled me outside when I answered, dragged me around the side. He had his arm pushed against my throat." I raised my arm, mimicking the position I could still feel on my skin. "He pushed his knee between my legs. I can feel it now. I was so scared. 'You're not gonna tell anybody about this,' he said to me.

"I promised, swore that I wouldn't. Then he said, 'That's right, I know you won't. You know how I know that? Because you won't be here. You're leaving tomorrow morning on that bus. If you don't, you won't have a father and that kid of yours won't have a father either. I'm good at what I do. Your father and my brother won't be around to take care of you.' Then he mentioned the yearly trouting trip that you and my dad were going on."

Lance stared at me blankly, his mind trying to reconcile his memory with mine.

"What do you remember about that night, Lance?"

He shrugged and ran his hand through his hair. "Not much. I've tried to forget everything. It's been such a long time, Kenny. I remember there was a man asking for Reg. He came by the house earlier and I told him Reg was out. I don't know who he was. I never saw him again. I've never even thought about it until now. I do remember that the RCMP were at our house. My dad had to go to the store with them. It was something about somebody seeing two men dumping a body into the ocean. Nobody knew who the men were. A body was never found. There's such a current by the dock. Nothing would stay in that area very long."

"So Reg was never found out?"

Lance shook his head and pushed himself out of his seat. He went to stand by the window again. I watched as he covered his face with his hands. "What did you tell your dad?" Lance asked without looking around.

"I didn't tell him about the threats. I just told him that I was going away to have the baby. He told me I didn't have to go, but I pretended it was what I wanted."

"What happened when you left?"

"I took the bus. I got off in Gander and flew to Halifax. I went to the address Reg had given me. The lady was expecting me. She had made arrangements in a home for unwed mothers. They helped me. I stayed there for months. Depressed most of the time. Scared all of the time. I didn't contact my dad because I was afraid. The lady Reg had sent me to came to see me when I was in labour. I told her I wanted to call my dad. She told me he had died the week after I left. My baby was taken away from me. I never saw her again. I never saw my baby.

"At first I thought I would die. I wanted to. I had lost everybody. My mother, my father, my baby and you. Everyone in the home was helpful. I pulled through, but I did a lot of thinking. If your family hadn't been rich, they wouldn't have treated me that way. Money is awfully powerful, Lance. I decided I was never going to let anyone push me around with money again. I decided that I'd get to university somehow, but it would be business. I decided that I was going to be rich. I was going to be powerful, powerful enough to protect myself. You have no idea how much I hurt and how determined I was. But instead I met Katrina and, because of her, B.J. and he taught me my reasons for wanting to be rich were the wrong ones."

I took a deep breath. My chest was so tight and my head was spinning. "I had a baby. Having my baby taken away from me was harder than going through labour all by myself. I didn't even know if it was a boy or girl. They said it was best for me, that it's easier to get on with your life if you don't know.

"Easier? Easier for whom? For seventeen years I wondered. I never knew until dinner at your father's that night, when she took off her baseball cap. That's when I knew I'd had a girl. She's our daughter, Lance. Our daughter!"

He stared at me, the tears still slowly falling down his face.

"I've spent my entire adult life in hiding," I picked up the wig and tossed it onto the coffee table. I was terrified of Reg. Still am, to this day. I wouldn't have come back if it weren't for my husband. We had time before he died. Time to talk, time to listen. He knew all my secrets, my disguises, and accepted the choices I had made to stay alive and succeed. Yet, in his final hours, he asked me to confront my past and gain the closure I needed to be happy. His last wish was that I come back here and say goodbye to my dad, as he had had to do with his own daughter."

"Unbelievable," he muttered. "Of all the scenarios I've pictured over the years, all the stories I've tried to patch together, I never, ever thought you had left under duress. Reg has always been smug about you leaving, rubbing it in, holding Asia over my head, but I never dreamed..."

"How could you? None of this is your fault, Lance. None of it."

"I never thought I wouldn't recognize you when I saw you

again. I thought I'd always know you." His voice had softened.

"It was the car accident," I said, rubbing my cheek lightly. "When Katrina died, I survived, but my face has never been the same. The doctors put me back together as best they could, did a pretty good job considering I was unrecognizable as even a human being when they started, but I've never looked like me. It's something that's taken me a decade to get used to."

"And the wig?"

"I've worn wigs so often that nobody ever questioned why. I always wore one when I felt vulnerable. Besides, I couldn't have come here without one.

"When I married B.J. there was a lot of press, press that continued once I started climbing the ladder at Tomtex. My hair was the only distinguishing feature left of Kennedy Warren. I was terrified that Reg would see a photo somewhere and put the pieces together."

"Holy God," he said with awe. "You really believed he was going to kill me. You truly believed that he would hunt you down."

"Yes."

"But, Kenny, what now? Now that I know, now that the truth has finally been said, what do we do?"

"I don't really know," I said honestly. I didn't have a clue.

"Do we just keep on pretending like nothing's happened? Will your plans continue with the fish plant deal? Will you leave again?" He looked like a kicked puppy.

"Yes, at some point, I will have to go back to Boston. My life is there, the company. But I don't know when. I don't know for how long. I don't know what I want, Lance. This is all so much. Now that you're back in my life, well in Kay Toms' life, I don't think I could ever not see you again. And Asia, how am I supposed to leave her here in Reg's care? He's a murderer and a sociopath." I could feel my own anger rising.

Lance turned around. "We can go to my father."

"No. We can't go to anybody. Your father may have been involved. Perhaps he was the third man—I never did see the third man's face. I don't know who it was, but they were familiar. When Reg gave me the money, he said it came from your dad. It must have come from him. There was so much. He must have known. No. We can't trust him yet. It's been so difficult, working with him over these past weeks, still not entirely sure what his part was in that night. He seems so kind, so honest. Yet, I know he gave Reg that money to send me away. What if he finds out who I really am and sends me packing again?"

I wanted him to hold me, to tell me it would be okay, but he just watched me and listened to me as if he was still figuring out the English language.

"Don't you believe me, Lance?" I finally asked.

"Oh, God! It's been eighteen years. Eighteen damn years. I've got to think. I need to figure this out. I don't think my dad was involved. I know I never forgave him for your going away. In fact I always believed he sent you away and he always denied it. But murder? No! Not my dad."

"Lance, we can't go to him. Not yet. If he knows who I am and he was involved, what do you suppose he'll do? If Reg knows who I am, then I am doomed. I don't exist anymore, so I can easily be disposed of and nobody will ever care. No. We can't go to your dad."

"I find it so hard to understand. When you didn't show up at the library, I finally went home. Next morning I said I was going to see you when my dad told me."

"'She's not there Lance,' he said.

"'What do you mean she's not there?'

"'She's gone away.'

"'But she couldn't have. She wouldn't go away. We talked earlier and you said it would be okay. You said you'd look after the baby while we finished our education.'"

Lance ran his hand quickly over his face. "Look at me, Kenny. I'm as devastated as you. I loved you. I asked him about the baby.

"My dad said that you told Reg you wanted out of the town, so he agreed to pay for you. I remember him saying that he always thought you had character, but then he said, 'It's amazing what money can do, Lance. She's gone, son. Forget her and get on with your life.'

"I can hear every word echoing in my head right now as if it just happened. When fall came I went on to University for one day. One day only, then I left and joined the Forces. I swore

I'd never come back again, but I did. When I came back I met Asia. I loved her at first sight. I was devastated at first. Then again if Reg hadn't brought Asia home we would never have known.

"I couldn't change what had been done, not without hurting Asia, so I plunged into my work and tried to spend as much time as I could with her. Even though she doesn't know I'm her father, she treats me like one. I know it upsets Reg at times, because we have a bond he could never have with her. I've been reminded over the years that Reg is the legal father of our child. He rubs it in when necessary. I stay away as much as I can from all of them, except Asia."

I shook my head. "Life is so unbelievably cruel. I feel like I'm frozen. I don't know where to turn now, where to go, what to do." My shoulders shook violently as I felt the sobs reverberating in my throat.

He sat down on the sofa and slipped his arm around me. I melted into his chest. He was so solid. So real. Yet, the whole situation seemed so unreal. Nervously, I played with his fingers.

"It's amazing," I finally said. "I started out at that home for unwed mothers with a dream of becoming rich. Under the weight of tragedy and pain, B.J. came into my life and made me realize that money isn't what makes the person. Money opens doors, but that's not what makes the person. He taught me tolerance and understanding. He taught me gratitude for everyone in my life and for all I had. He reminded me of the values my father had instilled in me.

"He was a wonderful man, Lance. When he died he left me an empire. I gave him the love and respect he deserved. It was all I had to give. Now I have more than I ever dreamed possible.

"I swore to Reg, and your father also, that I'd never come back. My dad's gone, but he can still hurt you and for that I'm scared."

"I'll be okay, but where do we go from here, Kenny?" He suddenly pulled me into his arms. I looked up at him and he wiped my cheeks, then pulled me even closer. "God, you're here. You're really here," he said softly. His lips gently touched my eyelids, then moved to my lips. It all came flooding back, the love, the passion, the years wasted, rushing between us. We feasted on each other as our minds took a break from all the worrying, all the thinking, all the planning. We feasted. He picked me up and carried me up the stairs to his bed.

When his body entered mine I knew I had found my place in time. The years were swept away and our bodies moved together as one connected in the future our past had destined us to have.

We lay in each other's arms, naked and panting. "Well," I said, still trying to catch my breath. "That should complicate things nicely."

We looked at each other and burst into laughter. "Yep, that should do," Lance said lightly. "God, how did we get here?"

"I have no idea, but it's a nice spot to be in," I said, playfully running a nail down his chest. "Can we solve all our problems tomorrow? I've missed you so much."

He ran a hand through my hair. "Tomorrow sounds good."

Chapter Thirteen

Tomorrow easily turned into the next day, as we lingered in bed, telling our secrets, our histories and our hopes. I left late Sunday night, knowing beyond a shadow of a doubt that I'd be back to Batty Catters again. It felt like a beginning. Lance and I were getting to know our adult selves, seeing if these older versions of us even fit together anymore. We did.

"Good morning, good morning, we talked the whole night through," Sean's voice trilled as I stepped out of my room at the Park Place Motel first thing Monday morning. I cringed slightly as he continued to whistle the tune all the way to the restaurant.

"Are you quite done?" I asked as we took a seat and flipped our coffee cups over.

"Hmmm, that depends," he said, leaning towards me mischievously. "Just exactly how many details am I going to get about *your* weekend?"

"Oh, not that many," I said bluntly as I raised the menu to block my face. I was actually dying to tell him every detail. Every morsel of what had transpired between Lance and me..

"Huh, gonna play hardball, are you? Right, the truth will come out, young lady, the truth will come out," he pointed sternly. "You and our host-with-the-most, god I could eat that man alive. He's stunning. I don't blame you one little bit for rip...Ester! Good morning," he said suddenly.

"Good morning, Sean, Mrs. Toms, how are ya today, then?" Ester asked as she poured our coffees. She wasn't quite as colourful, in either attire or personality, as we had become accustomed to.

"We're fine, Ester. How are you?" I asked.

"Oh, maybe not my best morning on record, but I'll do fine," she tried on a smile and failed. Her normally brilliant lips were pale, her hair only somewhat bouffant. Everything was just slightly off.

"You sure, sugar?" Sean asked as he patted her hand gently.

"Yeah, yeah, I'll be fine. Just a bad weekend, is all." With that, she collected our breakfast orders and scurried off to the kitchen.

"I wonder what that's all about..." Sean whispered loudly.

"My lord you're nosy this morning!"

"What do you expect? You've left me stranded in a teeny, tiny town, all by myself, for two whole days. I need the gossip. I'm used to a bustling office of whorish secretaries and executive playboys. Monday mornings are normally a binge of useless information and tidbits. Tell me about your weekend, please? Please?"

"Not much to tell," I said, watching his hopeful face fall. "We pretty much stayed in the whole time." I couldn't stand to see him suffer.

"Oh my god! I knew it, I knew it, I knew it!" he nearly yelled, then caught the looks of the other patrons and hushed himself. "You and Lance, that gorgeous hunk of man meat...it's about time you got a little action!"

"All right, all right, that's it. That's all you're getting from me on the topic. Now, can we move on to business?"

"Oh, fine, that'll be enough to sustain me for a day..." he winked. "So, what's on the agenda for this week?"

"Well, we'll need to video conference with Boston this morning, go over the next steps with Raj's team. Then, we'll sit down with the mayor, makes sure all the permits are on track, and we should stop in and see if Melissa Young's made a decision."

"Oh, no need!" Sean said with a small clap of his hands. "Since you were off gallivanting all weekend, Melissa invited me for dinner last night. It was amazing. Honestly, she's a genius in a kitchen! She told me she and Tom had discussed our offer and she's said yes."

"That's fantastic! Oh god, this is really happening. We're really making a start. Good work, Sean." I felt a surge of sheer exhilaration, with a nice side dose of fear.

"I told her I'd start the paperwork. Jennifer in legal should have everything we need by the end of this week." He beamed with a sense of pride I had rarely seen in him over the years. It was a look I had a feeling I was going to see a lot of in the future.

"Right, well, I think it's time we asked the mayor to call a meeting then," I said. "By the end of this week, we'll be ready to officially announce the program and reveal our plans for the plant." My stomach fluttered nervously. By the end of the week, Reg would know, without a doubt, what I was doing in Englee.

After breakfast and a very productive conference with Raj, Sean and I decided to check on the house on the hill before our meeting with the mayor. Tom Young had been working steadily and I was curious to see the progress. As we walked by past the General Store in the midmorning drizzle, we spotted Bob Pearson, Reg's manager, sitting on a bench looking at the old fish plant.

"Good morning, Bob," I said. We hadn't seen him since the disastrous dinner at the Richards house.

"Oh, mornin' missus," Bob said with a slight nod of his head. "G'mornin' Mister Chen."

"Good morning, Mr. Pearson," Sean replied. "Day off?"

"You could say t'at." He looked at his feet.

"Why is everyone so glum around here today?" Sean said quietly to me.

"You okay, Bob?" I asked. His shoulders were slumped over his portly belly, as the collected rain dripped from the brim of his hat.

"I'll get by, missus, always 'ave," he said slowly.

"Get by? You mean this isn't just one day off, don't you, Bob?"

"Yes, missus. Reg fired me, straight out. Not laid off, not let go. No, he couldn't see to be t'at kind. Just straight out fired me."

"But why?" Sean gasped.

Bob looked up and met his eyes, then turned them directly back to his own toes.

"What? Because of the other night? Because of me?" Sean's right hand went to the centre of his chest. "Oh, Bob!"

"It's alright, b'y. Alright. Like I said, I'll get by. And, for the record, I'd do it all over again. Reg was out of line, well out of line, talking t' you the way he did. I knows him well enough to know where his twisted mind was goin'. It wouldn't 'ave stopped at name callin'."

Sean looked at me, his dark brown eyes on the verge of tears.

"How can I ever repay you, Bob?" His voice wavered with emotion. "I didn't realize you'd lose your job over that! Why would you risk it?"

Bob stood up slowly. "I've worked for Reg for years. He's a mean son-of-a-bitch. I think I just got used to it. But seeing himself picking on you, well, reminded me t'at I used to hate him." He walked over to Sean and clamped a big hand on his shoulder. "You should meet my son Kevin sometime. Nice lad. Studyin' art history at McGill." Bob winked, patted Sean's shoulder twice and walked away.

"But, but, Kay! This is all my fault," Sean said as we turned and watched Bob lumber down the street.

"No, Sean, it isn't," I said, taking his hand. "It's Reg. Bob's right, he's a true ass. A bully."

"But what about Bob?"

"Bob'll be alright. Don't you worry. He's a good man, from all accounts. Getting out from under Reg's thumb might just be the best thing that ever happened to him."

The house on the hill looked great. Tom had obviously been working overtime, pushing his trades to get the job done. I walked through the house as he and Sean chatted at the front door. My hand ran along the wall as my eyes took in every detail. It was the house of my childhood, before life's tragedies had started. Before my mother died.

"Should be ready for you to move in sometime next week, missus, if not sooner," Tom reported proudly.

"It's incredible, Tom, thank you." I turned my head quickly to cover the tear that threatened to fall.

"Now, Tom," Sean said, seeing me falter. He took Tom's arm and pulled him outside. "What about this roof?"

"Well, we've reinforced the beams by using..." their voices trailed off as Sean started walking around the perimeter. I stood in the middle of my mother's kitchen and took a deep breath. She would have loved the colour, the newness of the appliances; the luxuries she'd never been able to afford. I could see her hazel eyes smiling as I fiddled with a few of the dials on the stainless steel stove. My memories of her were faded, hazy, but they still remained.

I shook my head, clearing the cobwebs, and joined the men outside. Sean was standing back, looking intently at the shingles Tom was displaying for him and nodding. He didn't have a clue what Tom was talking about.

"Ummm..." I spun on my heel at the sound of Charlie's voice. "Mornin', missus. Tom, weather's poorly t'day." Charlie stood four feet back from the rest of us, his hand rubbing his woollen cap nervously.

"T'at's right, Charlie," Tom said. "Weather's not gonna let you work t'day. Why don't you spend some time on your nets and come back t'morrow?"

I looked at Tom.

"Oh, I've asked Charlie to paint the outside of the house, now t'at the new boards is up," he explained to me.

"Oh, right," I said, turning back to Charlie. "Good."

"Yep, glad for the work, missus," Charlie mumbled. "Specially with Reg kickin' off."

"What's that?" I asked, taking a step closer.

"Oh, Reg, hittin' the fuc..." Charlie caught himself and took a second to rethink the sentence. He might have been a bit slow, but rude Charlie was not. "Been hittin' the bottle t'is past week. Hittin' it hard, missus. Makes the work for 'im unsteady. Figured I might as well pick up some hours for Tom. Paint your house."

"Oh, I see. Yes, well, you might as well, Charlie. I'm sure Tom will be glad for the help."

"Sure am," Tom said kindly. He was the sort of man who took in every stray he met. "You come on back the morning t'en, Charlie. Hope the rain gives us a break."

"Sure, b'y. Sure t'ing." Charlie's eyes flicked up to meet each of ours for the briefest of seconds, before he turned and started walking home.

"Is it me or is there something, well..." Sean let the sentence hang.

"Special? Special about Charlie?" Tom finished for him.

"Yes, that's it."

"Always was," Tom said. "Born like that. Just slow. His parents weren't the nicest people, from what I hear, either. They died just after Charlie turned eighteen. Been on his own, scraping a living ever since. He always seems to manage."

"Is that the damn motto of this town?" Sean asked in exasperation. "Manage? Just manage to get by?"

Tom looked at him and just smiled. "Has been. Has been exactly t'at for years, decades, generations. Be patient, Mr. Chen. We're ten steps behind you, but some of us are tryin' to catch up."

"So then I said to him, oh yeah," Sean prattled on as we made our way back to main street, recounting the tiff he'd had with his boyfriend Scott Saturday morning. Apparently, Scott wasn't a fan of long distance relationships, even for a short amount of time. As we reached the mayor's office, my heart fluttered at the sight of Lance's Jeep parked down the block at the motel.

As we stepped into the reception area, the door to Mayor Gina's office opened suddenly. Dressed in a pair of jeans that seemed custom made for his body and a thick, dark sweater, Lance walked out, with Gina right on his heels.

"Oh, hello, Kay," he said casually. "Sean, nice to see you again."

"Oh, it's *always* nice to see you, Mister Richards," Sean nearly purred. Behind Lance, Gina's head nodded unconsciously in total agreement.

"Mrs. Toms!" she finally said, snapping herself and Sean out of the same daydream. "Hi, hi, hello. Please, won't you come in?"

"Thank you."

As I slid past Lance, I felt his hand brush my hip and thought I'd swoon. There was a playful twinkle in his eye, just for me.

"Good day, Kay," he said, making his way to the door. "I've got some...stuff to do..."

"Right, well," I wanted to tell him to meet me in my motel room. "You should stop by the motel." The mayor's mouth was slightly ajar. "To see Ester," I added quickly. "She didn't seem herself this morning."

"As off as cashmere in July," Sean tisked.

"Right, I'll do that then," Lance said and with a quick nod was gone.

"So, Madam Mayor," I said, turning my full attention to the situation at hand and forcing my mind to focus on anything but the sight of Lance's perfect ass. "We're ready to move forward."

"Wonderful!" Gina said with an excited clap. "That's fantastic news. With both projects?"

"Yes," we said. The office was stuffy with the humidity of the morning.

"Right, then, permits!" she jumped up and found a rather large file. "I've been working with your development office in Boston and it looks as though everything's in order. Just a few i's to dot and t'at. We'll have it wrapped up any minute now. What can I do for you today, t'en?"

I looked to Sean and smiled. "Call a town meetin'!" I said with a giggle. "Sorry, Gina, that's just one of those things you rarely get an opportunity to say in real life. I couldn't resist."

"Ha! Don't get the chance to say? I hear t'at from old Missus Johnson almost every week! She seems to think that the only way to get what she wants, whether it's a new road sign or a pothole fixed, is to call a town meeting. We all know she just wants the free coffee and cookies!"

"Well, we'll have to have plenty of those. You decide the time, Mayor, and the place—the school, probably—that would best suit the majority of the adults in town. I want every able bodied man and woman there. We'll announce the micro-bank program and the re-development of the fish plant."

"Oh, Missus Toms!" I thought for a moment the mayor was going to burst into tears. She pulled herself back from the brink, but just barely. "Right, best time for a town meeting's gonna be Wednesday night. Alt'ough, with all the speculation about what's happening, I think you can expect a full house no matter when you have it. No one's going to want to miss this!"

"The Event of the Year," Sean said, splashing his hand through the air above his head. "We'll bring all the promotional materials and arrange for catering. You just be ready with that speech, Missus Mayor! You'll be the star of the whole event!"

I was fairly certain Gina's cheeks paled by at least three shades.

"Yes, a star!" Sean said as he stood quickly and opened the door, holding it for me. We swiftly exited, leaving poor Gina staring, wondering how she'd ever gotten herself into this situation.

"Lord almighty!" Sean burst out as we stepped onto the road. "Could it have been any hotter in there? Orchids would melt!" He waved a hand to his face dramatically.

"Oh, Sean, I can't tell you how happy I am that you're here," I said as I fanned my own face. "This wouldn't have been the same without you."

"Ah, that's nice," Sean said, taking my arm as we made our way to the motel. As the parking lot came into view we stopped dead in our tracks.

"Fuck you!" Reg raged, as he bobbed and weaved in front of Lance.

"I said go sleep it off, Reg." Lance's face could have been etched in stone.

We advanced slowly, unsure of what to do. Reg was obviously drunk and utterly dishevelled. The stubble on his face told of at least a three day binge. The dirt on his clothes said they had been a difficult three days.

As we stepped closer, I could see the faces of the restaurant patrons pressed up against the glass. They were getting coffee and a show.

"Fuck you and you're holier than thou…she's my goddamned wife and that's my goddamned business. I'll talk t' her any way I want, where I want." Reg jabbed a finger into Lance's chest. "Come ta t'ink of it, get off my fuckin' property!"

Lance grabbed Reg's finger and in one swift motion, twisted his hand down, around and up his back.

"He must have gotten lessons from Bob," Sean whispered to me.

"Didn't need Bob, Sean. Military."

"Military! You're telling me he was a soldier! God, I'd love to see him in uniform."

Reg stumbled forward, almost falling to the ground. He regained his footing and his eyes met mine. He sneered. I remembered that sneer. It sent shivers down my spine.

"Oh, there's your little whore now," he said, his eyes never faltering from mine. "All over town, everyone talkin'. Knows she spent the weekend with ya. In your bed."

Lance pushed him forward roughly. Reg continued to stare at me. Then he smiled. For a just a moment, before he raised his foot and kicked back, hitting Lance's bad leg right in the knee.

"No!" I yelled and tried to run forward. Lance winced in pain, losing his grip on his brother. Sean held my arm tightly.

Ester burst through the door of the restaurant. "Don't you dare..." she started to yell.

"Get out," Reg said to her. "Get the hell out of here, out of my house, out of my life!"

Ester's face crumbled. "Reg, you're just drunk..."

"Yes, yes, I am." He wiped a hand across his mouth. "Drunk and finally seeing sense. You get the fuck out of my life. Seventeen years I've suffered with your foolish self. Seventeen years I've known I needed you, but hated you every minute."

"That's enough," Lance shouted. "You little bastard, how dare you talk to her like that?"

"I married her, gave her a better life than she deserved..."

Lance's fist flew, landing squarely on Reg's face. The crack of contact could have been heard a mile away. Reg laid flat out on the ground. In the moment's peace, Lance walked to Ester and whispered in her ear. Ester could barely take her eyes off her husband, bleeding on the gravel. She shook as she stumbled into the motel, coming back out only a second later with her purse and car keys.

As she started the engine, Reg tried to regain his feet. In a flash, Sean was gone from my side and standing over him, with his foot planted firmly in Reg's back. He waved to Ester to go quickly.

"You won't get a dime!" Reg yelled, spitting small pieces of gravel.

"Thanks, Sean," Lance said, clamping him on the back with one hand, as he rubbed his wounded leg with the other. "Can you hold him there a minute?"

"All day, my friend, all day," Sean said as he applied more pressure. "A decade with a first class gym membership has finally paid off!"

"Thanks," Lance said with a small smile. "Give me the key to your room?"

"Sure." Sean dug it out of his pocket.

"Kay, go, now, get all your stuff. Sean's, too. You're not staying here." He held out Sean's key. I ran to my door. "Get everything."

I ransacked the rented room, throwing everything I could into my bags, leaving the small stuff. Then I did the same next door.

It took only a couple minutes, but by the time I made it back to the parking lot, a crowd had gathered.

"Get in your car and go to Batty Catters. Get Asia on your way. She's at Dad's," Lance whispered. "Sean will be right behind you, and so will I."

"Right, right," I nodded as we threw the luggage into my trunk. I peeled out of the lot, leaving Sean standing on Reg's back and Lance trying to control the crowd. I sped across town, racing for the Richards. Throwing the rental car into park, but still running, I bolted to the front door and started pounding.

"Lord t'underin'," Janine said as it flew open. "What the hoppin' hell is goin' on?"

"Asia," I panted. "I need Asia."

She saw the fear in my eyes and turned quickly. "Asia!" she yelled up the stairs. "Mrs. Toms is here for ya, hurry!"

Asia came bouncing down the stairs, her hair tied loosely in a low ponytail and fresh face smiling. Then she saw me.

"Mrs. Toms? What? What is it? Has something..."

"Your uncle Lance wants you to come with me to his house." I had almost managed to catch my breath. She stared at me blankly. "Now, Asia, now. Go, pack an overnight bag, quickly." I heard my own voice, but didn't quite recognize it.

As she disappeared upstairs, I looked to Janine. "It's Reg," I said. "I don't know what's happened, really, but he's drunk and yelling. Kicked Ester out of the motel. Out of the house. Kicked Lance, hard. Out of control..."

"No good bastard," Janine said under her breath. "T'is day's been comin' a long time. He's no good when he's drinkin', Reg. Been startin' trouble across the county all weekend, throwin' his money around, tellin' anyone who'd listen t'at t'ey're worthless.

Talkin' bout movin' for good. Good riddance!" She took my hand then and patted it warmly. "It'll be alright, love. Just stay close to Lance, keep Asia close, too. I'll tell Mister Richards when he gets home. You'll see him later, too."

Ester paced around Lance's kitchen, tapping a nail against her teeth, while Asia and I sat at the island counter watching. She muttered to herself, as though trying to argue two sides of a disagreement.

"Mrs. Toms, should we?" Asia looked at me pleadingly.

"Um, yeah, yes, right," I stumbled, trying to figure out where to start. "Ester, let me make you a cup of tea." She didn't respond as I waited for her to pass by, then made a dash for the kettle. "Do you want to talk about it?"

She looked at me blankly, then to Asia. "I don't know where to start..." her voice was raw from the tears.

"Well, you can skip the part about Reg being an ass," Lance said as he and Sean walked through the open backdoor. "We all know that part."

"Uncle Lance!" Asia said.

"Oh, Asia, you're old enough to have figured that much out about him yourself," Lance said as he stopped and kissed the top of her head. "The truth's the truth."

"Are you okay?" I asked. He was limping heavily.

"I'll be alright," he said with a thin smile. "With Sean's help, I managed to get Reg back to his place, threw him inside and told him to stay put until the whiskey wears off. Doubt he will though."

"Thank you, Sean," I said. "Thanks to both of you. I was really scared back there."

"It's fine, Kay," Sean said, puffing out his chest a bit. "Nothing we couldn't handle."

"You're a good man to have in a fight, Sean," Lance said.

"How about that? You learn something new about yourself every day!" Sean said daintily with a slight flutter of his lashes.

"Ester?" Lance looked to me for an explanation as to why his sister-in-law was wearing a path in his tiled floor. I shrugged.

"Ester, dear, come sit down." He took her by the shoulders and glided her to a seat. She looked at him as though he was a mirage. "Sit. I'll get the brandy."

"Oh, okay," Ester said quietly.

"Lance! Lance! Asia?" Jack Richards' voice boomed through the house from the vicinity of the front door.

"In the kitchen, Dad," Lance yelled back. He took another glass from the cupboard and poured a full round.

"What the hell is going on?" Jack demanded as he burst into the room. "Everyone in town talking about you and Reg punching each other's lights out in the middle of the road! What the hell hap..." his voice dropped as he looked at Ester. She was a shell of the woman he'd known for seventeen years. A paled copy of the vivacious spirit who had raised his granddaughter. "Ester?"

She looked at him and crumbled. Jack caught her quickly and hugged her close, patting the back of her head and rocking her softly from side to side. I could remember him holding me like that when I cut my knee as a child. It was the best possible place for Ester to be. Sean pulled a seat over for Jack. He settled into the embrace, ready for the long haul, if necessary. A member of his family was hurting; Jack would sit there all night if she needed him to.

"Jack, how could he have never loved me?" she said finally. We were all sitting around the table, sipping our brandies and not making eye contact.

"Oh, my girl, now, come on," Jack lulled. "You know that isn't all true. You know it was a marriage of convenience at the start, but there had to have been love there somewhere."

"No, Jack, he said there wasn't. He said that he had despised me every minute of our marriage. There've been other women."

Asia winced, but kept silent. This wasn't news to her.

"Lots of other women—some he's dated, some he's paid. Whores. Girlfriends. In the city. That's why he was always going there to work. That's why." This was all, however, all news to Ester. "I never thought..."

"How did this all start? What happened? Asia said when she came over Saturday night that Reg had been drinking and yelling, but she didn't say what about. Tell us, dear, we're here to help. We're your family." Jack's kind eyes glistened with tears as he looked between Ester and Asia.

"He came home Saturday night, stinking drunk. He'd been gone since the night before. Reeking, he was. I asked him where he'd been and he started yellin', sayin' it was none of my business where he'd been. That's when I sent Asia to yours."

"I thought he'd just pass out," Asia said quietly. Lance took her hand.

"Then what?"

"Maybe you should go upstairs, Asia," Ester suggested.

"No," Jack said firmly. "She's old enough to know the truth." Lance and I locked eyes.

"Tell me, Ester," Asia pleaded. "I know my father." It was Lance's turn to wince.

"Well," she wiped her eyes, now completely naked of mascara. "As soon as you left, he started goin' on about how I had no right to send you away. No say in your life. I was nothing more than the nanny, he said." She took a deep, shuddering breath. "The nanny. I couldn't believe my ears. I told him he was wrong, that I had been like a mother to you."

"You have," Asia, Jack and Lance all said in unison.

"I said that I'd not hear him speak to me that way. He laughed. Ugly. Laughed and called me an idiot. Said he'd been sleeping around since the day he met me. That he only married me so I'd look after Asia for him. Said that with her mom..."

Asia's spine straightened.

"Well, he said all kinds of horrible things. Then he left. I sat up all night, waiting for him to come home. Scared he'd come home. Sunday I went to work at the motel, tried to keep busy, not knowing if I still had a marriage. How could it all be over just like that? How?"

A shiver ran through her and the tears flowed. "Sunday night, I went home, expecting him to be asleep in the bedroom. I thought maybe we could talk about it all, work through it. But, he wasn't there."

"Oh, Ester," I said. I could feel her heart breaking.

"Then this mornin' he shows up at the restaurant, lookin' rougher than ever. When he sees me, he yells at me to get out. Get out of the restaurant. He wants a divorce. Says he's going to leave me with nothing." Her voice cracked under the pressure.

"You'll not be left wantin'," Jack said soothingly. "No matter what, you'll be taken care of by us."

"I just don't get it," Lance said. "He's been drunk before, been mean before, but nothing like this. What the hell set him off?"

"Me," Jack said simply. We all looked at him.

"What?"

"It was me, I'm afraid." He looked ashamed and tired. "Last week, I went to see him after I found out he'd fired Bob Pearson. Couldn't believe he'd be that stupid, or that cruel. Bob's a good man, didn't deserve that for his trouble."

Sean looked at me sheepishly.

"I went to see Reg and told him he was acting like an ass.

That he needed to sober up and come back to reality. So what, he sold the fish plant and made a bit of money. That didn't mean he didn't have responsibilities. He started yelling at me, telling me to mind my own business and get out of his life. Said he'd been shouldering his responsibilities, and those of other people, for decades and was tired of it. I called him a coward and said...well, I said he was just like his father."

The room went silent. Ester, Asia and I looked frantically from Lance to Jack, trying to figure out what he'd just said.

"Oh, my, God," Sean said, his mouth agape. "Sorry, sorry, family business, maybe I should go?" It was a rhetorical offer. There wasn't a hope in hell Sean would miss this. It was too juicy, too sordid.

"What?" Asia finally asked. "But, Grandpa, you're his dad."

"No, Asia, I'm not," Jack said gently. "Reg is my sister's son."

"Uncle Lance, did you know about this?"

"Yes, I did. I've always known, but it never really meant anything. Reg was always my older brother."

It still wasn't registering. I was trying to place the pieces, but they wouldn't work. "Did he ever tell you?" I asked Asia.

She shook her head. "No," then turned to her grandfather. "Then what is his real name?"

"Martin. Reg Martin."

"But don't worry, Asia. What's on your birth certificate and passport is correct. You are a Richards."

"How can that be?" she asked.

I stared at Lance with dawning awareness of how awful the whole situation had been for him.

"No one outside the family really knew," Jack continued and Asia's question was left unanswered. "It was just taken for granted that Reg was my son. He has always gone by the name of Richards.

"The wife and I never adopted him. His mother, my sister, Dolores, got involved with some guy, got pregnant, then he ended up in jail and she was left all alone. But she was just as bad as he was. They say there's always one in the family. Well, I guess it was Dolores. Daisy and I had just been married a few months when it happened. We talked about it and then went to Halifax and took the boy. It was to give her a chance to get her life back on track.

"Thing is, she met somebody and she asked us if we'd keep him. We were already attached to the little guy, so we didn't mind. Turns out she never told the new guy that she ever had a baby. She's been married for years now. I don't think her family knew anything about Reg.

"He was four years old when Lance was born. Lance adored his older brother – at least for a while. Turned out that Reg was jealous of Lance. I think it happened the day he found out he wasn't a Richards."

"Did you ever want to adopt him?"

"No. Daisy wasn't that keen on it. Besides, there was no need. To us he was still our son. To him, however, we didn't want him to be family or we would have adopted him. I don't think adopting Reg would have changed anything. There's always been a jealousy there, a wild streak. Guess it's in the genes. He didn't go anywhere beyond high school. He just wanted to get in there and work with me. Couldn't convince him that his education was more important. Then, when Lance made something of himself, Reg would make himself the underdog because he didn't have the education. Adopting him wouldn't have changed his character. I kept my fingers crossed all these years that he wouldn't get into any more trouble than he did."

"What happened to his father?"

Jack ran his hand over his face before speaking. "I don't know how Dolores got tangled up with that guy. He was abusive to her. He was a conman and he was finally caught in an armed robbery. Went to jail after Reg was born. I never met the guy. Can't say I wanted to."

"Does Reg know about his father?"

Mr. Richards stared at me and I felt suddenly that I was asking too many questions. "Reg asked. I told him. He wanted his mother's address years ago. I gave it to him. After all he was an adult. I don't know if they ever met. I didn't ask.

"I have no idea what happened to his father. I heard from my sister that he had been released from prison and was heading this way to see Reg, oh, that was years ago. Never saw him. Never heard of him again. That would have been just before Asia was born. Guess we'll never know what happened to him."

"Why didn't you tell me?" Asia asked. "All this time, Grandpa. All this time and now you're saying you're not even my grandfather? Uncle Lance isn't really my uncle?"

I swallowed hard.

"We're still family, Asia, that doesn't change. Those, those are just titles, nothing more. I'm the same man you've known all your life. So's your uncle. Knowing this changes nothing."

"But, it does, Grandpa. It changes everything!" Asia's voice rose a full pitch. "Ester did you know?"

"No, Asia, I didn't," Ester said. "This was kept from me, too. Makes sense. Reg wouldn't have ever admitted to me that he wasn't a Richards through and through. Always held his 'station' higher than mine. So many lies. So damn many..."

"Ester, I'm sorry," Lance said gently. "I'm sorry we never told you. I honestly didn't think it would matter. I've never thought of him as my stepbrother, or cousin, I guess. He was just my brother."

"I don't know how much more of this I can take," Asia said, pushing her chair out as she started to pace. "Our whole family, our whole lives, have been lies! Secrets. Is there anything else I should know?"

We all looked to each other. Each one of us asking a different silent question. Is now the time? Should she know she's not Reg's daughter? Should she know her mother?

"You're right, Asia," Ester finally said aloud. "There have been too many secrets. Not anymore. There is one more thing you should know..."

Chapter Fourteen

"What?" Asia snapped. "What else could there possibly be for me to know?"

Ester straightened her spine. "Your mother's not dead." She met her stepdaughter's stare and held it.

"What?"

"Your mother didn't die in childbirth. To the best of my knowledge, she's still alive. You should have the chance to find her. You should know." Ester tore her eyes from Asia and looked to Lance. "Shouldn't she?"

"Uncle Lance? Is this true?" Asia asked, her voice oddly calm.

Lance downed the last of his drink and contemplated the bottom of his glass. "Yes," he said finally. "It's true."

"Oh Lord," Jack muttered, looking to the ceiling. "Tell her, son. Tell her everything. It shouldn't have been kept from her this long."

I watched as the idea of the truth settled on Lance's shoulders. As he squared himself towards Asia, I knew he was ready.

"Asia, Reg isn't your father," he said.

"What? But you just said that Reg wasn't Grandpa's son. Now he's not my father either? What the hell is going on?"

"I'm your father, Asia."

From across the wide table, they stared at each other for what seemed an eternity. The rest of us sat, frozen in the moment. Ester's mouth hung even closer to the floor than Sean's. I could feel my body starting to shake.

"What?" Asia finally asked, quietly.

"I am your father."

"But...what?" Her voice shook. "But, uncle...how? Why?"

"We should have told you. Someone should have spoken up, but the timing never seemed right. We wanted you to be happy and, well, for the most part, you always were. With Reg and Ester raising you and Dad and me nearby, we figured there was no point rocking the boat."

"Happy? Happy? You thought I was happy?" Her voice steeled as the information began to settle. "All my life, I've lived in that house feeling like an outsider, feeling guilty for not caring more about my father, for not feeling a connection to him. I've spent hours in front of the mirror wondering where this hair came from." She pulled a lock of her red curls roughly. "Why I was different. I knew Ester wasn't my biological mother, but it was more than that. I dreamt, wished, that I could be your daughter. That I could move to this house and we'd be a family. I've hated myself for that dream."

"I'm sorry," Lance said meekly. "We thought it was the right thing."

"We?"

"Your grandpa and I. Reg," he explained. "I don't think anyone else knew."

"I didn't," Ester said. "Though, to be honest, I've always suspected."

"So, wait," Sean chimed in with a wave of his hand. "If you're Asia's real father, how did Reg end up with her?" We all turned to look at him in unison. "Sorry, I'm curious. You can't just tell half the story..."

"Sean," I started.

"No," Jack interrupted me. "He's right. We're in this now, might as well see it through. Go on, son."

"Well, we were young, Asia," Lance started. "Younger than you are now. We were in love. Truly, hopelessly in love. When we found out she was pregnant, we made plans. Plans to run away together, then plans to stay in Englee and raise you here. Then, well, circumstances took your mother away. It wasn't her fault, she had to go."

Jack's mouth opened as though to protest, then closed again.

"I was out of my mind with grief. I didn't know where she had gone, didn't know if you were okay, if she'd delivered you safely or not. I couldn't stay here. I was half out of my mind. I left Englee and joined the forces.

"When I came back, years later, I found out that Reg had somehow adopted you. He had married Ester and they'd been raising you as their own. You were still young, but old enough to have formed a bond with them. I couldn't rip you away from your home."

"But, but, I...holy fuck, Uncle Lance!" Asia blurted. "What the hell am I supposed to do with that? Oh my god, I can't. I can't deal with this!" She slammed her fist on the table before turning and walking out the backdoor.

I knew Lance wanted to run after her. I wanted to run after her. Ester simply rose and poured herself another drink. Sean followed suit.

Lance and I stared at each other, wondering what we should do next. Silently, the question loomed. Should Asia know everything?

Jack watched us.

"That was very kind of you, son," Jack said softly.

"Sorry?"

"The way you made her mother seem noble in leaving town. The way you protected Kennedy."

He was talking to Lance, but his eyes were on me.

"Jack..."

"Are you going to say it, or am I?" he asked. This man was still a force to be reckoned with.

I swallowed the lump in my throat and held his blue stare. "My name is Kennedy Warren."

Ester and Sean's chatter ceased. Jack looked almost relieved, yet there was a layer of thinly veiled rage boiling just below the surface.

"Kennedy Warren?" I heard Sean whisper to Ester behind me.

"*Asia's mother!*" Ester whispered back through a shocked inhalation of breath.

"Oh...my..." Sean turned to the sideboard.

"I suspected it," Jack said. "It was you, Lance. The way you look at her. I put two and two together and I knew. I was just waiting for you to tell me."

"But, but," Ester tried to find her voice. "You don't look anything like the girl I've seen in the pictures. You don't look one bit like Kennedy Warren. Do you?" She reached a hand forward as though she needed to pinch my cheek.

"No, I don't. I don't look anything like the girl who left this town. There was an accident and the doctors had to reconstruct most of my face." I ran a finger down my nose, where the telltale Warren bump used to be.

"Oh..."

"Who cares what you damn well look like!" Jack exploded. "Why? I need to know why the hell you did what you did. Why did you run away and drive a wedge between my son and me for all of these years? I have a grandchild caught in the middle. Why the hell did you do what you did?"

"Dad, let me ask you something first," Lance interrupted. "What do you remember about the day Kenny left?"

"Why? We've been over this a hundred times. I told you I had nothing to do with her leaving. I gave Reg the money. Nothing else. Why?"

"I saw Reg kill a man," I blurted out.

Jack's face went white. Ester's glass dropped to the sideboard with a thud. "What?"

"I saw Reg kill a man," I repeated.

"You saw my son kill a man," he said slowly.

"Not your son. Reg. Reg is not your son, Mister Richards. Yes, I saw Reg kill a man."

I watched his hand shake as he put his glass on the table. He sat back and closed his eyes. I wanted to cry again.

He opened his eyes and stared at me. "Who? Where? When? When did all of this happen?"

"I'm sorry. I saw him kill a man the day I left. That was why I left."

"Why didn't you come to me? Who was this man?"

I shook my head. "I don't know who he was. I couldn't come to you because he told me you knew about it. He gave me money, told me to leave town or he'd kill my dad and Lance."

He put his hands in his head. "Oh, dear God!"

"But? Kill? Reg?" Ester stuttered as she fell back into her seat. "He's not capable..."

"Isn't he?" I asked her, point blank.

"Oh," she said at the realization. "Oh God."

"Oh, Kay, you poor thing!" Sean sighed, clutching a hand to his chest.

"God, Sean, I'm sorry, I never meant for you to get caught up in all this," I said. I was embarrassed and flustered and felt like I was drowning in the details of it all. "Asia. Someone should get Asia."

"Yes, we need time to talk this through, the four of us," Jack said, pointing to Lance, myself and Ester. "This will be too much for the girl right now. Too much for us, let alone...."

"Sean? Can you go make sure she's alright?" I asked.

"Of course, sure, no problem. I'll go sit with her for a while, keep her busy," Sean said as he grabbed his coat. "Oh, and mum's the word, of course. She won't hear any of this from me."

"Thanks, Sean. You and I'll talk later, okay?"

"Sure, Kay, whatever you need," he said with a sympathetic smile.

He disappeared out the backdoor and the room seemed nearly empty. The four of us sat, facing one another, unsure of where to go, what to say, next.

"Kenny Warren?" Ester finally asked. "As I live and breathe. I never thought I'd get the chance. Kennedy Warren?"

"Yes, that's me," I said shyly. "Although, it's hard to remember exactly who that is, after all this time."

"I should think so," Jack said. We all took a minute, unable to move the conversation forward without letting some of the information sink in.

"So you believe me?" I asked.

He lifted his head and his eyes were filled with tears. "I don't believe you have a reason to make up such a story. I remember that day. The RCMP were there. I went with them because they had gotten a call saying somebody had been stabbed on my property. Nothing was ever found. Reg came and asked me for money because Kenny, you, wanted to leave town. I wasn't even thinking properly. I was with the police all evening. I gave him the money for her, for you. Oh dear God."

He looked at me. "You left to protect your dad and Lance."

I nodded.

"And you thought I was involved."

I nodded. "I haven't been myself since the day Asia was born. I couldn't help the changes to my face, those were necessary, but the rest I chose. I covered my hair and took a new name. I hid from Reg and the world in plain view as I built up the company. I thought—still think—that if he figured out who I was, he'd stop at nothing to destroy me. He will. I know it, know it in every fibre of my being. I've hidden who I am for so long."

Jack looked at me, his eyes softening. "You know even though Daisy and I were disappointed that you were pregnant, we had decided that we'd keep the baby while you two went to university."

"You want us to believe that?" asked Lance.

"It's the truth, son."

Lance turned to me. For the first time ever there was doubt in his eyes.

"It's all my fault," Mr. Richards continued. "Reg must have

overheard the conversation between Daisy and me about you being pregnant and our plans for both of you."

"Reg?" We both echoed.

"I didn't know until it was too late. I only knew the next day that you had gone, but I didn't know it was because of Reg. Your dad came to see me the day after you left. He couldn't understand why I had given you the money to leave. He wanted to know where you had gone and what was going to happen to the baby. I told him what Reg had told me, that you wanted to go away."

All these years I had blamed him. All these years his secret had driven him apart from Lance. I looked away. There was silence. I finally got the strength to ask.

"Lord forgive me, I never wanted you to come back, Kenny," Jack blurted.

"That's nice, Dad, super," Lance muttered.

"You may not believe me, son, but I believed Reg at first. I thought you were the one who couldn't see what was real. Then I felt like I had betrayed everyone. I confronted Reg. He was surprised because he didn't think your dad knew you were pregnant. I told him your dad knew I had given you the money to leave. I said I'd try to find you. I swore to him that I'd bring you back. Then, a few days later, Reg came to me and said that I didn't have to worry about finding you; that there was no need because your dad was dead. I asked him what had happened and he told me about the boat going down. It happens. Boats go down here every year. I felt so bad because you had gone, your dad had gone and I knew that I would lose Lance. I didn't know he had killed anybody but I realized that he had sent you away."

He wiped at the tears falling down his cheeks. "I went down to the old mill. I sat on a rock and I cried. I think that was the only time I ever thought of suicide. I could not believe what was happening to our family, the most prominent family in town." He took a deep breath. "I realized that night that Reg was going to be a problem."

"What did you do?" Lance asked.

"After I sat and cried Reg came to me. He hadn't said he was responsible for your dad's death, but I had assumed it. I thought that by his sending you away, your dad had no reason to live anymore. I blamed Reg and I blamed myself. I was debating what to do but he said he had decided to go away. I thought it was a good idea. I needed time to think. I didn't know what to do. I didn't hear from Reg for months. Then one day he appeared with his new wife and child. He had gone to Halifax, swept you off your feet, Ester, and adopted the baby."

"It seemed so simple, so easy at the time," Ester said. "He needed a wife and I needed, wanted, a better life. Reg had money and promised me a fresh start. When I saw Asia, when I saw that precious babe, I knew I could be a good stepmother to her. He said she was an orphan."

"You did nothing wrong, Ester," I wanted to console her,

take away the pain Reg had caused her. "And you are a good stepmother to Asia."

Jack reached out and patted her hand warmly. "When he came back with his new wife and baby girl I was trapped. What could I do? You were gone from my life, Lance. I couldn't have Reg arrested or committed on suspicions only. I thought I'd do the only thing I could. I'd be the best grandfather I possibly could and I'd help Reg get established and leave the past in the past.

"I always wondered about your dad's death. It just didn't look right. I hate to think this, hate the thought. Reg was responsible for your dad's death." He looked at me. "And that's why you don't want anybody to know who you are."

I shook my head. "I only came back to visit my parents' graves. I had no idea I'd run into Lance or my daughter. But I can't let Reg know who I am. I can't let anybody know. I'm a witness to a murder and I don't know what to do."

"What exactly did you see that night?"

"I was walking past the plant and heard a noise. I thought it was the ghosts from the Indian burial ground rattling around. I didn't want to be afraid of them anymore. It was silly, but my entire childhood I had lived in fear of those spirits. So, I turned back, to look in the alleyway. There were three men. One was in the shadows, holding a stranger by the arms."

"What did the stranger look like?"

"Tall, older, probably about my dad's age at the time. He

was thin and blond, yet somehow his face was dark—etched with deep lines."

"What else did you see?" Jack asked, trying to probe my memory.

"Reg. Reg was in front of the stranger. He punched him in the gut and the stranger pushed back into the man who was holding him." I closed my eyes and the vision flooded my mind. "They both grunted and the man pushed the stranger forward, towards Reg, roughly. He grumbled, Charlie..."

"Charlie?" They all asked.

"Oh my God," I exclaimed as the third man's voice rang in my ears and his face pushed out of the shadow ever so slightly. "The third man. It was Charlie!"

"Oh no," Jack exclaimed. "Reg has been leading that boy around by the nose since he was a child."

"Keep going, Kay, tell us the rest," Lance urged, knowing his father needed to hear the whole story.

"Charlie pushed the stranger forward. Reg smirked. He smirked and told the stranger he should have never come looking for him. That's what he said, 'You never should have come lookin' for me. You should have stayed invisible.' Then there was a flash of light, a glint on the blade of the knife, as Reg flipped it open. He didn't even flinch as he stabbed the stranger right in the gut. The man groaned, screamed. Reg told Charlie to hold him and pulled the knife out. There was blood. He straightened the blade and stabbed again. The stranger slumped forward and Charlie threw him to the ground. That's when I ran. I ran home, terrified and shocked. Reg followed me and that's when he told me he'd do the same thing to Lance and my dad if I didn't leave town for good."

Mr. Richards reached out his hand and took mine in his. "Kenny Warren, Kay Toms, I don't know what to say. I wish you could have come to me that night and told me everything. We would have saved a lot of heartache over the past years. Was I such a monster that you couldn't trust me? Did you ever think that I could do something like that?"

"Jack, I was seventeen years old; naive and scared. You were the richest man and the most powerful man in town. I was scared for my dad and for Lance. I would have done anything to protect them. I could never let anybody hurt Lance."

He stood up and walked to look out the window. We watched him. Then he slowly turned around and I stood up and went to him. He put his arms around me, pulled me close and kissed me on the head. "We'll make it right, Kenny. We'll make it right."

I pulled away and Lance went to hug his dad. Mr. Richards squeezed his eyes shut but the tears trickled down his cheeks. He patted Lance on the back and pulled away and wiped at his cheeks. "You've got her back, son. Now we've got to keep her safe."

Chapter Fifteen

"She needs to see pictures," Sean said as he lead Asia into the kitchen from the backyard an hour later.

"What?" I asked.

"Lance, you must have a picture of her mother. She needs to see her." Sean stood firmly in front of the girl whose eyes were swollen and red.

"Sean...no, it's all..." Asia tried to mutter.

"Don't get all shy on me now, child. Go with Lance. See her. Go, now." He pulled her forward. She stared at the floor.

"Oh, right, right, of course." Lance fumbled his way out of his chair. "Upstairs..." he reached a nervous hand towards her, but she sidestepped around him and made a beeline out of the room. He limped behind her, favouring his bad leg.

"Thank you, Sean," Jack said as he gestured for him to take a seat.

"No, no, there's too much to do," Sean said and looked at the screen of his smartphone.

"To do?" Ester asked.

"Yes, I know you're all wrapped up in this. I know the timing is atrocious, but we have a town meeting in less than two days."

"Oh, but you can't really expect..." Jack attempted.

"Oh yes I can," Sean retorted with a slight waggle of his

head. "We've been working our behinds off on this project. Knowing this town, and the mayor, word has already gone out that there's going to be an announcement. We can't stop now."

"But, Reg..."

"But, Reg? We're going to let that thug ruin our plans?" He looked at me deadpan. "Kay, pardon me for saying this, but it's time to man-up here. We can't let him put a hold on everything. Evil little sod. I might not know the whole story, frankly I'm not sure that I want to know the whole story, but this town needs to move forward. Now."

Jack and Ester looked at me. I looked at Sean. At the vice-president. Suddenly, the frivolous boy I had hired all those years before was a man to be reckoned with.

"You're right," I said. "You're absolutely right. Business doesn't stop, as B.J. used to say. It's a machine that keeps working, even when our emotions threaten to shut it down. The meeting will proceed."

"But, what about Reg? You know he's not going to stay away, Kay." Ester bit her fingernail.

"No, no he won't," Jack concurred. "We'll need security at the meeting. We should call the RCMP, about it. About everything."

"Already on the line," Lance said as he hobbled back into the room with a cordless phone to his ear. "We can't let this go on. We know Reg killed one man and suspect he may have played a part in killing another. Your dad." He looked me dead in the eye. "This is a matter for the cops."

"Where's Asia?" Ester asked.

"Upstairs with my old photo albums. She said she needed some time alone."

"Of course," Jack nodded.

"But, the police, I'll have to tell them..."

"You'll tell them exactly what you've told us. Lance is right here. Everyone you care about is right here and safe." Jack patted my hand warmly. "He can't hurt you. Can't hurt us."

I knew it was the right thing to do. I knew it had to be done, but the thought of the whole truth coming out made my stomach do cartwheels.

"Asia? I don't think she's ready..."

"You're right there. She doesn't need to know who you are. Not yet. You'll go with Lance to the RCMP, the nearest detachment is in Roddickton. You'll talk to them there, tell them everything and arrange for security at the meeting. They'll pick Reg up and hopefully hold him."

"Hopefully," I repeated. All eyes were on me. Sean, Jack and Lance stood united. Men. Men ready to do the right thing and protect me. I should have felt secure in that. I should have, but the terrified girl I had been was screaming in my head to run. Run away.

"Jack and I will stay here with Asia. We'll be safe. You need to end this, Missus Toms. You need to end this now. You've hidden for half your lifetime because of my husband. If he finds out the truth there won't be nothing that'll stop him. End this." Ester's naked eyes pleaded with me.

"Good lord, Ester, you can call me Kay," I said with a smile. "My friends don't call me Missus Toms."

Her face lightened for the first time all day. "Right, then, Kay, get your butt out that door and to the RCMP." She was up out of her chair. "C'mon, skoot, out with ya." She grabbed my arm and started tugging. "If it's my friend you say you are, you won't be sitting around here cowering."

"You go girl," Sean said with a snap. "Tell her."

"T'at's right, up, out and march," she said as she shooed me out of the kitchen and to the front door.

"But, can I just freshen..." I tried as she threw my coat into my arms.

"Oh, what? Ya gotta look pretty for this?"

"I'd do what she says." Asia's voice came from the top of the stairs. She had poked her head out of Lance's den. "I don't know what she needs you to do, but trust me, I know that tone. She won't stop till you do it."

Ester turned to look at her. Asia smiled warmly and gave her a wink.

"Who do you think taught me to be so hard-headed?"

Ester nearly melted on the spot, big floppy tears welling, as she smiled at her child. "T'at's right," she said, turning her attention back to me. "Now, out t'at door and get it done. T'won't hurt a bit, you'll see."

She was right. It didn't hurt. It was nerve-racking and hard as hell, but it didn't hurt. Lance sat beside me the whole time, holding my hand and filling in details where they were needed. The constable listened, taking notes diligently and looking like he had just been presented with a feast. This was, without a doubt, the most excitement he had ever seen in his long career on the Northern Peninsula.

With our report filed, and promises from the constable that he'd be investigating immediately, we left the detachment. They would start by picking up Charlie and searching for Reg. It had been hours since Lance had left him and we knew he was still drunk. He could be anywhere.

The constable assured us that there'd be a patrol set at Lance's property, discretely, and that there'd be plenty of officers on hand at the upcoming meeting. We drove back to Batty Catters in silence. It was as if we had used all the words. All the words possible, in one day. Yet, we knew we'd have to say more. Asia needed to know the full truth eventually. Once the meeting was over and things had settled down, we'd tell her. Together.

It was fully dark as we pulled into the driveway. The moon was a sliver in the sky. Someone had left the front porch light on, but the rest of the house was dark. Lance took my hand as we walked to the front door and lead me into the house, up the stairs, and into his bedroom. Still we didn't talk.

He stood silently in front of me and undressed my body

slowly, gently. As he ran his hands up my face I closed my eyes and felt his fingers slide my wig off. It dropped to the floor. He worked the pins out of my hair, one at a time, and let the long curls fall to my back.

Completely exposed, I finally opened my eyes. I expected to see passion, fire, but instead was faced with sheer tenderness. I nearly gasped as he scooped me into his arms and laid me down on the bed.

I watched in the dim light as he undressed and slid between the sheets. I curled into his side and felt, for the first time in nearly eighteen years, that I was truly safe.

The next day was chaotic. In the living room, Sean had set up a makeshift office, with papers and files spread everywhere. His cell phone seemed permanently braced on his shoulder, as he typed on his laptop, multitasking his way through the mountain of work that needed to be done for the meeting the next evening. There were a million details to attend to and he seemed to be handling it all.

On the other side of the room, I was set up at my own work station. Raj's team was ready to start small test markets for the products and needed my approval. Jennifer had a stack of legal points that needed my attention, and it seemed that the world was simply moving forward, regardless of the previous day's events. Sean and I video-conferenced in on four separate team meetings, while Jack worked at the kitchen table on his own business.

Lance divided his time between working in his den and checking in on Asia. We'd hear him limp down the hall once an hour, on the hour, to poke his head into her bedroom. It didn't take long for her to start telling him to leave her alone, in such a stereotypical teenage tone that we'd all smile.

We had all agreed to stay in the house until the meeting. There would be no going out, no excursions. There was safety in numbers, we had decided. Asia was a bit confused by this, but went along with it, unsure of what else to do. The adults in her life had obviously lost their minds.

Ester busied herself around the house, trying to tidy up around the rest of us, and endlessly cooking. By the time we all put away our computers for the day, there was enough food amassed in the kitchen to feed a small army for about a week.

As we sat down to dinner, the phone rang. Lance managed, just barely, to pick it up before his daughter. She pouted fiercely. Jack raised an eyebrow in her direction.

"Yes, yes," Lance said into the receiver as he stood and went out onto the front porch. Asia didn't seem to notice the looks the rest of us exchanged. The RCMP hadn't contacted us all day and we were on pins and needles waiting for news of Reg and the investigation.

Ester immediately started passing bowls around the table, insisting that we eat everything she had made.

"Oh, Tom Ford forgive me," Sean said, rolling his eyes to the ceiling. "I'll probably never wear a pair of trousers the same way again." He crossed his chest, then happily accepted the potato salad on offer.

As he continued to entertain the table, I quietly excused myself and made my way to the front porch.

"Thank you, Constable," Lance said as I stepped out and pulled the door shut.

"Well?"

"They've had Charlie at the station all day. He's told them all about the murder, confessed his part in it. They've charged him, but it's with a minor misdemeanour, considering he wasn't the one to pull the knife or plan the attack. Plus, with his diminished capacity, they're pretty sure they wouldn't be able to make any serious charges stick."

"Oh, well, that's good." I was still processing. "I didn't really want to see Charlie go down for it all. It couldn't have been his fault."

"True. And he's given the RCMP everything they need to charge Reg. They've issued a warrant for his arrest."

"A warrant? You mean they don't have him in custody?" Shivers played up and down my spine.

"No, they haven't been able to find him. Yet." He gathered me in a hug. "They will, Kay. They will. They'll find him and when they do, they'll be able to put him away for a long, long time."

I turned my head against his chest and looked down the driveway. At the end of the road, there was an unmarked RCMP car sitting, waiting presumably. We were all waiting. Waiting for Reg.

Chapter Sixteen

"Ma'am," the young officer said in his Toronto accent, with a nod of his hat. "Right this way."

I followed him as we made our way into the school auditorium. It was an hour before the meeting was to start. Sean went straight to work, setting pamphlets out on the tables and rearranging chairs. Asia followed behind him, determined to help. I had told her my plans for the plant that morning and she was thrilled. Her friends lived in Englee and jobs meant that their parents could survive and provide for them. She loved Englee; it was home.

"Whaddya mean identification? Can't you see my hands are full!" Melissa Young's normally calm voice rang out from the entrance way. "Stop lookin' at me like I'm a terrorist, young man, and give me a hand."

"Oh, Melissa!" I ran to take one of the many baskets from her hands. "What on earth have you been up to?"

"My first catering job," she said proudly as she sidestepped around the young officer posted at the door.

"Your first..."

"That's right!" Sean chimed from the stage behind us. "I hired Melissa to provide all the refreshments for this evening."

"Yes," Melissa struggled to lift the rest of her cargo onto the table. "He did. Called me up yesterday and said to make enough food for the whole town."

I nearly choked. "He said?"

"Food for the whole town. Said there was going to be a heck of a turnout for this." She beamed from ear to ear. "Now, can someone give me a hand with bringin' in the rest?"

"The rest? How much food did you make, Melissa?"

"Enough for the..."

"Whole town," I finished with her. As she rushed out to her truck I turned to look at Sean.

"Perhaps I could have been a touch more specific," he said with a low chuckle.

"Just a touch," I agreed as I looked at the overflowing baskets of cookies, cakes, and scones in front of me. "Well, looks like it's going to be more of a party than a meeting."

"Hum, seems fitting, wouldn't you say?" Lance smirked. How on earth could I be angry while looking at his charming face?

"Hmmm...yes. But, no dancing. Alright?" I wagged a finger at Sean and Asia.

"Yes, Missus Toms," they said in unison, then proceeded to wiggle their hips and hum *Celebration*. Behind me Jack absentmindedly joined in, humming along with the tune as he began unstacking chairs.

"You've all gone mad," I tried to scold as Tom Young followed his wife into the hall with an armful of trays and did a little two-step across the gym floor to the tune. "Really, Tom?"

I asked with a raised eyebrow.

"Sorry, Missus Toms, I'm a sucker for a good tune," he said quietly with a smile. Melissa slapped him lightly on the arm.

"No, it's alright, Melissa. Perhaps these fools are right and this does need to be a celebration. We've been all business since I arrived in town. Tonight is about good news!"

"Hear hear!" Jack saluted. "And not a moment too soon. Sounds like the guests are starting to arrive." From the other side of the entrance, we could hear the voices of people as they started to gather outside. Lance and Jack had insisted the RCMP officers stand at the doorway, but I was adamant that they not impose. If people were showing up to hear about her plans for the plant and put their names forward, then they needed to feel free to join in.

The young officer by the door quietly moved inside the gym, to stand near the door, but not right at it. Everyone would know he was there and that there were other officers around the building. They wanted to be visible. Catching Reg was a priority, but even more important to me was getting through the event without any trouble.

I took a moment to sneak backstage and straighten myself up. I ran a hand over the deep red jersey-silk dress I'd ordered for the occasion from Boston. It fit beautifully and felt wonderful as it skimmed my hips from the belted waist and rested mid-calf. I glanced in the mirror to make sure my wig was set and makeup not overdone, then squared my shoulders. The noise from the auditorium was growing steadily. Butterflies began flapping in my stomach.

Lance poked his head around the door and smiled. "You ready for this?" he asked.

"Oh, I think so." I knew my nerves were showing.

"You'll be fine. Remember, it's a celebration!" With that, he was gone, back into the crowd.

"Right," I said to the mirror. "Right." I had a few minutes to review my notes and prepare myself for what was about to happen. I was about to change the future of Englee. Jack would introduce me, then I'd step on that stage to say...what? I turned from the mirror to grab my notes and nearly screamed. Two feet in front of me stood Charlie. He was tall, taller than I ever remembered noticing, and strong. When did Charlie get so many muscles? My eyes flew around the little room, looking for anyone to help.

Charlie didn't look happy.

"Charlie! What, what are you doing here?" I gasped. He raised his hand. My heart nearly stopped. He reached up and pulled off his woollen cap. "Oh God," I stammered.

"Missus," he said quietly. He was looking right at me. Something I had never known Charlie to do. "You's her, right?"

"Sorry?" I was frantic and confused. No one in the gym would be able to hear me if I screamed. They were talking and laughing, as crowds around food tend to do. I was on my own.

"You's her, right?" he repeated.

I stared at him blankly. "Her?"

"Kenny Warren. You's her," he said, still looking me straight in the eye.

"Now, Charlie, I don't know what you've heard..."

"Oh, I hear plenty. Plenty enough. No one t'inks I listen, but I hear it all. The RCMP, they talked to me a lot t'day." He rubbed his stubbled jaw.

"Did they?" I tried to keep my voice calm, the way one does when trying to coax a bear away from their tent.

"Oh yes, Missus, t'ey did. Told me how a witness to a crime committed seventeen years ago had shown up back in town. How t'at witness had made a statement to t'em and wanted charges pressed, t'ey said."

"Oh?" was all I could think to say.

"Yes, Missus, t'ey said as how I should confess to me part in it all."

"Did they?"

"Yes, Missus, t'ey did at t'at. And I did. I told them everyt'ing I knew. But, then I gets to thinkin' whiles I'm sittin' t'ere. T'is witness just showed up in town. Showed up and told 'em everyt'ing. After all t'is time. See, Missus, t'at's what got me head workin'."

"Really?" I asked as my eyes scanned the room for a weapon. Anything I could strike him with and run like hell. That was my only plan.

"Yes, got t'inkin' pretty good and figured a few t'ings out," he said, his tone flat. He stepped forward. I jumped. There was less than a foot between us and I had no way of getting around him. "I'm sorry." He held out his hand.

"What?" Nothing made sense.

"The way I figure it, I owes you an apology." His hand was still outstretched. I looked at it like a live bomb.

"An apology? For what?"

"You's her. The witness. You're Kennedy Warren."

My jaw must have hit the floor.

"T'ere was only one witness. Reg told me. Told me t'at night t'at Kenny had seen everything. Said he'd take care of it. I offered, I did, but I was glad when he said he'd do it himself. I didn't like the t'ought of hurtin' a girl. T'at's you, right?"

My heart was still racing, but I was listening to him intently. If there was a threat in Charlie's voice, I couldn't hear it.

"But, how did you know?"

"T'ey said t'at the witness had shown up in town. You're the only woman who's come to Englee in years. Knew it couldn't be t'at gay fella. Had to be you, even though you don't look like you. 'Cept the eyes, maybe."

"Oh my God, Charlie! That's it, you wanted to apologize? I thought you might be here to...to..." I could feel my cheeks flushing.

"Hurts ya? Na, but I do owes ya, Kenny. You and yours were always nice to me. Your dad would come down to the twine loft and help me mend nets. He'd talk and talk; even took me huntin' with him. I even remembers your mam. I was just young when she went, but I remembers her being kind to me, always askin' after me and takin' me on walks. T'at's where you get the eyes, only part of you I recognize. Don't suppose t'at it's just me though. You's had every one fooled."

I stared at him.

"Anyways, I wanted to say I'm sorry, for everyt'ing. I didn't know what Reg was gonna do t'at night. I didn't know. He asked me to come w'it him and I followed, like I do. T'ought maybe he had a bit a work for me at the plant. Even back then I was lookin' to Reg for jobs. Over all he's been pretty good to me, ya know? But, t'ere's t'ings. T'ings I didn't want any part of..."

He looked sad, weighted and for the first time I noticed Charlie's age. He was nearly ten years my senior and that decade showed in the lines of his face.

"It's okay, Charlie. It wasn't your fault," I said, reaching out to touch his arm. He didn't flinch as I made contact, but took a step back.

"You don't know it all yet, Missus," he said, his eyes round as saucers. "I's told the cops everyt'ing, but I t'inks you need to know it more. I might get locked up, I don't know. Don't matter. I did all of it."

"All of what?"

"Everyt'ing Reg asked me to. Your dad." We both froze.

"My dad?"

"Yes, Missus. Your dad. He was a good'un. Good sort. But, see, Reg had me 'tween a rock and a hard place. Few days after t'at night, what you saw, your dad's boat goes missin'. I's worried sick. Knowing what I do. He shoulda been back t'at afternoon and t'ere it was gettin' dark and no sign. I see Reg and tells him I'm calling Rescue. Reg says no, t'at I won't do t'at. When I asked him why not, he says how if I even think of raisin' ta alarm that he'll tell the cops that I stabbed t'at guy. He still had the knife. My knife, w'it the guy's blood all over it."

"But, that's not your fault, Charlie..." I wanted to reassure him. The picture of how Reg had manipulated this poor slow man was forming clearly.

"See, your dad, he'd asked me to help fix his boat. He had a hole in it and I helped him fix it. It wasn't all finished, but it was gettin' late, so we called it a day. But when I went to check on the boat in the morning, your dad said it was all done. I shoulda checked meself. I knew Reg'd made the original hole. He wanted t'at boat to sink. N'ver dawned on me that he'd go back and make another hole. Your dad had no chance out t'ere on t'at ocean. Not wit'out someone sendin' out a rescue." He pulled his cap between his hands and stared at the floor. "I'm sorry, Missus Kenny."

"Oh God, Charlie," I wanted to cry. Cry for my father, cry for the pain Reg had caused and cry for Charlie. He'd never had anything handed to him in life and Reg had taken full advantage of that. "It's okay." I took both his hands in mine.

"It wasn't your fault. It was Reg. You couldn't have saved my father. You couldn't have saved me. It wasn't your fault and this is all going to be okay."

He looked at me then and I hugged him. It was obvious he didn't know how to respond or what to do, so he just stood still till I was done. When I pulled back and looked at him, he asked. "Why's don't you look like you?"

"Oh, Charlie, that's a very long story. Very long, but I'll tell you the whole thing another time, okay? Right now, I've got to get out there and talk to those people. They're waiting. You know what this meeting's about, Charlie?"

"How you've bought the old plant and are turning it into a new business. Jobs, t'at's what it's about."

"Huh, you really do hear everything, don't you?"

"Yes, Missus," he sounded almost proud.

"Right, well, in order for there to be jobs, lots of new jobs, everyone out there, the whole town, needs to believe I'm just Kay Toms, not Kenny Warren. Can you keep my secret, Charlie? Just for a little while?"

He took a moment to put his cap back on. "Yes, Missus, can't see the harm in t'at."

"Good," I said with genuine relief. "And thank you, Charlie. Thank you for telling the RCMP everything. And for telling me. My dad would be proud."

Charlie's head shook back and forth as he shuffled out of the room through the backdoor. I took only a moment to collect myself, then stuck my head out the front door. I caught Jack's eye and nodded. It was time for a meetin'.

Chapter Seventeen

"Ladies and gentlemen," Jack said into the microphone. "If you'd find your seats, we're ready to begin." He looked at me and winked. I was seated just to the left of the microphone, still trying to steady my nerves. It seemed all five hundred and seventy one souls of Englee had converged for the meeting. The room was packed to standing room only. I noticed the young constable at the door as he said something into the walkie-talkie on his shoulder. Another uniformed figure on the side wall responded. They both then stood at attention.

"Citizens, friends, I'd like to formally introduce you to Missus Kay Toms," Jack said once the room had settled. "You've probably all met her, or at least seen her, recently as she's been settling into town. She's been working diligently with Tom Young and his crew to restore the house on the hill." He swept a hand to the audience to point out Tom Young. I clapped along with the crowd.

"But, she's been doing more than that," Jack said, drawing their attention back. "Now, I've gotten to know Missus Toms quite well and I have to say, she's an impressive businesswoman. As owner of Tomtex Worldwide, she runs a multi-billion dollar corporation. More importantly though, she runs it well, with morals and high standards." I forced myself not to blush. "Now, I've reviewed everything Missus Toms is about to tell you and

I have to say, I couldn't be prouder. Listen and make up your own minds, but do so knowing I think what she's proposing will, literally, save this town. Missus Kay Toms," he finished with a flourish to a smattering of weary applause. The people of Englee would not decide anything on one man's endorsement.

"Thank you, Jack," I said as I took the mike. He took his seat on the stage beside me with Sean and the mayor. After I spoke, Sean would field questions about the micro-bank and Gina would round off the evening with her speech.

There was no turning back.

"Hello, everyone, thank you for coming tonight. As Jack said, my name is Kay Toms and I am the owner and CEO of Tomtex Worldwide. Over the past few weeks, I've had the opportunity to meet most of you. Getting to know you, your families, and this town has been a privilege. What I see in Englee is opportunity. Opportunity for those who are willing to take a risk."

I looked across the crowd, trying to gauge their reaction so far. Nothing.

"Well, I am willing to take that risk. In fact, I already have taken most of it."

"What by dating Lance?" a man yelled with a laugh. The crowd responded to that. They chuckled, then seemed to lean forward in their seats, waiting for my answer. To the left of the stage, I spotted Asia and smiled. She gave me a wink and an encouraging nod.

"Touché, touché, getting mixed up with a Richards is a pretty risky proposition," I said lightly with a nod towards Jack. "In all seriousness though, the Richards' family has been extremely helpful to me in my endeavours. Without Jack Richards' support, I may have gone home weeks ago, without having made an impact or change to this town at all. And without Lance..." they waited... "well, you'll see shortly how important Lance has been."

They let out a muffled awe.

"Tonight we have two announcements. The first is that I have, that Tomtex has, bought the old fish plant."

A lot of nodding and I-knew-its.

"We plan on remodelling the facility entirely, almost from the ground up. The new, modern plant will open this summer to produce a full line of ready-to-eat meals and food products featuring L.B.C. shrimp. The Roddickton facility owned and operated by Lance Richards, will be expanding their own production in order to keep up with Tomtex demand. If our projections are right, and they usually are, we expect that the Englee facility will be a year-round operation, offering permanent employment."

"How many? How many jobs we talkin' about?" a woman yelled from one of the back rows.

"It's hard to say exactly at this point, we're still in the planning stages here, but we estimate nearly 150 permanent positions, as well as part-time and seasonal jobs, too."

You could have heard a pin drop. The whole room went dead silent. I turned to Jack. He shrugged. Then, suddenly, the whole crowd burst into applause.

"Thank you, thank you," I said, trying to settle them down again. "In the meantime, there will be plenty of work available to those who want it in the reconstruction of the facility. We'll be bringing in a commercial contractor from the mainland, but he'll be hiring locally. Anyone who's interested can get an application from Mister Sean Chen at the end of the meeting."

Again, more applause. I took a moment and looked at their faces. Written on most of them was relief, genuine, pure relief. They had finally seen the light at the end of the long tunnel.

I took a deep breath.

"Alright, that was announcement one. Now, did everyone enjoy the refreshments before we started?"

"Yes!"

"Oh, yes, very nice!"

"Well, that was thanks to the efforts of Tomtex's first micro-loan recipient, Melissa Young!" There was hesitant applause. "Our second announcement for the evening is the creation of a brand-new Tomtex endeavour. I know what having stable jobs in this town means to all of you. I know what having a major employer can do for your families as this town grows. But, I wanted to see more than that. I want to see Englee flourish, thrive, and become independent. It doesn't take a genius to see that Englee has been dependant on others for too long—the government, the fishery, heck, Mister Richards..." Jack laughed along with the crowd.

"Tomtex Worldwide Micro-Bank will work to provide zero-interest loans to applicants who want to start their own businesses. This is a new venture for us. We've never tried anything like this before."

"So we're an experiment?"

"An opportunity. Toxtex will lend ten entrepreneurs up to fifty-thousand dollars each, payment-free for their first year of operations, and with virtually no interest. This will allow those among you with ideas to get a start, a foothold. Be as creative as you'd like, think of ideas that could bring tourists to Englee, keep tourists interested once they get here, and most importantly, ideas that will enrich the community.

"Tourism is a growing industry here on the island. Parts of Newfoundland are flourishing because of the oil industry. But oil is not here. Although you do have benefits from the industry, you must initiate your own prosperity. Take advantage of the fact that tourism is an upcoming industry. Other towns have started and I think this is one of the prettiest towns on the Northern Peninsula. The long-term economy of Englee is dependent on diversity. Melissa Young was brave enough to take her first step. The loan we've approved for her will allow her to open a restaurant and cafe on the hill. Her lifelong dream will employ at least two full time positions, with the potential of more in the future. Already, she's employing contractors for the renovations, and those people are then able to spend more money in town. It's cyclical. I believe, in my heart, that Englee can thrive again. We just need to make a start."

In the first row, I could see Melissa blush as she clapped with all her might.

"I know you have questions, probably many questions, so I'll ask my associate, Mister Sean Chen, Vice President of Philanthropic Operations at Tomtex to join me. Mister Chen will be overseeing the micro-lending program in Englee long term. Sean?"

"Thank you, Kay," he said as he stepped to my side. "And thank you, Englee, this has been..."

A woman screamed. Outside the door to the gymnasium her voice rang. Terrified. We looked frantically around, trying to sort out what was happening. The RCMP officers rushed to the doors and flung them open.

"Fire!" she yelled again. Out the doors, the whole crowd looked, to see the flames engulfing the old fish plant across the road. "Fire! Fire! Help!"

We ran. We all ran out the school doors and across the street, to see the massive flames shooting up the sides of the plant. We ran right where Reg had wanted us to.

Chapter Eighteen

I felt his hand on the back of my neck. Rough fingers digging. I stopped dead in my tracks, snapped back by the force of his grip. Everyone else was in front of me, racing to the fire, grabbing buckets, hoses, anything they could find. No one was looking at me.

"You bitch!" he spat into my right ear. He was behind me, one hand holding my neck. I couldn't see the other.

"Reg, please..." I tried. I had to try.

"Don't even think about screaming. We wouldn't want anyone to get hurt," he said quietly. Around us, chaos swirled. It felt like time had stopped, slowed, and I could feel my heartbeat thumping. I saw a glimpse of Lance as he raced towards the flames. The RCMP officers were at the front of the crowd, trying desperately to retain control. Every fibre in my being wanted to scream.

"You fucking bitch, who the fuck are you? Coming into this town, stealing my plant out from under me? Land developers? I don't fucking think so. Not from what you just said in there."

"You, you were there? At the meeting? But..."

"What? The cops? Don't forget, I've lived in this town my whole goddamned life. I know that school like the back of my hand. Easy enough to sneak out of, back in the day, easy enough to sneak into now." He pulled my head back, forcing me to take a step backwards, further away from the crowd. The voice of my self-defence instructor from ten years before rang in my head—*never let yourself be taken to a second location. You die at the second location.*

"Come on, Reg, it was business, that's all," I tried. "I got the feeling you wouldn't want to sell to me, so I had my people fib a little."

"Oh, is that all? Just fib a little? You made a fucking fool of me!" His mouth was right on my ear. I could feel the sweat from his upper lip. "Told the whole town land developers had bought it. Now, turns out that I was faked out by a skank from the mainland. Stupid bitch, why the fuck did you ever come to Englee?"

"I, well, I heard..." His finger moved on the back of my neck. He stopped pulling me as he felt the ridge of my wig, felt the stitching.

"What the fuck..." he ripped the wig from my head roughly. He had to pull hard several times to free it from the numerous pins. Pain shot through me as the natural hair tore from my scalp in clumps.

In the flickering light cast by the fire, he looked at the wig now in his hand. Then he looked at me, my hair. "You! You can't be. Holy shit, Kenny Warren! You're not supposed to be here. You're not supposed..."

"What? To be alive? You never said I had to die, Reg. Just that I had to give up everything and everyone that mattered in my life and leave."

"I warned you..." he threw the wig to the ground and spun me around to face him.

"What? That you'd kill my father?" I had to fight. I couldn't let him drag me off into the night. This time, I had to fight. "Oh, but you've already done that, haven't you?"

A sadistic grin spread across his sweaty face. "Didn't take much. Old man went down on the Cross Rocks like a mainland fisherman."

"You son-of-a-bitch!" I yelled. He still had a grip on my hand, but the slight distance between us made me feel brave. "You did it, you killed that man in the alley and you killed my father..."

"I gotta say, if I had to choose, I'd say I enjoyed killing my father more than killing yours. I enjoyed seeing him die."

"Your father? The stranger?" I tried to process the information quickly. "Oh God, that was your father? You just stabbed him in cold blood and dumped his body? Why?"

"He was gonna make trouble. Showed up sayin' he thought this would be a good little town to set up shop in, start conning the good people of Englee. Thought I'd join him. Thing was, I had plans. I didn't want to be a low-life conartist, the former son of the richest man in town. I wanted to own this town and everyone in it."

"You'd kill your own father?"

He laughed. "God, you're not much smarter than you were

seventeen years ago. I *did* kill my father. Think how easy it'll be for me to kill you..."

I screamed. I couldn't help it. I screamed with all my might at the top of my lungs, as I twisted my arm violently, trying to get free. The bone in my wrist snapped. Searing pain shot up my arm and through my whole body. For a moment, I saw only darkness.

As I came back to my senses, I could hear myself yelling even louder. I couldn't concentrate to see if anyone was coming. All I could see was Reg, looming over me, twisting my broken arm. There was panic in his eyes and a glint of steel in his hand.

A knife, I thought. The knife. Oh God.

I pulled frantically to get away, but his hand held. "Shut up! Shut the fuck up! You've ruined everything! Stupid little slut," the words were hurled at me.

"Monster!" I yelled. It felt like my vocal cords were ripping from the strain and the smoke in the air.

"Kay?" someone yelled from the crowd. "Kay!" the voice was scared.

"Here! Here!" I yelled back.

"You should have stayed away," Reg said through clenched teeth.

I looked towards the voice in the crowd yelling my name. It was Sean. I could see his face in the burning light, as he ran towards me. He looked scared.

"No!" Sean yelled, just feet from where I struggled. I didn't see Reg pull the knife back. Sean's face collapsed at the moment the blade struck my abdomen. I felt the metal rip through my flesh, tearing inside my body. I looked down and saw Reg's hand on the hilt. Then he let go, as a blur passed in between us. I saw the woollen cap before the whole world went black.

Chapter Nineteen

The sounds came back first. People yelling, screaming, fire sirens blaring, mingled sounds that blurred. They didn't make sense. I tried to focus. Focus on one. Just one. I just needed to tell someone what had happened. My stomach hurt, throbbed. My arm burned with pain. Burned. Smoke. I smelled the smoke of the fire. For a moment, I thought I was burning in the building. I snapped to consciousness.

I pulled my eyes open and tried to make sense of the scene. Charlie was kneeling in front of me. I could only see his form in the darkness, framed by the light of the fire across the road. He had his back to me, only an inch from where I laid on the ground.

"No!" he yelled. "Not this time, Reg! I won't let you kill her like you did t'at man!"

I shifted slightly and saw Reg standing in front of him, blood dripping from his hand.

"She ruined it all!" Reg yelled as he grabbed Charlie's shirt. "Get the fuck out of my way!"

"No!" Charlie yelled and punched Reg in the gut.

"Kenny!" Lance's voice rang in my ears as I saw him running from the fire. Reg hit Charlie again and punched him in the face. Suddenly Sean was by my side.

"Kay, Kay? Kay, can you hear me? Oh god, Kay..." I looked

at his precious face. He was looking at my stomach. I followed his gaze and saw the knife, the handle of the knife. The blood.

I swooned, but grabbed myself back from the brink. "Stay with me, Kay. Stay with me," Sean pleaded.

"Kenny!" Lance screamed again as he ran into my line of vision. "No!" He spun on his heel towards Reg and Charlie. "You bastard! What have you done?"

Reg stopped struggling with Charlie and straightened himself to face his brother. "She ruined everything. She...that stupid little no-name slut...ruined me!"

People were gathering. I couldn't see their faces clearly. Couldn't figure it all out. I focused on Lance, standing tall above me, shaking with rage.

Reg turned to look at the crowd. "You've all been taken for fools! Don't you see? Don't you see who she is? Kennedy Warren! She's made fools of all of you!"

"No, you're the only fool here," Lance screamed. "Murderous, lying, evil fool you are!"

"It's her," Reg pleaded with the onlookers. "Don't you see? She's nobody. Kenny Warren! Not Kay Toms. She's lied to all of you. Just a nobody—the fucking handyman's daughter!"

Lance's fist flew. The crowd yelled. I couldn't tell what, the screams melded. Reg fell to the ground. Lance jumped on him, throwing blow after crippling blow. The edges of my vision darkened. They were all moving further and further away...

Then, suddenly, there was Asia's face, just inches from

mine. "Kennedy Warren?" I saw her lips form my name. Felt her fingers touch my hair. "Kenny? Kenny? Mom?"

Then it was all gone. Darkness enveloped me as I felt myself slip away.

Chapter Twenty

There must have been noise. There must have been screaming, yelling, clamouring. There had to have been, but I couldn't hear it. Swimming in darkness, I struggled to grasp reality.

There were hands, I felt them as they smoothed my hair back off my forehead; as they lifted me, fingers dug into my back, arms and legs. A lot of fingers. Many hands.

Bright lights of all colours in flickering segments as I tried desperately to open my eyes—blinding white, flashing red and blue...

Asia! my mind screamed. *Asia, I have to find Asia! She can't be taken from me again...not again...*

I struggled, fighting my way back, towards the lights, towards the noise I knew must have been there. I pried my eyes open. Chaos swirled around me, swarmed my senses as I tried to figure it all out. I was on a bed, *no, a gurney, it's a gurney.* Beside me, a young man in a uniform was pressing down hard on my stomach. I moaned, feeling the weight of his strong hands.

"Stay still," he said as he looked up and saw I was awake. "You're going to be okay. Just stay still..."

I tried to speak, but my palate was so dry my tongue was stuck to the roof of my mouth, my lips sealed shut. I opted for groaning as I dropped my head back down to the thin mattress.

"Kay? Kay, you're awake!" Sean was at the paramedic's elbow, peering around him and over him, trying to see my face.

"What? What's happened?" I heard Jack ask from a short distance away, his voice filled with panic. I turned my head, trying to spot his face in the crowd.

The light was all wrong. Flickering, glowing...*the fire!* I arched to my right, hoping to see the fish plant, only to be pushed forcibly back down.

"Please, Missus, stay still. You've been stabbed, you're losing blood," the paramedic said very calmly and firmly, the way you would speak to a hyperactive child. "We're going to get you to the hospital, just stay still."

I worked my tongue back and forth frantically, trying to get the saliva flowing again. With just enough moisture, I managed to pry my lips open. "Fire?" I croaked.

"It's okay, Kay, the fire department's here now, they're taking care of it," Sean yelled over the din. "I've been told they have excellent volunteer firemen." All around us, people were milling about, covered in ash, dust, and debris. Sirens and lights from the fire brigade flashed and water flowed. "Asia!" Sean yelled into the crowd. "Asia! She's awake!"

"Asia?" I asked weakly.

Suddenly, her face was floating above me, worried and panicked. "You're awake! Oh, thank God!" She grasped my shoulder and searing pain ripped through my arm. "Oh, sorry! Your arm's broken pretty badly, they say," she fumbled, unsure of where to be or what to say.

As I looked at her blushing, dusty face, I smiled. "You're here. You're okay?" I asked, each word ripping my vocal chords.

"I'm fine, just fine, you don't need to worry," she said, obviously relieved. "We're all okay."

"I couldn't bear to leave you again. Not again." Tears stung the corners of my eyes. "Asia, I'm sorry."

The paramedic stabbed a needle deep into a vein in my good arm, forcing me to wince. "Hang that bag," he ordered to his cohort. They looked identical in their pressed whites, like one person working double-time.

"It's okay," Asia said as she brushed the matted, sweat soaked hair off my forehead. "It's okay, we'll have plenty of time to talk, once you're better."

"We gotta roll," one of the uniforms said behind her.

"No, wait," I begged. Through the noise, somewhere in the background, there was a voice. Lance, yelling. *What's he saying?* Words wriggled through. "No. Not now. You'll let me. You'll let me, now…"

"Kenny!" He roared suddenly. I turned my head to see him pushing his way through the crowd that was splitting its time between watching me and watching the blazing fire. Behind Lance, two RCMP officers trailed, waving their notebooks and pleading with him to stop.

"Lance," I smiled. As he came closer, I took in the damage. His face was battered, under all the soot and sweat. His limp was even more pronounced than it had been and his knuckles on both hands were bleeding. "Oh, Lance," I muttered as his hands cradled my face.

"Mister Richards, please," one little RCMP officer pleaded behind him. "Please, just a statement…"

"Give me two minutes here, then I'll tell you everything you need to know," he said soothingly, never taking his eyes off mine. "No way," said the paramedic beside him who was still pressing on my abdomen. "We're rollin' now. She needs to get to the hospital. Right now."

"Okay, okay," Lance responded, rubbing a thumb across my temple. "You're going to be alright. I just have to go talk to these cops for a bit. You need to get to the hospital, Kenny. You're going to be fine." Tears welled in his dark, bloodshot eyes. "Reg can't hurt you anymore. Never again."

"What? Where…Lance, what have you done?" A vision of him lunging at his brother, fists flying, flashed in my mind. He wouldn't stop. He looked like he wouldn't stop for anything. "Oh God, Lance, did you…"

"No, no, he's alive. He's alive. The RCMP have him now. Charlie and Sean pulled me off. Stopped me. I could have…" he looked from me to Asia. "For you, the two of you, I could have."

Asia lowered her eyes. "Holy sh…"

"Alright, folks, let's wrap it up." I felt something click under the gurney and it rolled a few inches forward, dragging Lance, Asia, Jack, and Sean with it.

"I love you," Lance said, then kissed me quickly. "You'll be okay. I'll get to the hospital as quickly as I can." He stepped back as an officer tugged at his arm.

"I love you, too," I said as loudly as my bruised voice would allow. "Asia, Asia?"

"I'm still here," she said from behind my head as the gurney rolled to the back of the ambulance.

"I love you," I said. "I've always loved you."

The gurney jostled and lurched as they rolled it into the ambulance. My eyes watered with the pain that shot through my torso. But, before they closed the doors, I lifted my head a few feeble inches off the bed and looked out the back. Jack stood behind Asia, holding her tightly, with Sean by his side. Off a little ways in the distance, Charlie and Lance stared at me as the officers talked to them. Behind them all, the whole town stood, staring at Kenny Warren against the backdrop of the old fish plant smouldering.

"Thank you," I said to my attendant as the doors shut abruptly.

"The wound's pretty deep and you've lost a lot of blood," he said as he fidgeted with the equipment around him. "But you're going to make it. Just rest, we still have a long ride ahead of us…"

I tried to listen, but felt myself swooning again. *They're all okay,* I thought as I felt myself slipping. *We're all safe.*

Chapter Twenty-One

It took surgery to repair the damage Reg's blade had done. The doctors had worked quickly to minimize the tear and sew me back together, again. I fell into the comfortable rhythm of the hospital easily in recovery. The hum of chatting nurses, the beeping of machines, the clanking of trolleys, cots and beds rolling down the hallways. In my dreams, B.J. was there, waiting by my side, patiently waiting for me to emerge once again. Floating in a sea of sedatives and dim lighting, I rested with him keeping watch, feeling utterly safe and secure. He was happy, settled in a way I had never seen him in life. Somewhere, somehow, I knew it was over. He was at peace and proud of me.

As the drugs wore off, I sensed full consciousness returning and felt B.J. leave me for the last time. His smiling, contented face faded as reality took over. I could still hear his deep baritone voice humming a familiar tune in my ear as I finally woke completely.

I opened my eyes, half expecting to find him sitting by my bed. Instead, I looked around a crowded room. Sean and Asia were curled into a big chair in the corner, sound asleep. Jack sat across from them in another, his head nodding to his chest. And on the end of my bed, there was Lance, sitting, guarding me.

"Kenny!" he whispered loudly.

"Shhh…" I said quietly. "You'll wake them." It must have been nighttime. The room was dark and the hospital as quiet as a hospital can get.

Lance moved gently to my side. "Are you okay?"

"Ummm, think so," I mouthed. Yet, I could feel the emptiness left behind by B.J. "Lonely," I tried to explain, as I shifted over slightly, as much as my stitches would allow. I looked from him to the empty space.

He grinned. "Yeah, you're okay," he said, gently sliding onto the mattress beside me, nestling his face next to mine. His breath felt warm on my cheek.

I stayed in hospital for seven days, giving my wounds time to start healing. It seemed as though I was never alone. If it wasn't the nurses checking in, it was Asia, Lance, Jack, Sean, Ester, or a random visitor from Englee. It seemed I was still the talk of the town. Yet, they all came by just to tell me how glad they were that I was back, that Kenny Warren was back, and how sorry they had been at the passing of my father, all those years ago. None of them had had any idea there had been foul play involved, let alone that Reg could have had a hand in killing him. Opinion of Reg seemed to be unanimous—what he'd done was unbelievable, yet no one was terribly, terribly surprised.

The phone rang constantly, keeping Sean busy every hour of the day answering questions from Boston, from Englee, and from the media. The scandal of Kay Toms' true identity had struck a chord with the public and continued to be the lead story on most outlets. "Fantastic advertising for Englee," I assured Sean as he had started fielding calls from magazines requesting interviews. "Line them up."

Jack and Lance had both stood, staring me down disapprovingly.

"Okay, alright, at ease, gentlemen," I said, raising my good arm in surrender. "Next month, Sean. Tell them I need a month to recover, then I'll decide who to talk to."

"That's better," Jack said with a hmph. "Crazy, one track mind…run herself right into an early grave…" he muttered as he threw down the paper he'd been reading and shuffled out of the room.

"You really do know how to get under his skin, don't you?" Lance asked teasingly as Sean turned his attention back to the phone.

"What can I say? It's a gift," I shrugged. "I think we all just need to get out of here. Everyone's going a little stir crazy. Tom said my house is all ready on the hill, so I can…"

"Nope." He shook his head and crossed his arms. "Absolutely not. You'll come to Batty Catters to recover. There's plenty of room and we'll all be there to take care of ya, night and day."

"But, what if I don't want taking care of?" I asked stubbornly.

The idea of a moment of peace was intoxicating.

"Oh, right, it's a want, now is it?" he asked smugly. "Put on your pants. Right now. I dare you."

I looked at the sweatpants Sean had set at the end of my bed and knew I was defeated. There was no way I could dress myself with one arm casted to the elbow and lord knows how many stitches in my stomach.

"Alright, alright," I said, surrendering for the second time in two minutes. "Batty Catters it is."

"Home." His voice was lighter. "I'm taking you home."

Everything about that sounded right. The words, the sentiment, him saying it. I was going home to Batty Catters at last.

Chapter Twenty-Two

Asia found me the following day, sitting on a deck chair Lance had placed at the edge of the lawn, watching the waves roll. The brine in the air filled my lungs and I felt nearly human for the first time since the incident. The morning had been blissfully quiet, after a solid night's sleep in Lance's bed with him by my side. Charlie had been the only visitor, ringing the doorbell, cap in one hand and a bunch of wild flowers in the other. He had said precious little, thrusting the flowers towards me as I'd shuffled to the door.

"Glad ye's alright," he'd said to the ground. "Cops says t'ey's not gonna press charges on me if I testify 'gainst Reg. Told 'em I's happy ta do it. Lock 'im up for good."

"Thank you, Charlie," I'd said. "For everything—for fighting off Reg. I owe you."

He blushed and started backing away. "It was not'ing, missus," he looked up briefly and smiled. "Kenny. Wouldn't say no ta a job, t'ough, if ya had a mind to hire me at the new plant."

"Consider it done," I said warmly. Charlie always knew how to take care of himself, that was for sure. "Go down there now and talk to Bob Pearson, tell him I sent you. Sean's hired him as plant manager and he's working hard to get the rubble cleared away from the fire. There was nothing left to salvage.

He'll need good help, Charlie."

"T'ank you, Miss Kenny. T'ank you," he had nodded, turned and walked back down the driveway. I watched from the doorway as he disappeared behind the trees and smiled.

"So, can we talk?" Asia asked once she had settled in the grass beside me. We both focused on watching the tide, comfortable in the slight distance it gave us.

"Of course," I responded as calmly as I could. On the inside, my stomach fluttered and flopped.

"I need to know," she said simply. "From you. I need to know from you. Uncle Lance has explained. Grandpa has explained. But they weren't there. It was you." Her eyes flitted from the far off distance to my face, then back.

I took a deep breath. "I can understand that. You know by now that I had my reasons. I was young—just the age you are now—I was pregnant, scared out of my mind, not just about having a baby, but for Lance and my father. I didn't know what else to do. At the home Reg sent me to, they made it sound so easy. Just hand the baby over and they'd give it a better life than I could ever hope to. Just hand the baby over."

I looked at her, but her features remained solid, unwilling to even flinch.

"It was the hardest thing I've ever done in my life. Letting you go. It felt like my soul was being ripped out. I didn't even see you. The second you were born, they cut the cord and whisked you out of the room. I couldn't bear it. I thought I would die."

The word hung in the wind as we sat looking towards the sea.

"But then, then they told me about the family that you'd have. That you'd be safe. That was all that mattered to me—that you and Lance were safe. My dad was already dead. I was still mourning him, without being able to come home and say goodbye. I mourned you, Asia, without knowing your name or your fate."

She turned her head then, my own eyes looking back at me. "Thank you," she said simply.

"Can you forgive me?"

"I've had a good life. I was safe. I am safe. You were put in an impossible situation, but you accomplished your goals. I grew up in a loving family, safe and secure, blissfully unaware of the evils in this world," she smiled softly. "I know what Reg has done. I know that he caused all of this, but I also know that he loved me. When I was little, he'd tuck me in at night, reading story after story. I have those memories, memories of good times, fun, a real childhood. In a weird, twisted way, it all worked out." She looked again to the ocean. "There's nothing to forgive. You made the only possible choice you could. I just needed to hear it from you…God! What should I call you?"

"It's okay, Asia, you can call me whatever you want. Whatever you're comfortable with."

She thought for a moment. "Think I'll stick with Kenny for

now. I've never used the name 'Mom' before, what with Ester and all. It might take some time."

"All the time you need," I said. "Is there anything else you need to know? Anything at all?"

She stared at me. "How come you don't have a bump on your nose like mine?"

I put my hand up and ran it over my nose. I felt myself blushing in embarrassment. "Cosmetic surgery. I was in a car accident and they had to repair my face," I explained.

She ran her hand over her own bump. "As much as I hate it, I think I'll keep it," she said thoughtfully.

"Good," I said. "It comes from your grandmother's side of the family, you know. I'll show you her picture sometime. You look just like her."

"I look just like you," she said shyly. "In the pictures Uncle Lance…" She rolled her eyes. "God, this is so strange. In the pictures Dad has of you in high school. The hair, everything. We'd probably still look alike if you hadn't had that accident."

I thought for a moment and smiled as I heard the backdoor of the house slam. I turned to see Lance balancing a tray with three very large glasses of iced tea. Butch ran around his ankles, trying with all his might to make the task of crossing the lawn as difficult as possible.

"If it hadn't been for that accident," I muttered, as Asia jumped to her feet and ran to grab Butch by the collar. His heavy golden retriever tongue lolled out the side of his mouth as he jumped to lick her face. She and Lance laughed in the sunshine as the glasses wobbled dangerously.

I turned to look at the ocean beating again the high cliffs. I had made it beyond the Batty Catters and I was finally home. It was a different Kenny Warren who had returned but inside, in spite of the pain, I was happier now than I had ever been before.

The town was getting a fresh start and Lance and I were starting life together with the child we had eagerly awaited years earlier.

The demons that had haunted me for years were gone. I was no longer afraid. I was home. "Thank you, B.J. You've given me everything."

Epilogue

It's been five years since I returned. It was a long painful journey but I've come home.

Our son will be having a birthday soon. He looks like his father but he has my father's name.

Asia adores her little brother. She gets to spend lots of time with him now that she has graduated from university and is working with her dad in aquaculture. She has settled into the house on the hill.

Tomtex is no longer mine. It caught the attention of another major corporation and I sold. Sean is now the president and CEO. Most of the staff remained with him.

It's our son's fourth birthday next month. The old group from Tomtex will be coming to Englee, not just for his birthday, but to see their instrumentation in helping what now is a thriving town.